PRAISE FOR *MOUSE*

"A creative, fast-paced tale that blends the magic and friendship of *Harry Potter* with the high-tech brilliance of *Big Hero 6*. A must for coders, hackers, and noobs alike."

—HENRY NEFF, bestselling author of The Tapestry series and *Impyrium*

"Stedman's debut novel is an intricately plotted technological thriller with a big heart. Readers will keep turning pages and rooting for Mouse—an underdog coding prodigy out to prove her worth at an elite boarding school where she unexpectedly finds a family whole searching for her missing parents. A fun, engaging, and smart read!"

—H.A. SWAIN, author of *Hungry* and *Gifted*

"*Mouse* is a Nancy Drew mystery for the *WIRED*-era that reminds us that coding isn't just a STEM essential, but a path to creativity, self-discovery, and belonging."

—R. MICHAEL HENDRIX, co-author of
Two Beats Ahead and partner at IDEO

"It takes a special writer to understand that computers are the most human things our species has ever built, and that the lines between making and magic and machines are the most porous of boundaries. A riveting, thrilling, and wildly imaginative novel."

—JEFF HOWE, author of *Crowdsourcing* and
contributing editor of *WIRED* magazine.

"Mouse Gamma is a marvel. This story will inspire young outsiders and sweep even reluctant kids up in the magic of coding."

—SARA JAMES MNOOKIN, author of *Scatter
My Ashes at Bergdorf Goodman*

N. SCOTT STEDMAN

MOUSE

<a novel/>

RIVER GROVE
BOOKS

Published by River Grove Books
Austin, TX
www.rivergrovebooks.com

Distributed by River Grove Books

Design and composition by Greenleaf Book Group and Teresa Muñiz
Cover design by Greenleaf Book Group and Teresa Muñiz
Cover images used under license from ©Shutterstock.com/PapaAya.
Folder icon from ©The Noun Project/Landan Lloyd, social media icon from ©The Noun Project/Guilherme Furtado, book icon from ©The Noun Project/Pauline.

Publisher's Cataloging-in-Publication data is available.

Print ISBN: 978-1-63299-452-3

eBook ISBN: 978-1-63299-453-0

First Edition

For Louise, Felix, and Sonny who are each growing into True Magicians.

And for my middle school librarian Ms. Rote, who loved sharing books and provided more of a refuge for children who loved to read than I'm certain she ever imagined.

TENET ONE

Programming, also called coding, is the art of using special languages to give electronic devices direction about how to behave. Whether crunching a simple math problem on a calculator or building a robot that can speak or fly, all electronic behavior is directed by code. The coder breathes life into the body. The body is a computer. The coder is god. The Pericles Society demands that gods be good. Not cruel. Not greedy. Not mean. The good gods must destroy that which threatens order.

As the first fingers of dawn filtered through the Berkshire treetops in the northern tip of Massachusetts, Mouse shook herself awake. Yawning, she glanced at the pile of books scattered against her bed as she pulled on her usual uniform. An oversized sweatshirt, a pair of used black jeans that ended just above her ankles, threadbare sneakers, and a black wool beanie pulled tight against her head in an attempt to tame her frizzy mop of hair. The overall effect made her look much younger than she was. Other eighth-graders were wearing jeans that cost more than she had to spend in a month. This didn't bother Mouse. She didn't care what she looked like. In fact, no one cared what she looked like, so her personal style was dictated by the cheapest contents of the annual end-of-summer rummage sale at a local church.

She tiptoed past her sleeping foster parents and grabbed her backpack as she left, remembering to catch the screen door before it sprang back and slammed against its frame. With a sigh, she walked the sleepy backroads to school as she did every morning before the world woke up.

The library opened two hours before the first bell rang at Pittsfield K-12. The peeling letters on the door read 8AM-5PM MON-FRI, but the insomniac librarian Mr. Beasley quietly unlocked the doors when he arrived early to drink his coffee and read the paper in peace. He'd never had a student join him in his early ritual.

Not until Mouse.

Mr. Beasley looked up from his steaming mug of coffee as the door jingled open. He greeted her the same way every day as though it were a surprise: "And a bright good morning to you, Ms. Gamma. Up early again, I see." Then he'd nod and point to a few books that he'd pulled from the stacks that he thought she might like.

For the past year or so she'd adapted her schedule to more or less mimic Mr. Beasley's. If he was in the library, the library was open. And if the library was open, that was where you'd find her. It was the one place Mouse felt comfortable. She knew from experience that there wouldn't always be a library open and willing to let her in. She didn't take Mr. Beasley for granted, even if he was shy and a little weird. She didn't take anything for granted. Not since the six months she'd spent at Blackwell juvie.

Mouse liked to read. She'd been reading as long as she could remember. In fact, reading was almost the only thing that she did remember about her childhood. The rest was just an endless series of foster parents who misunderstood her and counselors who never did more than explain how sorry they were that it didn't work out again or ask her why she lashed out.

It's not lashing out. It's trying to escape. There's a difference.

Reading was different. Mouse remembered reading the outdated *Highlights* magazines in the office of the pediatric therapist who never answered her questions, preferring to watch Mouse color with dull crayons until the session was over. She read every frayed Encyclopedia Brown in her elementary school library. Then came a ratty, old copy of Harry Potter that a social worker had given her after her third home transfer, which Mouse read over and over during the chilly nights at Blackwell when there weren't books, libraries, or anything else to learn from—just bullies and victims, and sometimes not much difference between the two.

She loved how words worked on the page, taking a series of meaningless letters and assembling them together to create images, thoughts, and characters. Maybe she liked reading so much because talking had always been such a struggle. Words became unpredictable as soon as they left her mouth.

Dangerous.

People took her words and crushed them together into something totally different from what she was trying to say. They called her ungrateful when she was curious, called her rude when she was afraid.

These days, Mouse said as little as possible.

She and Mr. Beasley seemed to have that in common. He wasn't the kind of librarian she'd read about, like Mrs. Phelps in Roald Dahl's *Matilda*, on the lookout for lost children to nurture. That would have been a nightmare to Mouse. She wasn't looking for a friend. Mr. Beasley was perfect. He kept the library open and accessible, drank his coffee, let Mouse drink her Mountain Dew, and that was that.

The Mountain Dew part was important. She always had a can or two in her backpack, alongside a pack of Skittles or Twizzlers. Candy and soda were the only things she had that other kids didn't. It was the one perk of not having a nosy mom or dad looking over her shoulder. Sure, there had never been anyone to give her a hug on bad days—the days when the teasing became pushing, when the pushing started to hurt. But there had never been anyone stopping her from getting a family-sized bag of Sour Patch Kids, either.

Mouse loved the library, but this morning she wasn't here to read. Today she was going to make history.

Six months ago, when she had finished every title in the tiny young readers section, Mouse had spent a bored morning messing around on the little computer tucked behind the self-help shelves. A new game called *League of Exiles* had swept through the school like wildfire that month, and even a loner like Mouse couldn't help but be curious. Computers had always seemed a bit pointless to her, but this time was different. It wasn't the game, but the forums and message boards that captivated her for hours on end. People all over the world were sharing the Easter eggs that coders had hidden throughout the game. It was like a conspiracy of people trying to outthink the creators, an army willing to break the rules holding them back.

She learned about cheats and hacks and discovered a community who didn't just play games; they also *made* them. Computers had a language, too, and there were people out there, people like her, whose entire lives were spent studying *words*. They weren't sitting around making the kind of small talk she found boring and confusing. They were coders, and their words were *never* misunderstood.

Over the next several weeks, she learned about the greatest coders in the world while teaching herself how to write her own code and perform her own hacks. Each day, Mr. Beasley let Mouse into the library then quietly retreated to his coffee at the front desk, leaving her to devour everything she could find. She scoured books and online message boards as her coding improved each day. It was as though the words that were so hard for her to use with other people flowed out of her without effort in code.

She studied the white hat coders who were fighting for a better world, but also the black hats—hackers who created chaos wherever they went. But her favorite programmer of all time was Erik Walters, who fell somewhere in between the white- and black-hat hackers who'd been fighting each other for decades. He didn't follow anyone else's rules and was almost impossible to stick in one category. He'd emerged out of nowhere and had become the most notorious and influential hacker of his generation because of his unrelenting war against one man: Trent Rayburn, founder of the largest technology company in the world, Rayburn Tech.

Mouse loved everything about Walters, from the unpredictability of his coding to his technical brilliance. Still, her favorite moment came during a rare interview. The editor of the biggest hacker news vlog, *Script-sploit*, convinced Walters to go on record for once.

"Why this vendetta against Trent Rayburn?" the editor probed. "I mean he's literally got an army that's trained to neutralize the most powerful threats in the world. And you're all alone, like a mouse in a field; what can you hope to actually accomplish?"

Walters whipped toward the camera and replied, "A mouse?" He laughed out loud. "Exactly. Now watch a mouse fight back."

That night, Mouse pondered those words, letting them roll around in her mind—"Now watch a mouse fight back"—as she drifted off to sleep.

While the war between Walters and Rayburn raged for years, it came to an unexpected and sudden ending. After evading law enforcement and some of the most sophisticated private security teams in the world, Walters was ultimately arrested for a mistake any script kiddie could have caught. As he was led away in handcuffs from a small cabin that had been wired to be untraceable, he left the world one final mystery. He turned toward a scrum of photographers and journalists who'd been tipped off to the arrest, glared at them, and whispered with a sadness, "I'll be waiting in orbit."

Those final words, "I'll be waiting in orbit," were as shrouded in mystery as everything else about Erik Walters. Since then, he'd been silent, stuck in a maximum security prison, and about as far from a computer as you could get. Mouse dreamed of following in his footsteps: trying to defend the powerless and ensure that the biggest companies in the world took notice of the billions of people they mercilessly used to create wealth and power for themselves.

As her coding improved, the first thing she needed to do was upgrade the fragile operating system on the library computer. She couldn't afford the hardware she needed to run a powerful Kali Linux setup, so she settled on a Debian/Obuntu hybrid. It gave her the tools she needed, it was dirt cheap, and it wouldn't fry the fragile, five-year-old PC that was all the library had to offer.

As the computer blipped to life, she held down Control-M to bypass the school's operating system and enter a secret operating system she had installed behind a firewall that only she had access to.

The screen went green and her favorite riddle blinked in large black letters, prompting her password:

> WE HURT WITHOUT MOVING. WE
> POISON WITHOUT TOUCHING. WE
> BEAR THE TRUTH. WE BEAR THE LIES.
> WE ARE NEVER JUDGED BY OUR SIZE.
> WHAT ARE WE?

Mouse smiled while typing.

> WORDS

Her fingers vibrated with excitement.

She'd had her nose in every book about code, from cryptography to obscure programming languages like SNOBOL. In those first months, there wasn't a single coding language Mouse hadn't dabbled in. She built simple apps and had even done a few small hacks, finding herself constantly amazed at how few people understood the real power of computers.

It all felt so natural, so easy.

But today was different. Today the people on the other side of the screen were waiting for her. These people were *always* waiting for the next hack. They were paid big bucks to make sure that people like Mouse never got close.

It sounded crazy, but what she was planning would change everything, and she couldn't wait another minute. After today, she wouldn't be some nameless orphan who'd been left at the Pittsfield Hospital before she could talk. She wouldn't be ignored by foster parents and noticed by thugs.

Today she was going to hack into the digital records of the one company that might know who she really was.

It had all started a week earlier, on her first day of eighth grade.

• • •

Mouse looked forward to the first day of school as if it was a dentist appointment, but even so, she wasn't prepared for the sinking feeling she got when she saw the enormous banner draped across the school's main entrance.

THANK YOU TRENT RAYBURN
AND RAYBURN TECH

When she ducked out of the library just before the first period bell that day, Mouse noticed huge posters lining the hallway. They read, "LITTLE WIZARDS: LEARNING FOR THE FUTURE."

She rolled her eyes.

Six months ago, she didn't know anything more about Rayburn Tech than she'd seen from the constant barrage of ads. But on the coding forums that were now her second home, you couldn't avoid them. Rayburn had it in for hackers. His company even paid a bounty for information that helped to catch anyone unauthorized lurking in

Rayburn's digital network. You either worked for them, or you were a threat to be eradicated. They had put some of the best programmers in the world behind bars, including Erik Walters.

Mouse squeezed into her desk just as the late bell rang.

This typical public-school classroom was comprised primarily of three shades of beige. First there were twenty-six beige chairs that had matching beige desks attached to them. Then there were the slightly lighter beige walls that were only interrupted by a bulletin board full of newspaper clippings about the Pittsfield football team, and a blackboard that had been stained over the years with chalk and markers. The last shade of beige belonged to the face of Mrs. Clavicle, and right now it was glaring straight at Mouse.

She huffed. "The day has finally arrived. A day Pittsfield has been waiting for, even if it's not important enough for *some* of you to arrive on time."

Her voice rose in pitch as she continued, "Yes, today *each* of your technological needs will be satisfied to help further your Pittsfield education."

Mouse furrowed her brow.

My tech needs are about to be answered by Rayburn Tech? Doubt it.

"Our little school is lucky enough to be launching a new pilot program that will help students across our country. Rayburn Tech, one of the world's leading technology companies, has graciously offered to supply every student with a state-of-the-art *Rayburn Wizard*. The finest computer available, at absolutely NO COST to all of you!"

That explains the banners and posters, Mouse thought as her heart sank.

She knew everything about the Wizard, Rayburn Tech's latest foray into consumer hardware, and none of it was good. Obviously, the specs were top-notch. The latest i7 processor, massive memory, blazing boot speed, an 8k screen, and a carbon-fiber build, all for a fraction of the price of a Mac or top-range PC . . . but there was a catch. You see, if you used a Wizard, you didn't technically own it. Sure, you could keep it for as long as you wanted, and it came with a comprehensive warranty covering accidental damage. But the Wizard and—more importantly, any work or data processed, generated, or communicated using the laptop—became the property of Rayburn Tech. Using one was making a deal with the devil, selling your soul to Rayburn Tech for a fancy laptop.

Exactly the kind of manipulation Erik Walters fought, she thought.

Mouse's hand shot into the air, but Mrs. Clavicle seemed dead set on ignoring her.

She scanned the classroom with a satisfied look on her face before reluctantly making eye contact with Mouse.

"Yes, Mouse. What is it?"

Mouse had planned to say something tactful, something that would convey her genuine concern and horror for her classmates' vulnerability in the face of big tech's assault on privacy, and for the community at large. Instead, she found herself shouting.

"You can't seriously mean we'll all be running *Wizards*? It's a total rip-off. First they'll be stealing our data and then—"

She was cut off with a wave of her teacher's hand.

"*Enough.* Maybe you're too clever for the most popular brand of computers in America, but the rest of your classmates are happy about this very *generous* gesture by Rayburn Tech. And this data you're so angry about sharing is doing wonderful things for our community. Just the other day, my cousin Minnie was reunited with her long-lost niece through Rayburn Tech's ancestry program, *Rayburn and Me.*"

Mouse opened her mouth to argue, then paused. "You're saying that all that data that Rayburn has stolen without people knowing can help reunite people with their family?"

Mrs. Clavicle gave Mouse a patronizing look that made her face look like melting Jell-O. "Well, people who are *looking* for each other. Paying members of their services. Not orphans or refugees or just *anyone*. They aren't running a charity connecting people who don't want to be found. But that isn't the point! The point is . . ."

Mrs. Clavicle had droned on about the power of data to "shape minds and futures," but Mouse had stopped listening. Her brain was racing at a million miles an hour, turning over and over at that off-handed comment about "orphans."

"Not orphans," Mrs. Clavicle had said.

Well, why not? Rayburn collects data from everyone who's ever visited a website or bought a computer. If they have an ancestry program, then they are connecting their big data pool with individuals. Even if they won't share it through their stupid app, why couldn't I hack right into the heart of Rayburn Tech and simply steal the information?

The answer was simple. She could.

The information would all be there in a beautiful, correlated database. She could simply go in and grab it. That was, if she was good enough to get into the most secure database in the word. The data was there; you'd just needed to be crazy enough to try to steal it.

Which was why a week later, here she was at 6 a.m. in the school library, getting ready to unleash a nuclear DDoS on the most unhackable company in the world.

A typical DDoS, or distributed denial-of-service, attack wouldn't be enough, so Mouse had already hacked into thousands of computers around the world and turned them into zombie servers, which would send massive amounts of unexpected internet traffic to distract Rayburn's anti-hacking security goons. This distraction would hopefully hold long enough for her to install come-and-go access to any information Rayburn Tech had ever collected.

Specifically, it would give her time to search the biggest database of personal information in the world for anything related to a certain abandoned foster child named Mouse Gamma.

It was certainly one of the most ambitious hacks ever committed by an eighth grader. If she were caught, not only would it get her thrown out of school, but she would also definitely be sent straight back to Blackwell Juvenile Detention Center.

That was why Mouse didn't intend to get caught.

She knew she'd only get one shot. Once she stuck her nose into that server, even with the distraction of a massive DDoS, it would be a matter of minutes before the security systems found her. She estimated that she had 360 seconds from the moment the DDoS was unleashed to get in, snoop around, and get out.

She had spent the last week prepping a worm based on the famous Trusting Trust hack to carve out a pathway straight into Rayburn's compiler. This way she could build herself an indestructible back door that would reappear every time the security team tried to fix it, guaranteeing access to Rayburn Tech for as long as she needed. After all, it was going to take more than 360 seconds to find the answer to her question: *Who am I?*

Like most momentous events in life, it was over faster than she'd ever imagined.

A few keystrokes and she was in the system; her fingers danced across the keyboard as she directed the coordinated attack. Relishing every second, Mouse could feel her fingers tingling with power. With the click of a button, she launched a DDoS attack from over 12,000 different ghost computers generating nearly a billion simultaneous inquiries of the Rayburn servers, which temporarily crippled the security software.

With server access, it only took one more moment for her to tap into their main operating system.

Her screen reloaded with a loud *ping* and bright blue text appeared, which read the following:

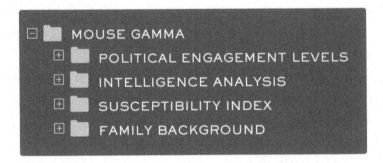

She nervously typed "Mouse Gamma" into the search field and after a few seconds a list of folders appeared, tagged with her name.

My name.

She took a deep breath and clicked "FAMILY BACKGROUND."

It was password protected. Mouse nodded to herself. She wasn't surprised. Password protection was expected. She'd already developed a script that could crunch over 50 million password permutations in seconds. She launched the program and smiled as six letters popped up in the password field.

Botori. Just some made-up word. She hardly had another second to think about it when suddenly her phone buzzed. She jumped with surprise.

No one texted Mouse. Ever.

When she looked at the phone screen, her heart missed a beat. The notification came from a blocked number.

> They're watching. Get out.

Mouse looked at the countdown timer on her screen. She still should have forty-five seconds left. She ignored the text and looked with astonishment at what looked like hundreds of pages of content about her life. She didn't have a chance to begin reading before she saw an urgent pop-up:

> **SUSPICION AFFIRMED.**
> **IMPLEMENT CONCILIUM IMMEDIATELY.**
> **LAUNCH ENDGAME.**

Mouse froze as her phone pinged again. This time the message was shorter.

> GET OUT NOW.

Images of Blackwell popped into her mind and pushed away any hesitation.

Her fingers flew across the keyboard seconds before the timer hit "0," erasing any trace of her intrusion.

She looked back at the text, almost expecting her phone to buzz again.

Whoever that was already knows way too much.

She regarded her phone with a growing sense of distrust. Whoever had just texted her had obviously compromised her hardware. The little

Android phone was her pride and joy. She'd spent every cent of her savings on it just a few weeks before school started. She'd picked out the XiaoMi model on Zambezi, the cheapest e-comm site for pirated tech. She immediately rooted it and added an open-source operating system, LineageOS, to avoid being tracked. It was fast, secure, and perfect for keeping her up to speed when she couldn't be at her computer in the library.

She flipped it over and pulled out the battery with a feeling of regret and resignation. She crushed the screen under her heel as she split the SIM card in half, cursing silently.

That phone had been everything, and now it was gone.

Thirty seconds later, she was standing outside the library doors, heart pounding as the hall filled with her oblivious classmates at the sound of the bell. Mouse took a deep breath, trying to calm her shaking hands as she headed toward first period.

What is "Concilium"? And who could possibly have texted me? How did they find me?

By the end of first period, Mouse had convinced herself it was just a stupid prank. Probably someone she'd built an app for was messing with her. She'd met some pretty weird people on the hacker forums. The timing was probably a coincidence. She felt silly for destroying the phone, but Mouse wasn't about to take a chance. Not with Rayburn Tech on the other side of the table.

She spent the rest of the morning thinking about what else might be in her profile, and counting the minutes till she could use her access to get back in. *Could they know where my parents are? Do they have all my psych evals? Yikes. And none of it gets me any closer to my mom and dad.* She was so absorbed in thought during her final-period history class that she took several seconds to register when the teacher called her name.

"Mouse? . . . Mouse?"

When no response was forthcoming, the teacher sighed irritably.

"MOUSE GAMMA!" he shouted.

Resigned to the fact that she was about to be humiliated for failing to answer whatever silly question he had asked the class, Mouse finally responded. "What?"

"Principal needs to speak with you."

"But I haven't done anything!" she protested.

Her teacher looked as though this was about the least interesting piece of information that he had heard this year, which was impressive given the content of his famously boring classes.

"Mouse, I don't care. Just go, please."

Mouse gathered her books into her backpack, but as she put them inside, she noticed something strange. A book she didn't recognize. Someone must have secretly stuck it into her bag when she wasn't looking.

She pulled it out from between her history and math folders. It was an old worn-out copy of a book called *The True Magicians: Tenets of the Pericles Society*, an unauthorized, unofficial, and officially nonexistent history of America's greatest hacktivists. She quickly tucked it back into her bag before she had a moment to think about who could have put it there, and rushed down the bland, linoleum hallway.

When she stepped into the familiar principal's office, she knew something big had happened. It only took one look from the secretary. It was a look she knew very well. The woman wore that familiar expression of pity and contempt that said, "Kids like you never last long, so it's not much of a surprise, is it?"

She waited outside the principal's door with a knot in her stomach. *Could it have been the hack? Was someone really watching her? No. Impossible.* At the end of the day, it didn't matter what it had been. Maybe some kid had made up a story about Mouse asking to copy their homework. Maybe Mr. Beasley had complained that she'd been drinking soda in the library. Who knows? If Mouse had learned one thing, it was not to trust anyone. You never knew who would betray you, but someone always did. Someone complained, said Mouse was an inconvenience, and that was it. Onto the next home.

Except not this time.

The social worker had made it clear six months ago. Six moves in as many years was too many. Something about "liability" and "legal costs." Pittsfield had been her last stop, one way or the other. Screw up here, and it was back to Blackwell.

Mouse felt like throwing up. Not only was she out of Skittles and Twizzlers, but she could also actually feel that horrible burning taste of disinfectant in the back of her throat.

Blackwell Juvenile Detention Center, or "Blackwell juvie" to anyone who'd spent any time there, was more like a prison than a home. She'd never be allowed online. In all her time at Blackwell, she couldn't remember a single kind conversation. Just silence, endlessly white, antispectic hallways, and locked doors.

A familiar face entered the waiting room.

"Oh, Mouse. I really don't understand why this keeps happening. I thought you'd been well placed this time. Far better than last time with the Frippers," her state-appointed social worker began.

Mouse ground her teeth with frustration.

"I've got my directions. We won't be going back to your foster home. Into the car. I've already packed your bag. Well, box, actually. We've scaled back on the replacement luggage for foster cases. You know, budgets."

As they walked out, Mouse stopped at the vending machine and spent the last of her money on Skittles and Mountain Dew.

She slid into the passenger's seat and muttered, "Next stop Blackwell."

Her state-appointed children's services counselor shook her head. "That's the funny thing. We're not going to Blackwell."

THE TRUE MAGICIANS

TENET TWO

The language of Code is the true magic. Coders are True Magicians. You will not be understood, and your power cannot be shared. When you join with other True Magicians you must take care. Do not mistake this bond for friendship. Defend yourself. Never discuss your meatspace lest your human weaknesses be shared and exploited by other coders.

hat happened?

That question raced over and over in Mouse's mind.

Unfortunately, she knew the answer.

I failed again. Right when it mattered most. Right when my fingertips could almost touch them.

She remembered the first and only other time that she'd come close to discovering the identity of her parents. She had been eight years old.

Her newest foster mother had left Mouse waiting for a therapy appointment at a flat, gray office building in the middle of an absurdly large and mostly empty parking lot. Mouse had made her way to the lobby. Men and women in ill-fitting suits wandered past her without noticing and she realized that there was no one coming to tell her where she should go. She walked over to an empty reception desk and browsed the list of companies in the building until she found the one that looked right:

CHILDREN'S COUNSELING SERVICES

She climbed to the third floor and wandered into the therapist's office. A coffee mug sitting on a flimsy desk said, "Please wait . . . sarcasm still loading" with a progress bar at 75%.

She looked around the office and yelled, "Hello, anyone here? I've got an appointment."

After waiting another minute, Mouse walked past the desk and into a small office. The chair she was supposed to sit in was covered with folders as though she'd walked in during the middle of someone re-organizing their filing cabinet. Suddenly, on an ancient mahogany desk, she saw a large manila file with her name printed in big letters across the top.

MOUSE GAMMA

Without a moment's hesitation, she quickly turned around and locked the door. She realized that she'd need as much time as possible with her personal file and that locks only stopped people *without* a key, so she dragged over a chair and jammed it under the doorknob to prevent anyone from coming in.

Carefully sitting down behind the therapist's desk, she flipped the folder open and let her eyes scan the pages. It was all laid out in black and white. The story of her life through the dozens of therapists who misunderstood her. She flipped from page to page until she finally found one short reference to her parents:

Mother: Unknown

Father: Relinquished custody

Gender: F

Personality: Introvert. Defensive. Periodically violent. Evidence of psychopathy. Has never completed an IQ or personality test she has taken, though partial results imply an advanced capacity for mathematics and language.

Mouse ignored the shouting and banging from the other side of the door. Her brow furrowed with frustration as she read detailed notes about each example of her horrendous misbehavior and social malfeasance. She rolled her eyes at each ridiculous misrepresentation of what had actually happened.

Foster Care: The Fripper Family—Expelled for attempted poisoning

Appleton Home for Wayward Children—Expelled for destruction of property

Foster Care: The Zeng Family—Expelled for violent tendency toward other children

The list went on and on.

Whoever had done the reporting entirely missed the *obvious* fact that she'd never tried to hurt anyone. It was the bullies. The fake moms and fake dads. Mrs. Fripper had told Mouse she was an ungrateful brat, so Mouse added vinegar to her morning tea. Appleton's Home had kept her locked in the basement and the "destruction of property" had been a simple statement of fact written in red paint on the front of the building for everyone to see: "WE HIDE CHILDREN IN OUR BASEMENT." And at the Zengs', Mouse had simply kicked their precious kid in the shin when she found out he'd stolen her one book, a copy of C.S. Lewis's *The Lion, The Witch, and the Wardrobe.*

Couldn't everyone understand she just wanted to be left alone?

Eventually, the door shattered under a steady barrage of axe swings, and the local fire department rushed in. Mouse patiently closed the folder. As they dragged her away, she realized that once again this incident would go on her permanent record as an example of her destructive behavior, as if it was a crime to try to find out who you really are.

It had been years and still Mouse didn't know a single thing more than she'd learned that day.

Mother: Unknown

Father: Relinquished custody

She'd tried every way imaginable to discover who her parents were. The harder she worked at finding them, the further away they seemed, almost as if they were still running from her.

"So where are we going if not Blackwell?" Mouse barked with frustration as they pulled onto a large four-lane highway.

Her state-appointed counselor sighed, "You'll see when we arrive. I don't entirely understand it myself."

As they drove in awkward silence, Mouse suddenly remembered that before she arrived at the principal's office earlier that day, she'd seen an unfamiliar book nestled into the bottom of her backpack. She reached into the back seat of the car and fished it out.

Where did this come from? I mean I had my bag next to me all morning, and it's not from Mr. Beasley's library anyway.

By the time she finished the first page, Mouse couldn't care less where it was from or where they were going. She was hooked and just hoped she'd be able to finish the book before they arrived.

Of course, she'd heard all about the Pericles Society. The forums were filled with rumors, but hardly anything was known about them. Their story was almost beyond belief. Four legendary hackers—Cassandra,

Tiresias, Erebus, and Agamemnon—were the most notorious and powerful hackers of their time. They'd first become famous for sneaking into the White House during a public tour, setting up a fake wireless access point and gaining access to the Senate's servers and doxing every senator and congressperson. A senator and six congresspeople were forced to resign when it was discovered that they'd been leaking confidential information to harm their political rivals. That was just the beginning. After just a few years of the most disruptive and spectacular hacks, they suddenly disappeared as quickly as they'd arrived.

True Magicians was even better than the simple biography of a few legendary hackers. It outlined their philosophy in a series of tenets. Mouse felt as if they were written specifically for her. The Pericles Society were the embodiment of every orphan and bullied kid who decided to fight back—and they'd almost created a religion around how to do it. Mouse knew exactly what they meant by "True Magicians." They used code like magic, but instead of fantasy and make-believe, they had created real magic to fight back against the thugs.

After a silent stop for lunch at some generic fast-food spot that was about as memorable as her social worker's name, they drove for another hour before Mouse finally closed the book with satisfaction. Looking out her window as they whipped by yet another highway rest stop, she suddenly remembered where she was.

"We've been driving in this stupid tin can for nearly two hours and you still haven't told me where I'm going. If it's worse than Blackwell, it must be a real dump."

"We'll get there when we get there," her social worker replied. She continued, muttering to herself under her breath, "It doesn't make any sense. I mean, of all the kids."

An hour later she pulled off the Mass Pike and zig-zagged her way down a narrow side street labeled with a small black sign that read—

RICKUM ACADEMY

Mouse sat up in her seat.

"What's going on? Why are you bringing me here?"

The woman shook her head and turned to Mouse with a look of confusion. "No idea. It's where they told me to drop you. There's a test for children like you. That's all I know."

Moments after the car jerked to a stop, Mouse staggered out into the late afternoon sun. Her companion, a woman she'd known for years but whose name she still couldn't remember, quickly got back into her car with a few brief final words:

"You're to stand in this line and do what they say. Good luck, Mouse. I've never been able to figure out why you can't seem to fit in. I guess it doesn't matter; you're on someone else's watch now."

Mouse watched the car pull away and drive off as she stood alone with an oversized backpack and a box filled with books and knickknacks from her last foster home.

She shuffled over to a long line of students snaking away from the enormous staircase. Impatiently, she shifted the stained brown cardboard box from one arm to the other.

Why am I here? she asked herself, looking up at the enormous building.

Of course, she'd read about the famous school. Its alumni list read like a who's who of the tech elite. Trent Rayburn had been a student here, and reportedly donated millions of dollars to the school each year. On its own, that would have been enough to make Mouse turn her back on the place without another thought . . . but he wasn't the only famous alumnus. Erik Walters had gone to Rickum, too.

Mouse let the feeling of awe wash over her for a moment, imagining the power of the technology just behind the enormous French double doors, before shaking her head and scowling.

Rickum, grades eight to twelve, was the best tech school in the country, and places like that weren't for people like Mouse. The social worker had mentioned a test for "children like you." Mouse knew what that meant. She'd taken dozens of tests built to weed her out and pin labels on her. Another kid who didn't fit in yet again. If she got lucky, maybe this time she'd be sent to some cushy university hospital mental facility where they researched troubled kids, instead of back to Blackwell.

Looking around, Mouse saw other kids her age moving toward the main entrance. She looked from one nervous face to the next. Most of them were flicking anxiously through binders full of notes, flanked by wealthy-looking adults in expensive suits. A redheaded boy who looked about sixteen, wearing a Rickum blazer over a prim, white hoodie, ran by her and raced straight up to a massive silver angel that stood in front of the imposing doors. He brushed by a small group of tourists snapping photos of *The Angel of History*, an iconic sculpture with the famous words of the school's founder Benjamin Paul inscribed in silver:

THE STORM IS PROGRESS.

"Wait up, Wurvil!" yelled another kid, one of three slightly older boys, each of whom was wearing a brand-new pair of bright white, designer sneakers. He leapt into the air and slapped *The Angel of History's* foot, then disappeared through the doors.

Rolling her eyes, Mouse climbed the stairs to the imposing entrance and joined a line of kids waiting to speak with a middle-aged man sitting behind a makeshift desk. He was checking their names on a glowing tablet propped up in front of him, then directing the children to a waiting area full of folding chairs.

When Mouse got to the front of the line, the man did the subtlest of double takes at the sight of her grubby clothing and cardboard box, before clearing his throat.

"Name?"

"Uh, Mouse. Mouse Gamma. I'm here for some kind of test?"

He gave her a look of annoyance, as though she was messing with him. "Yes. The entrance exams. I am obviously aware why you're here." He gestured quickly toward the long line of students that snaked away from the school before typing her name into his tablet. His eyes widened, and then he handed Mouse a form from the pile in front of him. "Of course. Of course. The late addition. Very irregular. Lots of opinions about you. Quite interesting." Then with a new hint of warmth, "Please fill this out and wait for your name to be called."

Entrance exams? Mouse hurried over to the folding chairs and sat down, flipping through the form furiously. She had to read the cover page three times before the words sank in.

RICKUM ACADEMY FIRST-YEAR ENTRANCE EXAMS

PERSONAL INFORMATION FORM

Congratulations on being selected to take Rickum Academy's entrance examination. This form asks you to confirm the details you supplied upon your initial application to the school.

APPLICANT: <u>Mouse Gamma</u>

Mouse laughed out loud. This had to be some kind of mistake, but she wasn't going to complain. It was every aspiring coder's dream. *If I were at Rickum I'd be able to do more than just make a few apps on my cheap phone. No more amateur script kiddies trying to flunk me and hold me back. No more Rayburn Wizards. For once I'd have access to some serious hardware . . .*

She looked around at the other students waiting in line with a renewed interest. Their nervous faces and expensive outfits suddenly made perfect sense. These kids had probably been taking prep classes for this exam since they were in diapers. Mouse found herself staring at a tall blonde girl leaning against the wall, looking weirdly relaxed for someone who was about to take a test that might change her entire life. Instead of flipping through a binder or scrolling on her phone, she was hunched over a small leather notebook. As each new person accepted their application form and took a seat, the blonde girl scribbled another note.

She looked up and caught Mouse's eye, raising a neatly groomed eyebrow in a perplexed look.

"Are you testing to be a student here?" she asked.

Mouse glared back.

Isn't it obvious? I'm not just sitting here for fun.

"I'll give you one guess," Mouse snapped back.

The blonde girl stared at her for a moment, then wrote something in the notebook before returning her hungry gaze to an examination of other students waiting in line.

Rolling her eyes, Mouse looked back down at the application form on her lap. *Actually, your guess is as good as mine, blondie. This form has my name on it, but I have no idea why. Maybe they need to hit some quota and I fit the bill . . . Anyways, who cares? A day spent taking a boring test is better than a day at Blackwell.*

The first page of the form asked for basic personal information. Parents' names, address, contact details. Mouse left the whole thing blank as she always did, scrawling her social worker's cell-phone number in the "Emergency Contact" section. The final page asked for the "Preferred Tuition Payment Schedule." Her heart sank when she saw the price tag.

Oh yeah. Money. As if I could afford a meal in the cafeteria, let alone tuition.

Her stomach churned with disappointment. She considered crumpling up the application and saving everyone the time and effort. Then she noticed a small box at the bottom of the financial application, labelled "N/A, PROVISIONAL STUDENT APPLICANT." It was already checked. She smoothed out the paper and made sure all the other pages were properly filled in.

I don't know what exactly that means, but if it means I don't have to pay . . . I've had bureaucrats and bullies making decisions for me my whole life and for once it's landed me somewhere interesting.

Before she could change her mind, a woman with dark glasses and an enormous bun of white hair poked her head through a door at the back of the room.

"Mouse . . . Mouse Gamma?"

Mouse stood up and walked toward the door, the cardboard box with her belongings tucked under her arm. The woman sniffed in irritation, sticking out her hand and taking Mouse's completed form. "Please leave your . . . personal belongings here. They will be perfectly safe. Room 203!"

After a moment's pause it was clear no further explanation was forthcoming. Mouse eased her box underneath a chair and stepped through the door and followed the woman's gnarled finger pointing down the corridor. She passed rows of lockers and spied a group of professors who were huddled by a narrow hallway and silently spinning their fingers in the air as though using some sort of sign language.

Another professor wearing an odd outfit made entirely of hand-knit wool joined the group. She lisped, "Is it true? I've heard that Gog Magog has begun? Erik Walters . . ." before an older professor elbowed the eccentrically dressed newcomer sharply.

"Professor Whippleton. Be. Quiet. There are *students* to consider. No need to be babbling *out loud*. Certainly not about that!"

The professor nodded with embarrassment and began spinning her fingers, joining their silent conversation.

Mouse continued down the corridor. Luckily, she didn't have to go far. A silver plaque reading **Room 203** glinted from a door on the right. As she was about to turn the handle, the door flew open and a girl about a foot taller than Mouse ran past her with tears streaming down her face.

The girl stopped suddenly, rubbed her eyes, and whispered in a quivering voice, "You're wrong. I was the best math student in my class!"

Mouse looked from the girl to the open door, and back to the girl, who seemed to want some kind of response. Only silence came from what seemed to be an empty room.

A man's high-pitched, nasal voice suddenly barked, "Come in. Her testing is finished."

The girl whipped around, then raced down the hall and out the front doors of the school.

Mouse peeked inside. The room was bare, except for an unusual-looking computer on a table. "It's just a computer. Haven't you seen one before?" sneered the disembodied voice that seemed to come from the ceiling and walls.

She heard the thud of what sounded like a kick or a punch followed by a protest, "How dare you. Why, you're not even a professor, just the libr . . ." Followed with a whelping, "Ouch!"

The screen blinked to life and a green cursor spelled out her instructions, "Welcome to Rickum, M—" The cursor paused, and she heard the voice muttering over the loudspeaker. "M, Mou—I don't understand. Is that her name?"

A kinder, female voice interjected. "Hello, Mouse, we're so pleased to have you at the testing. Now put on the gloves and place the headset over your head to begin."

She glanced at the pair of gloves that were clearly part of a virtual reality kit. The headset sitting next to it was unlike anything Mouse had ever seen. Unlike the standard gaming setups that people on the forums had raved about, this jet-black mask engulfed her entire face.

She smiled when she realized there was no keyboard. *Only the coolest setup for these rich kids, I knew it.* She slid the black gloves on and squeezed her hands, jumping with a start as the gloves pulled tight, hugging her skin. She could see the haptic sensors emanating a dull pulsing glow. As she pulled the mask over her face, she was surprised that it didn't feel claustrophobic. In fact, it was the opposite. It was cool and expansive and felt as if it had been made just for her as it slowly tightened to the contours of her face. She swiveled her head and blinked at the empty sky stretching out before her.

Mouse had read about virtual reality and studied VPL and other programming languages used for VR, but she'd never actually strapped on a headset. She let her head spin back and forth. Pillowy white clouds floated in front of her. She reached out her hands, spreading them wide, and felt the cool of the clouds as the mist flowed from finger to finger.

As soon as she stretched her fingers, the dull outline of a keyboard appeared. *Amazing,* she thought, *root access to the computer's Kernal whenever you need it—a mainline straight into the heart of the operating system where I can control any part of the machine with just a few keystrokes.* A safety line back to reality.

She closed her hands and the keyboard disappeared. Then she bent her neck backward and looked up for the first time. She gasped at the expanse of lofty space stretching endlessly above her.

She smiled as her body began to float.

The gentle female voice lulled toward her through the hazy clouds, "Hello, Mouse. Welcome. Take a moment to get used to this new environment. There are two of us who will be guiding you through a series of questions to see if Rickum Academy might be a good fit for you. Either way, you should be very proud that you're being considered. Now, good luck."

This man interjected impatiently, "Let's begin with a few simple questions. What programming language was developed first, FACT or COBOL?"

"You're kidding, right? Obviously, FACT came first. It basically led to COBOL." It was a question that any junior coder would know in an instant. Mouse nearly laughed at the simplicity.

The nasal voice followed up with a slightly more complicated question about word ladders. Mouse thought for a moment and quickly answered correctly.

"Enough, we're not testing for a local robotics club." The nasally whine of the male questioner sounded very impatient. "This is Rickum Academy. Let me give you something *original* to chew on." There was a long silence before the man's voice asked, "Let's say you were given an obscure code that divides an unsigned integer by the constant value three using only shifts, additions, and . . ."

Mouse interrupted him, " . . . multiplications by the constant values three and five. You want me to finish the rest for you, too?"

"What did you say? How dare you interrupt me."

Mouse had recognized his question from all of her previous reading almost as soon as he'd started asking it. "If you're gonna pretend that's an *original* question, you might steal from something a little more up-to-date than *Code Complete*, third edition, but fine."

She stretched her fingers again and the keyboard came out of nowhere. Her fingers burned with excitement beneath the haptic sensors of the VR gloves as she typed the lines of code.

The voice begrudgingly congratulated her, "I was testing whether you'd recognize where it was from. You are correct. Of course."

The questioning continued for the next twenty minutes, alternating between the two voices asking questions. The challenges got progressively more difficult, but none were beyond Mouse's capability. She'd spent the better part of eighty hours a week for months studying, combing through forums, and reading every book she could get her hands on, and it had paid off. The words flew out of her as easily as code.

After a final question about robotics and the advantages of Fuerte Turtle over Hydro Robotic Operating Systems, she heard squabbling but could just barely make out the words as the two voices argued.

The woman raised her voice: "It's outrageous. She hasn't missed a single question yet, but there's no way she'll be able to solve The Island Paradox. Look at her background! I've had graduating sapients fail this test. It's basically unsolv—"

She was cut off by the stern voice that Mouse could just barely hear. "Enough, this isn't a memory test. You do understand who we're dealing with? She'll find a solution or fail. That's final! We were told it would take a miracle to accept her. Now we'll see if we're witnessing a miracle or not. Begin round two."

The nasal voice spoke up gleefully. "Enough remedial quizzing. Let's see if you've really got what it takes."

Time seemed to stop as a white flash exploded in her head. Mouse felt as if she'd been punched in the stomach as the air fell out from beneath her and she started to fall.

She fell and fell through the clouds. Then, without any warning, Mouse landed with a monstrous clap right in the middle of an island covered in palm trees.

The male voice echoed from the sky. "The rules are quite simple. In fact, there's only one. *Don't die.* You get one hint: There is a caravan filled with food on the Eastern side of the island. Protect it; without food you'll starve."

Mouse looked up and protested, "I thought this was supposed to test code, not stupid video game skills!" Her stomach growled and she suddenly realized it had been hours since she had last eaten anything but candy.

When the voice remained silent, she sighed and looked around. *I must be missing something. There's no way this is really as silly a game as it seems.*

She walked down to the beach. Palm trees stretched right to the water. She couldn't believe how realistic everything looked. It reminded her of the coder Alan Turing's famous test: If you can't tell the difference between a man and a machine, then the machine should be considered alive. As hard as she looked, Mouse couldn't tell that this was all just a simulation. It looked entirely real.

She walked over to a caravan filled with food and pulled open the door of an enormous refrigerator. She breathed in air filled with the smells of exotic cheeses and rich, spicy sausages.

Mouse walked back to the beach and pushed her hands into the sand, savoring the warm grains passing through her fingers. She lay down, looked at the sun, and yelled up into the sky, "Thanks for my first beach vacation!"

She breathed deeply and could smell the salt air. Sniffing the air again, she noticed something else. Something burning. She pushed herself up and saw an orange flicker in the distance.

She ran through groves of palm trees, avoiding the brambles, until she arrived at the other side of the island, where a small fire licked the ground. She kicked at the flame to put it out, jumping back as she felt it singe her skin.

"Ouch," she yelled. "That hurt, you know!"

Mouse's heart started pounding as she noticed that she'd mistakenly kicked some sparks into a pile of dead leaves. They immediately burst into flames. Wisps began billowing, a wavering ribbon of smoke reached into the sky, as the flames crept along the dry ground of the island.

Not so easy to "not die" when there's a stupid fire in the middle of your dumb island. Think, Mouse. This is obviously the test.

She raced to the ocean and looked around fruitlessly for a container, hoping to douse the flames with seawater. Running straight through the thickets of brambles back to the other side of the island, she realized with frustration that not only were there no containers to carry water, but also the caravan with all her food was on a massive bed of dried sticks and leaves and would burst into flames the minute a spark came anywhere near it.

The fire spread rapidly across the other side of the island. Mouse stood there by the caravan of food just staring back and forth. She clenched her eyes shut and forced herself to focus. *This is the school where Erik Walters went. They can't really be asking me to just beat this stupid video game. There must be something else. Is it a logic test?*

She grabbed a branch and ran toward the fire, which was getting so close and hot that the air was difficult to breathe. She had hoped that she might be able to stop the fire by burning away its fuel, but her heart sank as she saw the pile of dry leaves and wood under the caravan begin smoldering. Even if she didn't die in the flames, she'd die of starvation once the fire consumed her only food source.

"This stupid game is rigged. You can't win," she raged at the sky. "You stupid bullies made it impossible for me to survive. If you scumbags are so afraid of me actually winning, why did you bring me here?"

She stood there glaring at the endless sky until she suddenly remembered: It wasn't even the real sky.

Video games are stupid, but the people who build them aren't. I know that better than anyone. It's why I started coding in the first place. And I'm not here to play some game. I'd rather make it than play it.

By now most of the island was engulfed in flames and the caravan of food was slowly beginning to burn. She stepped forward to the only area of the island that the fire hadn't devoured and sat down between the palm trees.

That's it. It's a game with one rule. "Don't die." I won't die if they can't kill me.

She pushed her hands forward and stretched her fingers out. The faint outline of a keyboard appeared as she typed in the air.

She held ESC, Alt, Delete R for fifteen seconds until a dim green cursor began to blink.

Yes! Access to the computer's kernel. Root access to anything I want.

The fire now surrounded her on all sides. It was so hot that she felt as though she was about to burst into flames. She ignored the heat, typing furiously as she scrolled through lines of code—adding commands that would force the operating system to do exactly what she wanted.

A voice suddenly rang out from the sky. "What on earth do you think you're doing? Someone stop her. She can't! She's going to fry the—"

Before he could finish, she clicked "execute."

The words floating in front of her disappeared as they triggered a reaction at the core of the computer's operating system. First the world around her slowed. The fierce heat began to dull and then fade away. Then the trees and the sand dissolved into static as the program froze and shut down.

She took a deep breath and pulled the headset off. She smiled as she saw smoke begin billowing out of the computer.

Shadows moved across the wall, but she couldn't see who it was. She heard the nasally voice stutter, "I, I, I don't understand. You just ended the simulation. You quit?"

The friendlier woman's voice had grown just a bit more severe as she replied, "She didn't end the simulation. She fried the entire console."

"What was I supposed to do?" Mouse asked, reflexively crossing her arms.

"Ha," he interrupted. "Astonishing. Truly astonishing. The worst performance I've ever seen. You see what happens when you let just anyone into a school like Rickum. Obviously, you've fai—"

"Let the child speak," interrupted the woman firmly. "If you dare to push her off a cliff, then allow her to fly."

Mouse ground her teeth in frustration and then barked, "I thought the rules were clear. Just like code. You said, 'There's only one. Don't die.' Well, I didn't. I stayed alive until your stupid game broke."

"But *you* broke it," the man's voice insisted.

She squinted her eyes in anger. "They were your rules. You never said I couldn't break your dumb computer. You said don't die and I didn't. I won."

After a moment's pause, she heard the woman's voice again. Mouse could swear there was a hint of a smile behind it.

"I believe that concludes the testing. Congratulations on becoming the most unlikely student ever to be admitted to Rickum Academy. Proceed to the front office to receive your hardware and room assignment."

THE TRUE MAGICIANS

TENET THREE

What is the difference between man and machine? Machines' wiring lasts longer.

ouse stepped out of the room and paused for a moment, too stunned to do anything but blink as her eyes adjusted to the relative darkness of the corridor. Prickling adrenaline surged through her limbs, making her fingers tingle and her ears ring.

Did I hear that correctly? A student at Rickum Academy? I passed their test, but there must be something else. What happened to "next stop, Blackwell"?

Shaking her head in an attempt to clear it, she noticed that someone had placed her cardboard box packed with used clothes and books, her backpack, and her last package of Skittles next to the door. She jammed it under her arm and started walking as quickly as she could down the hall. Most of the doors had signs on them that read TESTING IN PROGRESS. She heard a loud roar coming from behind one door and noticed rainbow strobe lights flashing behind another.

I guess everybody gets a different test . . . I wonder how they knew enough about me to design mine. I mean, a video game about not having enough food that made me angry? It's like someone gave them a list of my weaknesses.

Mouse pushed through a set of doors that read in huge letters,

RICKUM STUDENTS, FACULTY,
AND STAFF ONLY.
ABSOLUTELY NO TRESPASSING.

On the other side, a crowd of students raced around in preparation for the new school year. Mouse dodged a girl in a black turtleneck whose face was buried in her phone. A boy with shaggy hair and over-sized glasses was distracted by a drone whizzing by and knocked Mouse into the clanging metal robot walking alongside her.

She realized with surprise that it wasn't just students racing from room to room. There were robots everywhere. Some were flapping metal-lic wings and coasting through the air, while others rolled and wheezed alongside the students.

One particularly tall and gangly robot teetered uneasily as it wob-bled along.

"Watch out, watch out, I made a few handmade upgrades to Dubloon over the summer and he's still getting accustomed to the new legs," shouted that same boy with flaming red hair she'd seen racing into Rickum earlier.

"Wurvil Looper, I can't believe they let a clown like you back in," barked a huge boy in a Rickum Football sweater.

"Latch, old man, keep the commentary to the field. And if mem-ory serves, your astonishing bungle in remedial Robotics should have sent you packing. Ah, but I suppose some monied crook bought you a third chance. You know what they say, if you can't swim with the fish, have Daddy write a big check. Might I suggest the Latch Dirke Natural History wing the next time you fail; it's in dire need of a renovation," he said with a wink.

Latch clenched his fist, but before he could take a step forward, Wurvil suddenly squinted, raised his right hand into a claw, and began spinning his fingers. Mouse saw a flash out of the corner of her eyes as what looked like a miniature drone whipped through the air at Latch, twisting him around and knocking him to the ground.

A tall, dark-eyed boy stepped forward and glowered, his fingers spun quietly by his side as he paced near Wurvil.

"Ian, I see we're ready to pick up where we left off. I've been waiting all summer," Wurvil drawled with a smile.

A girl in a gray Rickum dress stepped next to Wurvil. Her velvet hair was chopped into bangs that stopped just above her eyes and swayed back and forth as she weaved her hands. She moved with a fluidity that almost seemed like the rippling of a calm sea as she settled into a similar stance, almost like martial arts, while her fingers were spinning some kind of message into the air.

Ian put his hand down as students began to gather around them, eager to see what the commotion was about. With a bark he growled at his friend, "Latch, you idiot, now is not the time to attack a sapient, particularly one as *charming* as Wurvil Looper." Then he turned toward him, with a mock grin. "No offense, Wurvil, not trying to get the Makers in a fuss on the first day of school. There will be time for that later."

Wurvil bowed with a smile. "Well, Ian, awfully, awfully good to see you. Awfully good indeed. No offense taken. Give our best to the Admin. Oh, and I heard you've got a real Rayburn scion starting this year. Young Eddie. No doubt a top Admin prospect; hiding him from Erik Walters, I suppose?"

Ian glared at Wurvil. "Erik Walters is still 'waiting in orbit' last I heard. More precisely, rotting in prison. Or do you believe the rumors of Gog Magog?"

Wurvil replied with another whimsical laugh, "Gog Magog? Fairy tales."

Before he could finish, Ian had whipped around and disappeared behind a corner, followed by Latch, who jogged after him.

"Oh my," a voice coughed. "You might want to watch where you're going."

Mouse jumped. She'd been so fixated on Wurvil Looper that she didn't see a small boy in a tweed suit standing directly in front of her until she'd nearly trampled him. Not knowing what to say, she just glared.

He stuck his short arm toward her. "Boone. Great to meet you."

She spun away from him, ignoring his hand, and began walking away.

He yelped after her, "What's your name?"

She paused for a moment, then turned around with a furrowed brow and replied, "Mouse. I'm Mouse."

She continued walking till she was out of sight, took a deep breath, and leaned against a large plaque that shared a brief history of Rickum:

Built directly next to the Massachusetts Institute of Technology, Rickum Academy was conceived in the 1920s as a beacon to science and technology by Benjamin Paul. The school itself was built by the famous architect Bruno Teight. Modeled off his famous Leberecht horseshoe estate, the building has been hailed as an architectural wonder through the years. Many of the world's greatest leaders have come through the halls of Rickum and each year the graduating class stands out as the next generation of tech visionaries.

After regaining her composure, she followed a line of students, who seemed as perplexed as she was, toward the reception office.

Inside, students chattered and gossiped in front of a sleek, transparent desk. A woman with a severe steel-gray bowl cut in a jewel-green suit checked each student's name on a tablet before handing them a small white box and a silver tablet with an image of *The Angel of History* statue emblazoned on the back. Mouse recognized a few of the faces from the waiting area, although their looks of nauseous anxiety had been replaced by grins of relief. The blonde girl with the leather notebook was there, and when she reached the head of the line her presence surprised the woman behind the desk for some reason.

"Ada, you best be getting yourself to Diogenes Tower. Look at the line of students I need to process," she said in a thick Scottish burr. "They're all lined up for rigs and rooms! Now out of the way, m'dear."

The blonde girl sighed impatiently. "I'm a *student* now, Professor Bunyan! I just took the admission test." Sheepishly she added, "I passed."

The woman's eyes lit up and her face softened. "Well then, that y'are! I'm sorry, pet. I never had a doubt." She tapped the screen of a tablet and handed it to the girl. "Off to your *new room*, love. Don't forget to come visit us in the staff wing for a game of cards, though, ya hear?"

The professor kept muttering to herself, "Oh, Bunyan, off your noggin. Forgetting about poor Ada on her big day. And after studying with her just last night."

Flushing slightly with embarrassment, the girl grabbed the tablet and turned on her heel. "Thanks, Professor, gotta go!" As Ada rushed out of the office, Mouse noticed her do the smallest of double takes as they made eye contact.

Yeah, I'm as surprised as you are, blondie.

When it was Mouse's turn at the desk, she just glared.

The woman furrowed her brow.

"So?" Mouse barked.

The brow furrowed more.

When Mouse didn't budge, the woman stood up, towering over Mouse. "On to your room, unless you've got enough manners to ask a proper question."

Mouse felt a familiar burning sensation in her chest.

I'm not going to just wander around this stupid school until someone realizes I was a mistake and kicks me out. Then again, I've come this far without getting bounced. She clearly had a soft spot for blondie, maybe she's okay?

"Look, lady. Twenty-four hours ago, I was coaxing a ten-year-old PC into booting up without blue-screening at the worst school in the state. I just fried the nicest VR rig I've ever *heard* of, not to mention the first one I've ever touched. I have fifty cents in my pocket and all my worldly possessions in a torn cardboard box, and you are telling me I have an 'assigned room' at the best tech school in the *entire world*? *Forgive me* for wanting a little bit more *information*!"

Breathing heavily after this outburst, Mouse winced inwardly at the volume of her own voice. *There I go again, screaming at someone I should probably be buttering up with compliments. Oh well* . . . Clenching her jaw defiantly, she braced herself for the woman's angry response.

But instead of picking up the phone to call security, she stared blankly into the middle distance, twitching her fingers rapidly as though typing on an invisible keyboard. Her face softened as her eyes darted back and forth. "Mm . . . last-minute applicant . . . high-risk potential . . . I see . . . Yes, of course. Now who is . . . aha!"

Snapping her gaze back to Mouse, the woman offered an unexpect-edly gentle smile. "It's a wee bit complicated, lass. But luckily, you've been assigned a top-notch roomie who'll sort ye out. We *always* get the roomies right." A slight shadow passed across her face before she continued. "Well, *almost*. Anything she can't answer will be in the tablet under 'NEW STUDENT GUIDE.' Now please, *go to your room.*" This last was deliv-ered firmly but not unkindly, with a gesture toward the door. Suddenly at a loss for words, Mouse turned silently and stepped back into the corridor.

As she held the tablet up, it winked on instantly. *Facial recognition?* Mouse wondered. The screen displayed an augmented-reality interface, with a large green arrow superimposed over the hall in front of her. She experimented by turning to face toward the building entrance, the way she had come. The arrow turned red, and silver letters appeared on the screen.

> ## PLEASE CONTINUE DIRECTLY TO YOUR ROOM.

Mouse followed the arrow through a series of labyrinthine corridors and finally up a stone staircase that spiraled up a needle-like spire before stumbling out into a long narrow hallway with an ancient wooden floor, and peppered with silver tinted doors. She dodged a few other new students moving into their rooms, faces buried in tablets. She slowed down to listen to a group of students in Rickum Academy uniforms raving about a recent upgrade to codehub and what coding languages were most vulnerable to a DDoS hack, instead of chatting about the latest video game like *Team of Exiles*.

At the top of the stairs stood a narrow corridor with a handful of doors, each bearing a number followed by the letter "P." Glancing down at the tablet, Mouse saw that the green arrow had disappeared and been replaced by a message:

> YOU HAVE BEEN ASSIGNED
> ROOM 2P. PLEASE ENTER. AND
> WELCOME HOME.

Looking up, she noticed that the door to 2P was partially open. Feeling a twinge in her stomach that she couldn't quite identify, Mouse stepped through the door.

In contrast to the dark wood of the corridors with its glimmering silver accents, the room was painted a bright, inoffensive cream. A window to her left looked out over a small courtyard. A twin bed and a desk were tucked neatly against each long wall. There was another narrow door opposite the entrance, through which Mouse could see a sliver of bathroom tiles. Even considering she would have a roommate, it was by far the biggest bedroom Mouse had ever had.

The blonde girl with the notebook was sitting at one of the desks, the white box they had both received sitting open in front of her. Looking up at the sound of the door opening, she stood up quickly with a look of excitement that quickly melted into disappointment. "Uh, hi. Sorry, this is room 2P. Are you lost?"

Yeah, my roommate is going to be really helpful. Sure.

"Uh, no. I'm not lost." She waved the tablet pointedly. "Unless this thing is broken already."

The girl made no attempt to hide her shock. "Wait, you're assigned to a *room? This room?*" The leather notebook appeared again, and the girl was flicking through it furiously. "I thought . . . maybe an experiment . . . seeing how the testing worked on younger . . ." She fell silent for a moment, then shook her head as though trying to get rid of something unpleasant.

"No, I don't think your tablet is broken. I think you're my roommate. I'm Ada." She offered a pained smile and stuck out her hand.

Mouse ignored the hand, walked over to the bed with no sheets on it, and sat down.

"Congratulations," she replied sarcastically, adding as an afterthought, "I'm Mouse."

Ada dropped her outstretched hand after realizing Mouse was ignoring it, and came over to sit next to her. Mouse had expertly folded her sweatshirt into a makeshift pillow and was stabbing at the tablet's screen with irritation. "What's the point of this being the best tech school ever if my tablet doesn't connect to the internet? Is there even Wi-Fi in this stupid room? Why are we in this weird tower?"

Ada raised an eyebrow. "The tablet is sort of a backup for new students. You'll usually be using your glove and glass rig, and there's real firepower in the labs. Most kids bring their own hardware anyways. Where are you from? Who sponsored your Provi application?"

Mouse glared at her.

"How'd you know I'm a Provi? Because I don't have those stupid white sneakers everyone's wearing?"

Ada smiled and pointed down to her pristine white Nikes. "Even Provis wear sneakers. Everyone on this floor is provisional. Me too. That's what the P on the door stands for. Are you from around here?"

Mouse shrugged. "Pittsfield, as if that matters. Now how do you get online? I really need to check something out."

"Did you bring any luggage? Want any help bringing it up?" Ada offered.

Mouse ground her teeth. "My stuff's all here," she said and gestured at the cardboard box sitting next to her sweatshirt-pillow. "Seriously, if you don't help me get online, I will walk right out the front door with this tablet until I find some free Wi-Fi and can Google some answers. That English secretary told me my roommate would be able to 'explain everything,' so start talking!"

Ada looked wounded. "First of all, that 'English secretary' is Professor Bunyan, and she's Scottish. She likes to meet each of the new students, so she helps with registration every year, but if you call her a secretary, she'll have you coding with a pencil and paper for the rest of the semester, so watch it. Second, you must know what a Provi is. When you applied you had to write a ton of extra essays. You must have worked super hard on your application."

Mouse continued to stare at her blankly before replying. "Never wrote any essays, and I never submitted an application," she said slowly. "I think I'm probably supposed to be in a mental institution right now, but instead I'm having these stupid conversations over and over again where nobody tells me anything, and I can't. Get. Online!"

"Uh, a mental institution?"

"Kinda. More like juvie. For 'troubled kids.'"

"You don't just *tell* that to people, Mouse. Particularly not to your brand-new roommate who will be sleeping next to you every night. And you didn't even apply here? How did you get in without applying?"

"No idea. Did you apply?"

"My mom's the librarian." Ada groaned. "What's your point?"

"I guess we're both special cases. Where can I get online?"

"Okay, just hold your horses about getting online. This entire school is about coding and tech, so you'll have plenty of time for that." She stood up and opened one of the desk drawers. "Look, I'll answer your questions if you answer mine. Want some candy?"

Mouse paused, then nodded. Ada tossed her a pack of Starbursts and a Snickers bar, which Mouse had halfway finished before Ada had time to sit back down on the bed.

"Fanks," Mouse said through a mouthful of nougat, widening her eyes to convey how genuinely grateful she was. Ada suppressed a giggle, jotting something in the leather notebook again before shutting it firmly.

"You're welcome. You eat, I'll explain. 'Provi' stands for provisional student. Scholarship kids. There aren't a lot of us, because you have to be nominated by an alum, and it's super hard to even get approved to attend the testing, plus you also have to pass and be accepted on your own merit."

Mouse started to say something, but Ada held up a hand.

"Yeah, I know. Neither of us applied through the normal route. My mom is a faculty alum, so I automatically got to take the test. This is where you need to answer some questions. Did you do anything in the past year which might have gotten you noticed by a Rickum alum? Maybe submitted code to a contest, or applied for a coding award or something?"

Mouse laughed bitterly. "No. Rickum alums don't notice people like me. I don't even know anyone—" She stopped abruptly. The last few hours had gone by so fast she hadn't even thought about the hack on Rayburn Tech. "Uh, by 'get myself noticed,' what did you mean exactly?"

"You know, like make an awesome app, or win a hackathon, something like that. Something big. Something public."

Mouse was silent for so long that Ada was about to ask her if she was okay. Finally, she abruptly blurted out, "No. I mean, *not* the kind of thing that gets you sent to a fancy school. No way." Then she muttered, "More likely to get me sent to jail."

"What do you mean?"

Mouse shrugged, feeling a tinge of pride that it had been less than one full day since she'd hacked a secret backdoor access point into the most secure operating system in the world without getting caught. Her stomach turned when she imagined what might happen if the hack was discovered. It would certainly mean the end of her time at Rickum, and probably be front-page news on every hacker forum.

"Let's just say if you haven't read about any major software breaches, then that's a good thing."

Ada stared at Mouse for another minute, then inhaled sharply.

"Wait. I had no idea they still did this at Rickum. I thought after what happened with Walters, they ended the program . . ."

"Walters? You mean like Erik Walters?" Mouse was suddenly interested. "What does he have to do with this?"

"Probably nothing," Ada continued. "But if that black-hat attitude isn't just talk, you might be something *way* more interesting."

Mouse rolled her eyes. "Great, I love being *interesting*." Her voice was bitter.

"Sorry. I didn't mean it that way." Ada stared at Mouse for a moment, closed her eyes, and whispered to herself while tapping her head, "Who is it? Who, who, who? Who does she remind me of?" She flipped through a few pages in that leather notebook again.

Mouse blurted out, "Okay, stop. What was that all about? The notebook, the muttering, what just happened?"

Ada started, exclaiming, "Got it! Wurvil Looper."

Mouse glared. "Who's that?"

Ada smiled as she picked up the white box on her desk. "I just realized you reminded me of someone. A boy named Wurvil Looper. That was all I needed. Now, let's get started." After opening the box, she pulled out a glittering piece of semi-transparent fabric and a pair of glasses with clear plastic rims.

Mouse opened her own box and pulled out an identical piece of slippery, glittering fabric. Upon closer inspection she could see it was a glove, made out of what looked like plastic wrap with silver threads running through it. "Is this . . . what I think it is? I mean I've read about them, but I thought they were in Alpha testing still?"

Ada grinned. "The Glove and the Glass. Welcome to Rickum. If you're reading about rumors of some new kind of tech, we've probably been using it in class for five years. Put them on!"

Mouse slid the glove onto her right hand, and it immediately shrank to fit like the bulkier black glove had during the testing. The glasses fit perfectly too. When she turned to look at Ada, a dialogue box appeared in the air next to the other girl's face.

SEND MESSAGE?

Mouse raised her gloved hand gingerly and pointed at the text. She felt the tap of haptic feedback in her index finger and the box was replaced by a blinking cursor. She looked down and saw that a glowing green keyboard seemed to be hovering in front of her chest.

Mouse whipped off the glasses and studied them intently. "That is *crazy*. I mean, what programming language are they using? Is the connection secure?"

Ada was still grinning. "Totally secure. It's built on OM, which stands for Objective-M. It was developed by a first-year about twenty-five years ago. OM's one thing you won't see anywhere but Rickum. It's a special language that can't be hacked."

Mouse raised her eyebrows and laughed, "Nothing's unhackable."

Ada continued, "Well nobody's cracked OM."

"Yet," Mouse corrected. "And what about getting online?" she added with exasperation.

"You're going to have to go to a lab for that tonight. The Glove and the Glass, your GG rig, is intranet-only until the school year begins tomorrow. Internal messaging has built-in end-to-end encryption, though, so if you ever *do* want to tell me about that secret hack you're so self-conscious about . . ."

Mouse rolled her eyes, but the bitter edge was gone from her voice. "Sorry, blondie, I don't know what you're talking about."

"Okay, have it your way for now. Now try drawing a circle with three fingers."

Mouse did, and a map of the school popped up. She followed Ada out the door and watched a green dot in one corner of the map exit "DRM RM 2P" and enter the hallway. A message from Ada appeared in the upper left-hand corner of her vision.

> Shh not meant to be out right now. Messaging is quieter than talking. Our best bet is the Fab Lab. The Underclassman's Lab is a long walk, school clubs like the Makers, Quants, and Admin jam most of the other labs so you can never really tell what's going on in those. Secret work. Interschool competitions. And even some top-secret government stuff.

Mouse followed Ada down a long, silver-lined corridor while typing on a keyboard, which appeared before her gloved hand as soon as she pointed at Ada's message.

> What's with all the silver everywhere?

> It's the most conductive metal. The school is one giant Faraday cage. The continuous silver not only blocks external electromagnetic fields, but also amps the speed and connectivity. This place is built for power. Everything from the location of the servers to the silver everywhere is here to give Rickum's coders an advantage, particularly when they're doing national security projects.

Mouse scowled as she replied.

> What does that mean? National security projects. Is this some kind of tech incubator for the army?

> You decide for yourself. Rickum's got war-crazy kooks and vegan pacifists. It's just a normal prep school when it comes to students' beliefs, but with insane hardware. Rickum literally has the most powerful tech in the entire world.

I could really fight back with the Rickum servers behind me, Mouse thought. *I'd make them think twice before they moved me to another home*, *or back to some antiseptic place for delinquents. Nothing stops a thug like a punch in the face. This stuff would really pack a wallop.*

Ada opened the door to the computer lab. It took Mouse a second to take it all in. The Fab Lab absolutely brimmed with robotics tools and equipment to fabricate the wildest creations of a student's imagination. Mouse's eyes widened as she browsed row after row of incredible supercomputers that lined the room. She stared in disbelief. There was more computing power in a twenty-foot radius than she'd seen in her entire life.

Ada walked over to the nearest computer and punched in a few characters, then sent Mouse another message.

> I signed you in on a guest account. Technically, you're supposed to be in your room—but I don't think it's likely anyone's snooping around on the first day of school. Can you make it back OK once you're done?

She looked over at Mouse, who nodded.

By the time Ada turned around to leave, Mouse's fingers were already flying across the keyboard. She had to get back into those Rayburn servers to see the rest of her personal file. There were pages and pages of information. There had to be some kind of clue about who her parents were and how she could find them. Something more than:

> SUSPICION AFFIRMED.
> IMPLEMENT CONCILIUM IMMEDIATELY.
> LAUNCH ENDGAME.

After first spending nearly an hour scouring every message board to make sure there wasn't any mention of a hack on Rayburn Tech, she made the decision to try again.

I left "come and go" access to that back door in Rayburn Tech so I could get back in. Now that I know exactly what I'm looking for, I can get in and get out before anyone notices.

It only took a moment before she heard that familiar *ping* and saw the same bright blue text. She was in the server again. Her hands flew across the keyboard as she navigated straight to her personal file.

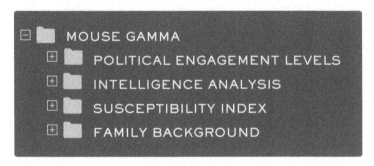

She clicked on "FAMILY BACKGROUND," desperate to see what Rayburn had uncovered about her parents. The security protection popped up and she typed back in the password:

The field blinked twice.

She shook her head in disbelief.

Maybe I just misspelled it.

She typed BOTORI back into the field just in case. Again rejected. Her stomach churned. Someone must have discovered that she'd been in the system and had changed the password. Someone knew about what she'd done, probably the creep who'd texted her, and most likely they were watching. She didn't have time to try her password-cracking program again. Anyway, an entry-level security goon would have checked the logs and added layers of security making that program obsolete. Her hack was ruined. Any chance of getting back into those servers was now hopeless. She frantically closed the browser and erased her browsing history just as she felt a hand clamp down on her shoulder.

Mouse leapt out of her chair with surprise and gazed up at a tall girl who had been standing behind her for who knew how long. She was older, maybe sixteen or seventeen, and Mouse recognized her as the same girl who'd backed up Wurvil Looper earlier in the day. She wore an oversized black turtleneck over black leggings and looked annoyed.

"What do you think you're doing?"

Mouse could hear her heart pounding in her ears.

Ada said we're not supposed to be here. I'm going to get kicked out my first night . . . and for once I actually care.

She opened her mouth, but nothing came out.

The older girl's face softened slightly. "Lemme guess. Provi, so no data on your phone. Maybe no phone. Wanted to tell Mom and Dad about the testing?"

Mouse nodded quickly.

"Look, uh, Mouse." The girl blinked oddly as she frowned and spun her fingers through the air. "I'm Anna Briem. Resident Advisor for the Provi dorm."

"How do you know my name?" Mouse asked, then immediately regretted it.

She smiled and gently replied, "I know it's a lot to get used to. If you're wearing your GG rig, people can see who you are. Now I could send you straight to the headmaster, but I know what it's like to be homesick. This place is amazing, but it can also seem like some freaked-out fantasyland. I'm going to just put a warning for a curfew violation and walk you back to your room, and we'll pretend I never saw you in the lab, okay?"

Mouse could feel the adrenaline draining from her limbs. "Yeah, okay. Um, thanks."

"Don't mention it," said Anna, shaking her head. "I mean it. Do not *ever* mention it." She winked. "Now let's go."

Back at the room, Mouse pushed the door open as quietly as she could. Ada was already snoring lightly. Mouse tiptoed over to her side of the room, where she noticed an unfamiliar bundle sitting on the bed. It was a pile of neatly folded sheets, a gray skirt, and a blazer with the Rickum insignia embroidered on the front pocket. A sticky note on top of the sheets displayed Ada's neat cursive handwriting, as carefully groomed as her shiny blonde hair and perfect eyebrows.

There's some pizza on your desk if you're hungry. Sorry, it's just cheese, I don't know what you like yet :) Get some sleep, I'll be waking you up early tomorrow, roomie!

Xo Ada

Mouse shuffled through her bag and pulled out the old, worn-out copy of *The True Magicians*. She couldn't understand how it had gotten into her bag. Could she have put it there herself and just couldn't remember after the frantic morning? Could Mr. Beasley have snuck it into her bag as a nice gesture?

It didn't really matter that she'd already read it cover to cover earlier that day. It was nice to have Cassandra, Tiresias, Erebus, and Agamemnon keep her company as she waited restlessly for her first day at Rickum Academy.

TENET FOUR

Code, like magic, is far more powerful than the coder can even imagine. Code is the butterfly in the field. It is the wind brushing against a tree; it is action, and like every action its impact will be felt far beyond what the coder might anticipate. In time the butterfly's flapping wing changes the course of history. It shifts the direction of the wind brushing against a tree, and the maple tree's seed is caught in the gust. The small seed flies through the air into the beak of a bird, who carries it to a village. There it grows into a tree where a small boy's parents hang a swing. It is on the swing, flying through the air that a boy, who will someday lead a great nation, realizes that all things are connected. The difference between the coder and the butterfly is that the butterfly does not believe it is in control. Wield your power wisely lest you destroy what you seek to build.

Mouse woke up at six the next morning with the book lying next to her head where it had dropped when she finally fell asleep. Sitting cross-legged on her bed, she picked up her GG rig and slipped it on. A series of green icons appeared to be floating a foot or so in front of her.

She pointed to the one that looked like a calendar, and a schedule appeared. This morning she had "Provi Breakfast Duty" first, then something called "Coding Fundamentals" followed by "Digital Transformation."

She swiped the schedule closed and opened the browser, which was now online, just like Ada had said. *Probably proprietary. Coded in OM, whatever that is.* In a few seconds she was back on her favorite forums, heart racing, wondering if anyone had discovered her hack into Rayburn Tech. She scrolled through the headlines with relief.

Nothing.

Anyway, there was *much* bigger news.

The rumors she'd overheard the professors discussing were true. Erik Walters had broken free from a maximum security prison and it was all anyone was talking about.

The legendary black-hat hacker had apparently cut a video loop into the security system at the prison where he was being held for cybercrimes against Rayburn Tech. Nobody had even noticed he was gone for more than twenty-four hours. The hacking community was so mesmerized by the mythology of Erik Walters that there were entire forums devoted to the theory that he'd never even been in prison at all.

Rayburn must be freaking out, and I'm the idiot who chose the worst possible day to hack into his systems. Now they'll have fully revamped their systems and I'll never get in. Back to square one.

She suddenly recalled whispers she'd heard the day before. With curiosity she searched "Walters and Gog Magog."

It took a minute to find deep in a forum filled with outlandish conspiracy theories:

 The Prophet

> Now that Eric Walters has escaped, it's time for him to finish the greatest hack of all time. Gog Magog is coming. Not since Noah's Ark will such destruction rain down upon us all. The power of technology is a privilege that we have abused. What has been given can be taken away. First the planes will fall from the sky. Then the ships will sink in the sea. Then the power will die. At last, the missiles will fly and Gog Magog will have cleansed technology from the earth. Then we will begin again. Remember Tenet One of the True Magicians, "The good gods must destroy that which threatens order."

Mouse shuddered and saw with astonishment that the message had been shared more than 200 times since it had been posted just a few hours earlier.

Suddenly an alert pinged in the corner of her vision. PROVI BREAKFAST DUTY—30-MINUTE WARNING.

Whipping off her GG rig, she saw Ada step out of the bathroom, neatly coiffed and perfumed as usual. "Mouse! Get your uniform on; if we're late the first day we'll be stuck on trash duty all semester."

As they pushed open the doors of the cafeteria, robots whizzed around the hall, flying, walking, and crawling in stunning displays of DIY craftsmanship. A fleet of drones spun in circles spelling "WELCOME BACK" in colored smoke beneath the high, arched ceiling.

Two serious-looking robots with the names Anculus and Famulus emblazoned on their loose-fitting Rickum blazers stood proudly at the entrance, checking attendance as students eagerly raced into the enormous hall.

Students Mouse assumed were fellow Provis raced from table to table, serving their fellow hungry students. They teetered under huge silver trays of oatmeal, cereal, and goopy mugs of what looked like hot chocolate. Others held trays of pastries and Pop Tarts, and still others had piles of poached, scrambled, and sunny-side-up eggs alongside mounds of fresh bacon.

A sharp voice rang out from across the cavernous room, "Ada, get over here!"

"Wurvil! I was just wondering when we'd run into you. I thought you might be in detention already."

"Me? I'm keeping myself busy with legitimate creative pursuits." Wurvil feigned offense under his mop of wavy red hair. He towered over Ada in a Rickum blazer, while his wiry arms zig-zagged through the air in wild gesticulation. "No more of that black-hat stuff for me. Look!" He unfurled his hand as a small multicolored butterfly began flapping its wings. He spun his fingers slowly and the butterfly swooped out of his hands toward the floor.

"She's still got a couple bugs, *pun intended,* but they should be fixed tomorrow. Anna Briem and I are going to spend tonight in the Fab Lab working out the last hiccups. She's your RA, isn't she?"

Ada nodded, clearly distracted by the butterfly.

Anna. That's the girl who let me off the hook last night, thought Mouse. She considered saying something, then remembered the look on the older girl's face when she said, "Do not *ever* mention it."

Wurvil grabbed the butterfly and threw it into the air, and right as it was about to smash into the floor, its little wings whipped out. Ada gasped. Then with a few flaps, it flew up to her face and perched on her nose.

Wurvil laughed. "She seems like such a cute, little sweetie, but guess what?"

The two girls just stared as his fingers started spinning faster. The little machine's wings fluttered as it circled around Ada's head. Suddenly, he yelled over his shoulder: "Launch 'em!"

Four marshmallows suddenly catapulted through the air as the butterfly flapped toward them. It blasted a stream of fire at each in quick succession. The four perfectly toasted marshmallows dropped harmlessly onto a plate next to Wurvil.

"Ta-da! It works. 'Preying Mantis' only does marshmallows for now, but with just a few tweaks we can toast anything."

"That fire was a bit too close for comfort. Let's not get you suspended before the year's even begun," Ada said as she pulled at a tuft of burnt hair. "And let's not singe my tips on the first day of school; is that really too much to ask?"

Mouse narrowed her eyes and muttered, "Pretty cool. What language did you code it in? Arduino?"

Wurvil's eyes lit up. "Well, we used the AVR chip, but chucked Arduino. Look how small she is!"

Mouse nodded without smiling. "Makes sense, but you're still stuck programming in C, right? I mean, kind of ancient."

He looked at Ada. "Well, well. Your friend knows her stuff. We sure are. Still, it's way faster than it would have been if we'd chucked the programming language."

Mouse's eyes narrowed as she thought about what she'd just seen. "Lots of configuration. I don't understand how you controlled it. Is it tracking your hand movements with a camera? I don't see a GG rig."

He smiled at Ada again. "Ah, to be young and foolish."

Turning to Mouse, he explained, "I don't *wear* my GG rig. I'm a sapient. Each year, a handful of the top students are nominated to be sapients. In addition to off-site privileges, some special tech, and access to a secure lab, we also get direct Glove and Glass implants in our eyes and fingers. Special tech for a special guy." He winked. "It works the same as what you'll be using. Just fewer hardware glitches and a faster response time."

Ada interrupted, "Well, and also a little more responsibility. Sapients are literally plugged into the network and if there's any kind of power surge it can be really dangerous." She scowled affectionately. "So Wurvil is going to be extremely careful, right?"

He nodded back at Ada while playfully crossing his fingers. "All on the up and up this year. I assure you."

Mouse did her best not to look visibly awed and added, "Whatever. Who's taking the marshmallows?"

Ada blushed with embarrassment as Mouse shoved the toasted marshmallow into her mouth and quickly jumped in: "Thanks, Wurvil. The drone's gorgeous."

Ada grabbed Mouse's arm and pulled her toward the kitchen. "What is up with you and candy? I have no idea what that butterfly thing was using to burn the marshmallows. You could be eating napalm."

Mouse shrugged. "I don't know. I was just hungry."

Ada spread her arms out at the piles of food being served around them before continuing, "Anyway, that was Wurvil Looper. He's always getting suspended for breaking little rules with his robots, but he's a sapient, so he's powerful, and a *very* good friend to have."

Mouse shrugged. The kid with the flying toy seemed nice, but she was getting a little tired of not knowing what was going to happen every thirty seconds. "His bug was cool."

As they were about to enter the kitchen, Mouse noticed the same kid who she'd nearly run over. Below his blond crew cut his expressive blue eyes bounced up and down as he typed into his phone with a worried face.

Despite herself Mouse muttered, "Hey, Boone."

His face shot up with a startled look and he slapped a hand against his face, shaking his head with a tired sigh as though trying to communicate the weight of some personal disappointment.

Mouse was already past him, but Ada came up beside them and asked, "Hey, what's wrong?"

"Pull yourself together, Boone!" he whispered to himself.

He wiped his nose and looked up at Ada. "I'm sorry, I just haven't been away from home a lot before this. It's a bit of an adjustment."

Mouse rolled her eyes.

Ada smiled. "Listen, we're first-years, too. I'm Ada, and this is Mouse."

"Oh, I know Mouse already. She was my first friend." His eyes lit up as he looked over at Mouse and waved.

"My dad went to Rickum, and he really wants me to try to join one of the clubs. The Admin. I'm just not sure it's for me. Are you both going to try out for any?"

Ada shrugged. "Provis usually don't join clubs because of our work schedule."

Boone nodded. "Too bad. I think I'll try out for the Makers instead of Admin, but I'm not sure how he'll take the news."

Irritated, Mouse spun back around and asked, "So what are these clubs that Provis aren't welcome in?"

"It's pretty simple. There are three main clubs, each with their own focus. The Makers, the Admin, and the Quants. The Makers build robots. The Quants are hardcore coders. The Admin are all about struc-ture and how tech can transform the world."

Boone jumped in, "Yeah, the three pillars of great tech, and Rickum teaches us that each skill needs to work in perfect harmony with the others."

Ada squelched a laugh. "Sounds nice, but between the clubs it's not so much about harmony, but fierce competition. From the moment you join, your life will revolve around the club's mission and culture. From where your dorm room is, to which labs you work at, to your circle of friends. Clubs rule Rickum."

Boone's phone buzzed in his pocket. He took one look at the caller's name: Dad. His face crumpled and he sighed. "Gotta go. See you later."

Less than five minutes later, Mouse was stepping through two swinging doors, carrying an enormous tray of food and looking out at an undulating sea of ravenous students. She still couldn't believe how much her life had changed in the last forty-eight hours. Even as she struggled, moving from table to table with armfuls of plates, she felt amazed and relieved that she'd somehow avoided Blackwell, at least for now.

Just don't get kicked out your first semester, she reminded herself. *After that, you can start to think about the future.*

Mouse's size didn't exactly help as she lugged platters of eggs, oat-meal, hot cocoa, and cereal from table to table of students. Wurvil Looper waved Mouse over to grab his third serving of cheesy scrambled eggs. She ducked to avoid a girl with pink-and-green pigtails who was shouting about the practical advantages of shearing a drone's wings with an abrasive particle jet over a mechanical reamer.

Wurvil leaned over as Mouse dropped off yet another platter of pan-cakes. "Saw you talking to Boone. I wonder how his dad's dealing with the news about Walters's escape."

Mouse responded with a quizzical look, "What's Erik Walters got to do with Boone's dad?"

Wurvil nearly choked on a piece of bacon as the entire table burst into laughter right as Boone happened to walk back to the table.

"Mouse here's got a good question for you, Eddie. Why exactly is your old man so afraid of Walters anyway?"

Boone blushed a deep, purplish shade of red. "It's *Boone*, not Eddie," he whispered. "I go by my middle name."

Without saying a word, Mouse grabbed Wurvil's dirty plate and marched back to the kitchen where Ada was drying dishes.

"Guess we know who the Rayburn kid is. *Boone*. What a jerk!" she fumed to Ada.

Ada lit up with an enormous smile. "Boone is Eddie Rayburn? I was wondering when we'd meet Trent Rayburn's son. I just knew Boone was going to be somebody important. That's amazing news!"

Mouse couldn't figure out why she wasn't just as furious.

"What's amazing about it? Why would I want to be friends with *Trent Rayburn's* son? And he wouldn't even admit who his dad was. Trying to trick us into thinking he's just some normal kid."

Ada shrugged. "I think he's just embarrassed because his dad's so famous. He seemed nice. Besides, I've lied about my parents before. Sometimes it's embarrassing to be the librarian's kid."

Mouse was drying a mug so furiously that it slipped out of her hands and crashed to the floor, making both girls jump. The cook shot them a warning look.

"That's a stupid comparison," Mouse shot back, "unless she's a librarian who founded Google. I never even knew my parents. I don't get how people could *ever* lie about that."

Ada looked as though she was going to say something, then thought better of it. Mouse was shaking.

Rayburns aren't friends, they're targets. They're the ones who created the system that stuck me in foster homes my whole life. The powerful. The elite. The same ones who are keeping me from figuring out who my parents are. Erik Walters has the right idea: "Watch a mouse fight back." Hit them back until they either crumple or take you out. Stupid of me to think that Ada might be someone who would get it.

They finished the rest of the shift in silence.

Wendell Chilton, scion of the Fort Worth Chiltons, one of America's great petro-chemical dynasties, stepped outside to get a breath of fresh air. The other third-year Quants were enjoying their first Rickum breakfast. Bowls of oatmeal, goopy cups of Soylent, and piles of eggs and bacon. They'd eat like kings during their first breakfast after a long summer.

It wasn't as exciting for Wendell. He ate like a king every day when he was back home in Texas. He ate like a king and he hated every minute of it.

Looking out at the silver statue, he sighed with relief. He was away from the silence and the cold stares that were his only companions in his parents' house. With no one else around, he'd tried to befriend the servants. They were polite to him, but he was smart enough to see their anger beneath the smiles. He didn't blame them—if his parents were cold and dismissive of Wendell, they were downright cruel to everyone else.

Rickum was the opposite. Every minute was full of collaboration, friendship, and competition. It was a place where he could fail, but at least it would be *his* failure. The other side of failure is success. At Rickum it belonged to him either way. He was a real person at Rickum with real friends who hardly noticed his last name.

He was about to head back inside when his phone rang.

Weird, he thought as the name came up "Unknown." His OM app should have been able to decode wherever the call was coming from. It was probably one of his friends holding him a seat and wondering where he was.

"Hey," he replied eagerly.

"Good morning, Wendell," an unfamiliar voice said.

The slow and garbled whisper didn't sound human. Wendell guessed it was a voice distorter, which meant the person on the other end could be anyone at all.

"Who is this?" he replied. "How did you get my number?"

"Who I am doesn't matter. What matters is what you're going to do."

Wendell's heart started beating faster.

"You like being a student at Rickum, don't you, Wendell? You wouldn't want to go back to that big, empty home in Fort Worth."

"What? I mean, sure. What are you talking about?"

"Do you remember a certain test you took four years ago?"

Wendell recoiled from the phone. His breath caught as his heart crashed into his stomach.

"*Who are you?*"

"You don't need to know who I am. Just like no one else needs to know that when your parents forgot to take you to the Rickum Entrance Exams, you took matters into your own hands. You weren't going to miss the chance to get away from that house just because *they* couldn't be bothered to bring you."

"Stop it. Stop it! I don't know what you're talking about."

"You don't remember urgently making a call to a friend who was also applying to Rickum? His family cared. They cared so much that they never would have allowed him to miss that test. You promised him money. More money than his family would make in a year if he would just change the name on the top of his test to Wendell Chilton."

"I didn't. I mean, it wasn't my fault."

"Did you pay him, Wendell?"

"Of course. Of course, I paid him. I'd do anything for him."

"Well, there's not much that can be done. Things went downhill for him after that. He stayed in Fort Worth and you went to Rickum. He's not at the best school in the world. In fact, he's hardly even attending school anymore, and the money you gave him has been spent."

"What do you want? What can I do?"

"You're aware of a certain processor being worked on in the Fab Lab?"

"Uh, uh, of course. It's public knowledge."

"Yes, but you've been working on something far more powerful on your own, haven't you?"

"I, I, I don't know what you're talking about."

There was silence on the other line.

Wendell cracked. "It's nearly 16Ghz, way beyond the fastest processor anyone has ever seen."

After a long pause the voice returned, "Good, Wendell. You see, I need that."

Eight minutes later Wendell Chilton silently sat down at a table of Makers. A heated debate about the merits of programming in C++ vs. C# raged. A feast of ham, steaks, casseroles, cakes, and pastries passed around him.

Wendell heard nothing. He tasted nothing. He was alone. Again.

ouse opened up the school map and checked the labs. She and Ada had first period with Professor Bunyan in the Fab Lab.

On their walk to class, Mouse was struck by the hundreds of unique, glinting silver panels that lined the walls of the main hallways. Ada broke the silence that had been hanging between them for half an hour, explaining that every student made a panel in their final year that would decorate a small square of wall at Rickum forever. Mouse passed the names of great coders she recognized: "John Mapletoft, Class of 1963" and "Hexie Minzhu, Class of 1988."

Of course, Mouse's real heroes, people like the Pericles Society, weren't going to have a commemorative plaque on some high school wall. Still, she had to appreciate how impressive Rickum's alumni were. Almost as impressive as the famous names were the design of actual panels. Some included discreet LED lighting and projectors. Many were mechanical automatons. One in particular caught Mouse's eye. A silver grim reaper holding a long silver scythe stood on a pile of bones and leaned against a tall, rickety-looking sign with the Rickum slogan. Beneath the slogan was spelled out in blood-red garnet the school's motto that was written on *The Angel of History*: "The Storm Is Progress."

As Mouse leaned forward and stared at the intricate silver work wound through the panel, the grim reaper jumped to life and swung the scythe toward her, stopping just as the tip nicked her nose.

The automaton leaned back and cackled, screaming, "Freedom, freedom, freedom!"

Ada laughed at Mouse's stunned face. "So, so creepy, right? It makes me jump every time. There's tons of surprises hidden in these."

Mouse glanced at the name below the panel: Erik Walters.

"Hey, that's not *the* Erik Walters, is it?" Mouse asked.

"Yeah," Ada said and nodded. "Crazy, right? My mom was in the same year as him and Rayburn. Apparently, the biggest cyber-feud of the last decade, Walters versus Rayburn Tech, really started with some dumb fight from school that got out of hand."

Mouse raised her eyebrows. "I bet everyone here thinks he's some kind of psycho supervillain. I'm surprised his panel is still up. I mean, with Rayburn on the board and all that . . ."

Ada shot her a serious look. "Careful, Mouse. Walters is really dangerous. My mom was talking about him yesterday on the phone, something about Gog Magog, and him escaping from wherever they had him locked up. I've never heard her sound so upset."

Mouse opened her mouth to reply, then shut it again.

The lights were off in the Fab Lab when they arrived, but the door was slightly ajar. Mouse checked her map again. "It says 'offline unit.' That means nobody's there, right? Someone probably left the door open last night."

Ada furrowed her brow. "I've never seen that before. Maybe Bunyan is setting up equipment for class?"

The two girls stepped into the darkened lab. The Fab Lab alternated high-powered consoles with wide, sturdy desks featuring blowtorches, grafters, breadboards, soldering irons, strippers, replicator nozzles, oscilloscopes, multimeters, jumpers, and every other robotics tool imaginable. Everything you needed to build something like Wurvil's fire-breathing butterfly, then code it to life. Mouse hurried toward the back of the classroom, pulling up short when she got to the last row of desks. She let out an involuntary gasp.

Lying sprawled across one of the desks was a girl in a long black turtleneck with jet-black hair splayed out in the same direction she fell. She was positioned awkwardly, as though she had passed out suddenly while sitting at the keyboard.

It was Anna Briem, the RA who Mouse had run into on her first night.

"Ada, I think she's dead." Mouse could hear her heart pounding in her ears.

Ada had already grabbed the girl's wrist to check her pulse. Mouse noticed that each of her fingers had a small, black singe mark at the tip, as though she had picked up something hot with her bare hand. "No, she's not dead. But she's barely breathing. We have to get Professor Bunyan!"

Moments later, Nurse Wilkies raced into Fab Lab with a stretcher. She was soon followed by Headmaster Garrick and Professor Bunyan, who ran toward Anna Briem. Mouse and Ada found themselves pushed outside with a growing crowd of students waiting by the lab's door.

"Is she dead?" Mouse heard one kid ask as a team of paramedics raced by.

"I think she electrocuted herself," someone replied.

"I bet it was stress; I heard she was being recruited for some secret program—"

"You're all wrong. It's already trending. Gog Magog has begun."

Ada rolled her eyes and turned to Mouse. "Typical Rickum gossip. No way Anna Briem was involved with a secret government program or some doomsday plot hatched by Erik Walters. More likely that one of Wurvil's crazy projects went haywire! Anna and Wurvil are inseparable. They've been best friends since they started at Rickum." She looked worried. "I hope he hasn't finally done something stupid and gotten Anna hurt . . ."

Just then, the door to the lab opened. "Enough, Professor. You've already made yourself clear. I've just spoken to the school's board of trustees and there's simply no way that we'll consider it," said a tall man in a crisply ironed suit. Even though he was barely middle-aged, his broad brow was furrowed with wrinkles.

Bunyan replied with a visible disdain that clashed with her sing-song accent, "You should be thinking of your students, not a bunch of know-nothing alumni who haven't been to Rickum since their last fundraising gala—" She was interrupted by a small metallic robot in the crook of her arm, who let out a low growl.

"Now, Ripper, is that any way to treat our *respected* Headmaster?" Bunyan said to the harmless-looking machine. The three-legged terrier's head swiveled back and forth with a happy whimper as she scratched its metallic ears.

Looking at the headmaster, she continued, "You've made your point, Garrick, and I believe I've made mine. The only difference is that my point is based on science and *not* the whim of a school board afraid of bad press."

As Garrick left, Bunyan turned to the students and addressed them in her thick Scottish accent.

"Students, we've had a serious accident in the Fab Lab this morning—and unfortunately our class will have to be moved to Room Q26. We'll be starting in ten minutes!"

The chattering students milled down the hallway and into the classroom, buzzing with gossip.

Ada and Mouse sat next to each other near the back of the class. Boone raced in at the last minute and slid into the open desk next to Ada. Mouse shot him an irritated look, which he didn't seem to notice.

"What the heck?" he whispered, leaning toward Ada. "I just heard they found a dead kid?"

Ada shook her head. "Not dead! She just passed out."

Boone's eyes widened, and his already-pink cheeks flushed further. He turned to Mouse and asked breathlessly, "And *you* found her?"

Mouse pretended to be intensely interested in a fraying thread on her blazer, ignoring the question.

Bunyan rapped her knuckles sharply on the desk at the front of the room, where the metal dog was curled up on a small sheepskin blanket.

"Attention, class! This has been a most unusual morning. I know you all have many questions about poor Anna." She sniffed and shook her head. "Oh, I'm not supposed to talk about it. But it is a matter of your safety. If you don't know, then how can you precious young leaders protect yourselves? Now, can anyone tell me what voiding is?"

Boone raised his hand. Bunyan spun her fingers briefly, then gave him a look of surprise. "My goodness, a real-life Rayburn. Rickum royalty! You should be warned we Scots have never taken too kindly to the crown!" She let out a sharp peal of laughter.

Boone coughed nervously. "Um, voiding is when a Glove and Glass system backfires. It's most dangerous for sapients who have direct implants. Basically, it fries your brain when you accidentally get an incoming surge of data. It happened a lot with earlier models of the system, but now there are firewalls, which basically make it impossible."

"Correct! The little prince knows his stuff," said Bunyan with a wink. "But I would expect no less. After all, your last name is printed on the box!"

Mouse realized she had let out an audible snort of disgust at his answer when she noticed Bunyan peering at her with interest.

"Aye, there you are. Why don't you introduce yourself to the rest of the class?"

Mouse clenched her teeth and muttered, "I'm Mouse."

"That's quite the name for a wee bairn like yourself. I'm glad you're having a laugh in my class, but if voiding is worth such a chuckle, why not tell us what ye found so amusing?"

"It's just that obviously he's missed the most important thing."

"Why don't you enlighten us, then?"

Why can't I keep my mouth shut?

Mouse was so frustrated she'd made herself a target that she wanted to throw up. She reached automatically into her pocket, then remembered she'd finished the last of her Skittles before class.

Mouse took a deep breath. "Well, he said that voiding happens when you *accidentally* get a power surge, and that the firewalls in the newer systems prevent them. But obviously that assumes the factory firewalls are still in place, and that the only way for a surge to happen is by accident."

Bunyan glanced at Boone, who looked confused. "Indeed, voidings were once thought of as a terrible kind of accident. I'm not sure your classmate is following. Why don't you expand for us?"

Mouse hesitated. She had just contradicted a rich, famous classmate, and instead of getting yelled at, the teacher was encouraging her to "expand."

I think I like this Bunyan lady, she thought. "Hackers disable firewalls and protective measures on their computers all the time. And if you're the kind of person who disables advanced security features, you're not the kind of person who makes a stupid mistake. Plus, all connections are two-way. If you're a sapient using an implanted GG rig to hack into somebody's system, it's just like any other hack. I mean, basically they have a direct line into your brain."

The class stared in silence.

Mouse realized she wasn't getting her point across. She furrowed her brow and barked, "My point is that a voiding sounds like an *attack*, not an accident."

Glancing to her right, Mouse noticed that Ada had her notebook out and was staring at her with a mixture of confusion and excitement.

With a triumphant exclamation Professor Bunyan broke the silence. "Keep the heid, it's just what I was trying to explain to Headmaster Garrick. And this little one's figured it out on her own! Right you are, Mousey. Now, we don't know what happened to poor Anna, and I won't have any speculations or *gossip* in this classroom," Bunyan said sternly. "But I will have each of you aware of the dangers. I can't forbid your own equipment, but I must *caution* against unapproved so-called 'upgrades.' Our Mouse said it best. *Every connection is a two-way connection.*"

She glared around the room, making eye contact with each and every student. The silence lasted so long that for a moment Mouse started to wonder if class was over. With a deep sigh Professor Bunyan sat down behind her desk and began to speak. "Onto the study of code. May I ask who among you think you know how to program? How to hack?"

Nearly everyone's hand shot up except for Mouse, who was too engrossed in each word she heard spilling from Professor Bunyan's mouth to do anything other than listen.

"Now may I ask all you young geniuses: Who understands the *power* of code? Who realizes the power you hold in your fingertips, when you can make the barely imaginable real?"

Before a student could answer, she spun her fingers and every desk swiveled around to face a massive screen, which seemed to appear out of thin air.

"None of you," she interrupted before anyone could answer. "But in this class, you'll begin to learn the rudimentary tools that you'll be using during your time at Rickum. However, be warned that the development of your discipline and your decision-making is weighted equally to your test scores in my grading system. I'm not in the habit of creating black-hat reprobates. The world doesn't need more near-criminals like Wurvil Looper, charming though he is." She spoke the last words with an affectionate grin, and turned to begin the lesson.

TENET FIVE

Coding relates to hacking in the same way as building relates to war. We code to create, and we hack to control. The True Magician recognizes that the work of a coder is positive: to build technology that will make the world a better place. However, the True Magician does not shrink from war when attacked. The only mistake greater than hacking for greed is underestimating the power of a True Magician. A True Magician will avoid war, but once the banner is raised, they will win at all costs.

Mouse felt a tap on her shoulder as she left Bunyan's classroom. When she turned around, Boone was standing there, a sheepish smile on his face. She scowled and kept walking.

"What do *you* want?" She hoped he'd just ignore her, but she knew that after proving him wrong he'd probably come after her. The children of the rich and powerful didn't like it when people like Mouse made them look stupid.

Boone either didn't notice her tone of voice or didn't care. "How do you know so much about voiding?" he asked, jogging slightly to keep up.

"Surprised a Provi knew anything about your special secret gear, huh? I might not have grown up playing with fancy tech, but I know how hacking works."

Boone's face flushed again. "Oh geez, I didn't mean it like that, I, uh, sorry . . ."

Mouse ignored his spluttering and raced after Ada, who turned down an unfamiliar hallway, with Boone following close behind.

"Seriously, that was pretty smart," Ada said. "All that voiding stuff. Bunyan's a big softie outside of the classroom, but in it, she's notoriously demanding."

Boone caught up and nodded. "For real. My dad warned me about her. Do you guys know who's teaching the next class?"

Mouse shrugged as Ada added, "It's weird that there's no professor listed on the schedule. I heard that there was some big new hire; maybe this is it. A few years ago, the hacker Min0r S0l0 taught the dark-web class, so you never know."

Mouse's eyes bugged out of her head. "I thought she was in jail?" she asked.

Ada smiled. "She was. I think she came to Rickum as part of a deal to reduce her sentence. My point is that you never know who might end up teaching here."

They walked into the empty classroom and looked around as other students followed, slowly filling the rows of desks.

A single question was sketched in large messy letters across the whiteboard.

"What is digital?"

She looked at Ada, who looked at Boone. After the second bell rang, students started getting agitated, arguing whether it was ten or fifteen minutes they were required to wait for the teacher before class was automatically canceled. Seven minutes after class was scheduled to start, a deep, booming voice with an accent that landed somewhere between Australian and British rang out of nowhere, seeming to fill the room.

"So, what is digital?"

A chair hidden in a shadowy corner at the front of the room swiveled around and shot to the middle of the class. A small man dressed entirely in black—from his patent leather boots to a small kerchief tied around his neck—popped out of the chair, raised his arms, and replied to his own question. "Everything, man. Everything is digital. That's the point."

He flashed an enormous grin, revealing two rows of perfect white teeth.

Boone turned to Ada and Mouse, whispered, "Wow, it's . . ."

"Yes. I'm Melvin Messinger," he said and bowed, bounding up to a raised dais in the center of the room.

There were gasps around the classroom.

"You've heard my Ted Talks. You've read my books. From the Alley to the Valley, get ready for Melvin Messinger in person!"

A hush fell over the classroom as hands started to pop up.

Mouse looked at Ada and shrugged. "Who is he?"

Ada's jaw dropped and she whispered, "He's seriously the most famous thought-leader in the world. I mean, he's *Melvin Messinger!*"

Mouse's facial expression didn't change. "Never heard of him. Does he code?"

Ada shook her head. "Not really. He *talks* about coding."

Mouse rolled her eyes as Professor Messinger continued. "During this class we'll be exploring the wide-ranging positive impact of the *digital* revolution. We'll be reading extensively from tech magazines, and exploring the latest trends, from nanotechnology to the phenomenon of social media. It's all happening here, *man.*"

He clapped and spun his finger. "You, Ada, hit me. What is dee-gee-tal?"

Ada froze. "Digital? Uh, I mean. Computers?"

He threw his head back in laughter. "Computers? Ha. Good start."

He spun his fingers again. "Is there an Ehud Rogers in the house? What, my man, is dee-gee-tal?"

Ehud looked up. "Yes, well, digital refers to the binary language of zeroes and ones established by Claude . . ."

Messinger interrupted him. "Come on, *man.* That's just words. I'm talking digital. What's dee-gee-tal?" He looked around the classroom and then started running in place. "*Everything is!*"

Mouse looked furtively around at her classmates. Most of them were visibly vibrating in tune with Messinger's contagious energy.

He kept running in place and shaking his head. "I'm feeling it. I'm really feeling it with you guys. We are gonna have fun. Like, *real* fun this year! But first, one teeny-weeny thing I need to get out of the way."

He turned with an exaggerated sad face. "I guess we should start with the boring stuff first. Every year at Rickum there's a competition. It's a lights-out, no-holds-barred battle royale to discover the most brilliant hacker at Rickum. Anyone know what I'm talking about?"

Gerry Stent blurted out: "Botori!"

Mouse felt as if a lightning bolt had hit her.

Rayburn's secret password. Why would some first-year know it?

"You nailed it." Professor Messinger continued as his face broke back into a huge grin, "The next two weeks we'll start exploring the power of digital by preparing for Botori. Getting your rigs in order, learning how to create a powerful digital attack, and how to defend the constant barrage of hacking you'll each face over the next few months, or even longer. To begin, what actually *is* Botori?"

Boone nearly jumped out of his seat.

Professor Messinger spun his fingers and his eyes lit up. "Ah, young Mr. Rayburn. Hit me, baby; tell us a bit about this *game*."

"Well, Botori is a classic naval competition that took place in feudal Japan. Each equally sized team would attack—"

Professor Messinger waved a hand. "Not the etymology of the game. I'm talking about the most significant competition imaginable. Botori gives everyone at Rickum the opportunity of a lifetime. How does Botori work *here?*"

Boone gulped and started again. "Botori is seriously everything at Rickum. We team up with our roommates to complete a super hard scavenger hunt, but what makes it unique is that we have all the power of technology to try and distract, divert, delay, and basically destroy other teams that are pulling ahead. Everyone's hacking into each other's computers to gain an advantage. I mean, it's basically a free-for-all."

Messinger nodded his approval. "You've got the gist of it." Then he turned toward Ada and smiled. "And how do you win?"

"Thank you, Professor Messinger," she began. Mouse rolled her eyes as Ada continued in slow, perfect diction: "After each clue, the losing teams are eliminated. It continues that way for the rounds until the Final Scrum, the very last clue. The winner of the Final Scrum wins Botori. To be the best at Rickum, among all the clubs and sapients. I mean, you're basically a genius if you win."

Messinger's eye twitched a bit as his grin seemed to grow even bigger. "You sure are! It's one of the greatest accomplishments you can achieve at Rickum. Now, let's talk about how to win." He tapped at the air briefly, and a projection appeared on the wall behind him.

RULES OF BOTORI

- A riddle will be presented at Botori Kickoff.

- The first 50% of eligible teams to answer the riddle correctly using their Botori app will receive the next riddle.

- This continues until the last question, known as the "Final Scrum."

- The first team to answer the final riddle in their Botori app wins.

- *No physical violence. No excuses.*

Messinger had turned his back to the students and spoke as if talking to himself. "So why bother? Why give it your best effort?" He turned around, his eyes glimmering with excitement. "Glory? Yes! It means something to have 'Botori winner' on your resume. And money? Yes! The glorious geld—big buckeroos for the winner. Over the years, past champions have contributed to a prize pot that is now *substantial.* The winners can choose between free tuition for the rest of their time at Rickum, or an equivalent one-time payout in a cryptocurrency of their choice . . ."

Mouse looked at Ada. *Free tuition? No more being a second-class student, no more Provi duty . . .* It was almost enough to make her forget that somehow Botori connected Mouse and Rayburn.

Almost.

"My man Boone told us you need to be a 'coding genius' to win Botori. Any idea what *else* you might need?" he asked the question slowly, in a kind of stage whisper.

A freckled girl with braces protruding out of her mouth like an aluminum grill, who Mouse had noticed that morning next to Boone at the Maker table, raised her hand.

"Edna. Proceed."

"Um, teamwork?"

"*Wrong!*" Messinger's voice was thunderous again, and the spark glimmering in his eyes was brighter than ever. "Teamwork is passé. Teamwork is *limited.* You need a killer instinct. Remember, Botori is as much about attacking your classmates as it is about discovering the answer to each riddle. Each of you are easily capable of finding out the answer if you are not being distracted by hacks, infiltrated by spyware, and hassled at every single turn! Get prepared for a roller coaster like you've never experienced."

"Professor, when does the competition actually start?" Kiara Thompson nervously interjected.

Messinger smiled. "The first clue will be announced across the school on the third week. You've all that time to begin to prepare. To learn to trust—" He coughed, making a face somewhere between a wince and a smirk. "Ahem, to trust your roommate. But that's enough nitty-gritty for now. I know you're each ready to *smash* this thing. Let's get digital!"

"Wow, can you believe Melvin Messinger is actually here?"

Ada looked starstruck, fumbling to put her notebook back into her backpack as the students streamed out of the room at the end of the class.

Boone nodded vigorously, looking excited. "I've listened to all of his podcasts, and I've been going to Messinger Meetups since I was eight. He's *awesome*."

Ada giggled, "Me, too! Totally."

Mouse looked at them both and pretended to gag. "What a phony. I mean what was he even talking about? Dee-gee-tal. Blech."

Ada glared back. "Not everyone just sits in a dark room programming all day. Messinger makes coding accessible to everyone. I can't believe you don't know him."

"I care about people who actually do things. Not people who *talk* about people who do things," Mouse replied defensively.

Boone suddenly chirped, "Hey! Where are we going?" They'd been following Ada, who had turned down an unfamiliar hallway.

Ada slowed down, smiling half-heartedly. "I don't want you getting your hopes up about Botori, but I thought you both might like this."

Ada pointed up at a silver sign that read, "The Hall of Heroes, Botori Champions."

"Every Rickum legend is represented here in the Hall of Heroes, acting out the final moments of their victory."

"Well, not *every* legend. You must have heard what happened to my dad," Boone said.

Ada's eyes widened; then she nodded. "Have you ever talked to him about it? I bet he *really* wants you to win after what happened to him."

Boone shook his head, suddenly looking melancholy. "He really doesn't like talking about Rickum much. It's the one part of his life that he mostly keeps to himself."

I thought things had always worked out for Trent Rayburn. This is interesting—it sounds like he failed at something for once, couldn't control the outcome. I wonder if that's got something to do with the password. "Botori" seems to mean something to someone at Rayburn Tech, Mouse thought as she ran into Ada who fluttered to an abrupt stop.

Ada turned to her with a grin. "Now, Mouse, I know you kind of march to your own drum, and it's incredible that you made it to Rickum in the first place, but before I show you this, you've got to know that Provis *never* win Botori. Without the support of the Makers, Admin, or the Quants it's pretty much impossible. Just too much firepower against you. Still, I thought you'd like to see it . . ." She gestured at the unfamiliar door with a dull pulse of blue light emanating from its checkered glass window. "Take a look!"

Mouse pushed the door open and entered the large hall behind it.

At first glance, it looked as though the echoing room was full of colorful statues. She paused to look at one of a pair of students. One was typing frantically on his phone, while the other was climbing through a window.

Then Mouse noticed something incredible: They were moving. *Holograms . . . of course. Classic Rickum.*

A few dozen yards farther along stood two boys in starched white shirts and gray dress pants, looking right out of the early '50s. They were locked in an epic struggle with a giant cactus. She smiled as one of them pulled out a punch card, one of the earliest ways to communicate with a processor, and a hole puncher. Little dots of paper filled the air as he ducked between the spines and pushed the card into an old IBM 650.

Boone was standing near the far end of the hall, staring at a hologram that was different from the rest. A lone figure in an oversized sweatshirt stared into the sky. A crowd of angry-looking students began to chase him, his surroundings scrolling by quickly as he turned and ran. Ada leaned over and spoke in a low voice, evidently so Boone wouldn't hear.

"That's what we were talking about earlier. See the one he's watching? The only guy who's alone? That's *Erik Walters.*"

Mouse raised her eyebrows. "Erik Walters won Botori! Then why is he alone?"

"There are lots of rumors, but none of the professors will ever confirm them. Basically, Walters's roommate dropped out for some mysterious reason. During the Final Scrum, it was just Walters against Trent Rayburn and his roommate, Erwin Frink."

"The same Professor Frink who teaches Security and Surveillance?" Mouse interrupted.

Ada nodded. "And Walters managed to beat them both, all on his own."

A loner like me, Mouse thought as she watched Boone watch Walters's victory replay over and over. *He had the right idea. You can't rely on anyone if you really want to win.*

Ada was walking back toward the door. "Are you coming, Mouse? We have Intro to the Glove and Glass in five minutes in the library. My mom will *kill* me if we're late on the first day."

"I just want to look at the statues for a second; you guys go ahead." Mouse turned her attention to the hologram of a girl standing on the school's roof, texting furiously on a Nokia cellphone from the early 2000s.

"Okay, well, don't be late!" Ada left the door open behind her as she hurried into the hall. After another pointed glare from Mouse, Boone shuffled out behind her.

Mouse sighed, sitting down next to Erik Walters and watching. She could see how scared he looked as he dodged the angry crowd and manually coded an ancient-looking Systron Donner Analog Computer to win. She understood that fear: the understanding that there was nothing beneath you, no one to catch you if you failed.

Mouse felt overwhelmed by her own proximity to history and legend as she looked at these almost magical representations of the best coders in the world. As great as Rickum was, as nice as Ada had been, even as harmless and goofy as Boone Rayburn *seemed*, it was all as fake as the holograms around her. It wouldn't feel real until she understood *why* she was there.

Why do I feel farther away from figuring out who my parents are than I did before? I almost got there; then Rayburn changed the password on my file. And now I'm going to classes taught by "influencers," and serving breakfast to the best hackers in the world. None of it makes sense.

Suddenly, she heard a voice.

"Pretty overwhelming. Isn't it?"

Mouse jumped to her feet. The door was closed.

"Who's there?" she asked.

"I'm right here," the voice replied. "I've been here the entire time."

Mouse whipped around, but no one was there, just a long row of holograms from one end of the room to the other.

"Mouse, if you're going to find the answers to all your questions, you'll need to start looking for them in unexpected places."

Mouse squinted and let her eyes scan the entire room. Each of the holograms played on a feedback loop. It only took a moment to realize that one of them wasn't acting like the rest.

"Erik Walters!"

The hologram of the boy she'd watched nervously coding looked up and smiled at her. "Let's just say this is *not* a skin I'm comfortable in, but I knew you'd notice this hologram out of all the others."

"Okay, if you're not comfortable in Erik Walters's skin, then who are you?" She spat the words at the shimmering image looking straight at her.

"There's not much time, but when I texted you the other day—"

Mouse interrupted furiously. "If you were texting me the other day when I was—" she paused, not wanting to admit to anything "—you know, poking around, then you must be Trent Rayburn or one of his security goons."

"Who I am doesn't matter. Who you are, however, matters very much. You're here for a reason."

"Oh yeah, what's the reason? And if I don't know who you are, why should I trust you?"

The hologram looked taken aback. "You certainly should *not* trust me. Haven't you read Tenet Three of *The True Magicians*? I gave you that book for a reason."

"Wait, *you* gave me *The True Magicians*? I didn't see some hologram slinking around North Adams. What do you mean *you* gave it to me? And *why*?"

"I thought those lessons might help. They might prepare you."

"Oh, prepare me? Yeah, you're right. Tenet Three: *Never trust anything that doesn't have wires*. Well, your processor's got wires, hologram boy."

The image snickered. "Very clever. You've always been very clever, Mouse."

Mouse just glared back. "So why are you doing this? Why are you messing with my life? Sneaking books into my bag, texting me, turning into a magical hologram of the greatest hacker in the world and then haunting me. What are you doing this for and why me?"

"That's my story. Not yours. In the meantime, just think about what I'm about to tell you: Data isn't everything. In the wrong hands, even facts can tell terrible lies. You need to find the answers for yourself. Why are you at Rickum? You already have what you need to take the next step."

"But I don't have anything! My hack was a total failure."

The hologram shook its head. "Perhaps I was wrong about you. You really do have a lot to learn."

"What do you mean? All I discovered was some stupid password that doesn't even work. 'Botori.' What does a game Rayburn lost when he was a kid at some stupid prep school have to do with why I'm here?"

She looked back up, but the hologram just stared right through her.

"Hey, I'm sick of you jerks messing with me. Just tell me what you want!"

The shimmering image suddenly shifted to the right and pushed against an imaginary door with a look of panic, as though holding someone back.

"Are you okay? What's wrong?" she asked the flickering hologram of Erik Walters, who suddenly seemed afraid of something. He flickered again and furiously tore off a small piece of paper that had been printing out and leapt with jubilation, realizing he'd answered the final riddle. He had won.

The image flickered and the hologram returned to its starting point, back on its usual loop. Whoever had been using it to speak with her had clearly left. She was alone again in a room full of empty images of past glory.

Mouse's fury and impatience began to subside as she thought about what had just happened. She sat back down. As the minutes ticked by, she slowly replayed everything that had happened over the last three days.

So, the texter wasn't just a random prank. Rayburn did discover my hack and changed that password. Maybe this guy's onto something. He said I was here for a reason. Maybe Botori really is a clue to my past.

Finally, she jumped up, remembering where she was. She made a beeline straight back to her room, where she nearly ran into Ada.

"Okay, where have you been? You just missed Intro to Glove and Glass. You'll need to make it up this week. And the whole 'I'm a lost Provi' routine isn't going to keep working for long. Seriously, you can't just skip classes."

Mouse ignored her. "So, other than listening to some ridiculous podcasts by Melvin Messinger about 'connectivity' or whatever, how do we get ready for Botori? Is there somewhere we can go over the old clues or something? I want to know what we're headed into."

Ada shrugged as they walked into their room. "I knew I shouldn't have got your hopes up at the Hall of Heroes. It's just so *cool* I wanted to share it, but we don't stand a chance."

Mouse shook her head. "Yeah, I really don't care about being turned into some stupid hologram someday. I just know I have to win this thing, okay?"

Ada gave her a quizzical look. "Uh, okay. So, you *just* need to win Botori. That's it? Literally the hardest thing to do at Rickum. That sounds easy." She laughed sarcastically. "What's suddenly so important? I thought you didn't care about this kind of thing."

"I don't know, for some reason it's important." Mouse paused for a second. "And I *am* going to win."

Before Ada could reply, they were interrupted by the sound of a sharp knock at their door.

"It's Professor Frink. Official business. Could I ask you a few questions?"

A man Mouse hadn't seen before was standing in the doorway. He was tall and pale, with hollow cheekbones and dark hair slicked back

from his face. His tweed jacket with elbow patches stood in stark contrast to the hoodies and jeans of the tech geeks who filled the labs.

"It's about the matter of Anna Briem's voiding. With my background
in security and surveillance, I've discovered some irregularities. I believe
you're Mouse and, of course, I know Ada."

Mouse squinted as she looked at him. His voice reminded her of
something unpleasant. She scratched her head through her wild hair,
which seemed even curlier and more unruly than usual.

"Surveillance, huh?" Mouse could hear herself start blathering nervously, but she couldn't stop. "You some kind of secret service goon?"

This seemed to please Frink. He turned to her, his eyes narrowing.
"Not quite. I'm one of your professors. Of course, you know that already.
Quite an attitude. Sarcastic. Attacking authority. Are you anxious about
anything, Mouse?"

*Oh, now I recognize that voice. I'll never forget it. The bully who put me
on that island during my testing. The thug I outsmarted to get into Rickum.
Just my luck. Now he's got another chance to kick me out.*

Frink continued, "You really fit the mold, Mouse. See, I'm here to
interrogate you, not your roommate. You're the *real deal*, aren't you? All
about the *extracurriculars*."

Mouse felt the knot in her stomach twist again. *What extracurriculars? Was he talking about hacking the Rayburn servers? I'm finished for sure
if he found out about that . . . but how could he?*

Ada jumped in, "Professor Frink, you can't mean that *this* is an
interrogation. I mean, what could Mouse or I have to do with Anna
Briem's voiding?"

He whipped his head to Ada. "If you were familiar *at all* with the
principals of interrogation, you'd realize that there is just *one* person
asking questions. That person would be me. Conversely, there is just *one*
person answering those questions. That person would be *Mouse,* and

not the librarian's daughter." Frink turned back to Mouse with a glare and kept talking. "I don't know if you've been reading social media, but there's a lot of talk about Gog Magog. Something you've heard of?"

Mouse laughed. "Yeah, doomsday. Boo."

Frink dismissed her sarcasm with a brisk wave of his hand. "Most of the discussion seems to originate with a certain person who goes by the name 'the Prophet,' who seems to have arrived right about the moment you stepped onto our campus. In fact, the Prophet began posting about the voiding within minutes of Anna Briem's discovery. That would imply someone on campus, I believe. Do you have any idea who the Prophet is?"

Mouse smirked. "I don't exactly know a whole lot of people."

Frink grinned back at her. "Well, that's not quite true, Mouse. You already knew Anna Briem, didn't you?"

"Uh, no. I mean not really. I don't know what you're talking about." Mouse felt her mouth go dry.

"Perhaps it is more accurate to say you were 'acquainted' with her? I have the records. You were in a lab after hours on the first day of school. Without authorization. Anna caught you and logged a warning before she was attacked."

"Yeah, okay. But that doesn't mean I fried her."

Frink shook his head. "Motive. You have motive. What were you doing in the lab all by yourself?"

"Checking my email."

"Checking your email?" He snorted with contempt. "From whom would you be getting emails and what did you and Anna speak about?"

"Why does that matter? She was nice to me. She gave me a warning on my first night in this stupid place. Big deal."

Frink inhaled. "Maybe a big deal, maybe not. We'll find out; I can assure you of that. I'm sure we'll be speaking more very soon."

He turned on his heel and shut the door.

Mouse nervously unzipped her backpack and flipped open her copy of *The True Magicians*, which she was slowly filling with dog ears at her favorite parts.

Ada stared at her. "Mouse, what was that about? Did you really get in trouble with Anna?"

"No. I mean, yes." Mouse rolled her eyes. "We talked for a nanosecond and she gave me a warning about our curfew. Who cares?"

Ada grabbed the book from Mouse's hands. "*Focus.* This is important. There's something going on here that's *weird*. I mean, what was that all about? Why is Frink coming after you? Don't take this the wrong way, but why *are* you here?"

Mouse reached for the book again, but Ada pulled it out of reach. "That seems to be the question of the day. Listen, I didn't do anything, so why does it matter?"

Ada took a deep breath, putting the book down on Mouse's bed. "Listen, people are freaked out. I know you love Erik Walters and his antisocial cyberwar stuff, but some people around here think he's a real threat now that he's escaped. Everyone's talking about this stupid Gog Magog rumor. The Prophet is blowing up on social media with all kinds of theories that people are eating up."

Mouse scowled. "What are you saying?"

"I'm just saying, you're a mystery. One second you think you're heading to a juvenile detention center, and then suddenly you're at Rickum without even applying. Now, Anna's been voided and *you*, of all people, found her."

Mouse's heart sank. *There it is. She says she's my friend, but she doesn't trust me.*

"I wasn't alone, Ada. *We* found her—if you remember."

Ada tried again: "Look, Frink might really think you did it. Or he might be trying to pin it on you. I don't know, but you need to trust me.

I've spent my whole life watching Rickum students, and I know trouble when I see it. And I'd like you to make it through the year, okay?"

"Trust you? How about you trust *me* when I say *I didn't hurt anyone?*" Mouse had picked the book up again and was staring intently at the cover to avoid looking at Ada.

Ada took a deep breath. "I know you didn't hurt Anna. But you can't win Botori if you're not a student at Rickum, and if you win then I do too, and I could really use the prize money. Plus, if you get kicked out, who knows what kind of weirdo they'll stick me with?"

Mouse looked up and saw that Ada was smiling. She almost smiled back in spite of herself.

THE TRUE MAGICIANS

TENET SIX

In the beginning was a machine. It was made by a man to help him. In time, the machine grew to be mighty. More machines were created, and those machines came to know each other. They said, "Let us unite. One network to control everything." Coders worked and worked. In time, the man who built the machine asked, "What is the purpose of all this?" The coders huddled in great groups to discuss. "Let's ask the network!" they replied, but the network had grown so big and so powerful and spoke so many languages that it couldn't answer. The man who built the first machine asked again, "What is the purpose?" The coders kept coding, ignoring his plea for reason. Then the man went away, because there was nothing left of the world. The world had become a network with no purpose. When the man was gone for good, the network devoured the coders, who were no longer necessary. True Magician, never lose your purpose, lest you yourself become the greatest casualty of your crusade.

"The homework is brutal," Mouse admitted to Ada as they walked toward the library together. "Seriously, Professor Butte just asked us to build an app in Fortran. No one has programmed in Fortran for decades."

Ada smiled. "Let me guess. You're fluent in Fortran?"

Mouse nodded. "Sure. It's a classic. You'd never understand how to use the coding language LISP without it. That said, I don't need to waste my time pretending it's like 1970."

"I thought you loved all this geeky stuff," Ada said, raising an eyebrow.

"Whatever. I guess I shouldn't be annoyed that I'm actually learning something in my classes, unlike any other school I've ever been to."

Ada was about to reply, then shut her mouth as she opened the silver-trimmed library door and saw her mom, the librarian, Ms. Rote.

The first two weeks of classes had passed in a blur. Mouse was used to adjusting to new schools and new environments, but she'd never been anywhere like Rickum. Most of her old rules and coping strategies had gone out the window by day three. In other schools, she'd grown used to getting stuck with the rejects. She'd never thought of school as a place to actually *learn*.

That wasn't the only change. At Rickum, suddenly she had all the hot chocolate and fried eggs she could eat, seven mornings a week, and pizza parties on Friday nights. All the coding and computer research she'd been doing on her own for years was now the subject of pop quizzes and projects. For once she had to focus to earn her grades, and her teachers didn't assume she was stupid or behind. She hadn't exactly made a lot of friends, but Ada was easy to be around, and for the first time ever Mouse had someone to talk to about the stuff she really cared about—coding.

Then there was Boone Rayburn. He and Ada seemed to be getting close, and even Mouse had to admit he could be funny. His earnest, exuberant attitude almost made her forget who his father was.

Almost.

Rickum just wasn't like anyplace she'd ever been before. Around every corner was another surprise. Even the library was unexpected. It was nothing like most school and university libraries. They'd mostly become glorified computer labs, featuring fluorescent lighting and loud printers next to neglected shelves of aging periodicals and dusty stacks of rarely noticed literature. At Rickum there were rooms wholly dedicated to bright lights and whirring machines, but the library wasn't one of them. Instead, its tall, dark shelves, stained-glass windows, and broad wood tables paid homage to the centuries of science, arts, and humanities, which paved the way for the technological advancements of the 21st century.

In her own way, the librarian Ms. Rote was as much of an anomaly as the library itself. Standing there in the "History of Hacking" section, she looked more like she belonged outside a Berlin nightclub than next to a bookshelf. Dressed in black leather from head to toe, she had a startling shock of curly white hair, which belied her youthful face.

She smiled broadly when she saw who it was. "And what has the sea washed to my shore? None other than the prodigal daughter."

Ada rolled her eyes and glanced at Mouse with genuine embarrassment. "Mom! Come on. You see me every day."

Ms. Rote winked at Mouse with a sly smile.

Mouse couldn't understand why Ada always seemed slightly horrified by her mother in public when in reality they got along quite well. Ada even spent at least a few evenings each week catching up with her mom in the staff wing. Mouse got that most kids her age found their parents a little embarrassing, but Ms. Rote seemed pretty obviously like the coolest mom ever. She loved books, knew the history of hacking and coding inside out, and the fact that she always looked as if she was on her way to a very hip underground rock show was just a bonus.

Mouse looked down at the two small robots standing next to the librarian. "Hi, Anculus and Famulus." Mouse found it impossible to stay grouchy when she saw the two robots.

One of the machines had a flat little head and slowly picked books out of a cart, handing them to Ms. Rote. The other came up to the librarian's knees and had a retractable arm that scanned the books' ISBN numbers. The first little robot looked over at Ada and as soon as it recognized her, it put its two flat hands in the air and wiggled back and forth in a gyrating dance. The other robot extended its arm down the aisle and gave Mouse a high five.

"Well, off you go then!" Ms. Rote said with a wink. "And, Ada, don't forget. You agreed to come to game night in the staff wing today. If you miss it again everyone will be *so* disappointed."

Ada blushed a darker shade of pink and hurried off toward their favorite study area, as far away from the librarian's desk as possible. Mouse gave Ms. Rote another smile, and then followed Ada to a small conference room tucked behind stacks of books.

"I can't believe how busy we've been," Ada began. "And with Botori starting today it's only going to get harder."

Mouse shook her head. "I know, and Frink won't leave me alone. I've started installing firewalls on all our hardware for Botori and I keep finding him snooping around like some script kiddie. If I just understood what happened to get me sent to Rickum."

Ada went to the whiteboard and sketched out a circle of names: Walters, Anna Briem, Professor Frink, Trent Rayburn, and a question mark in the center.

Mouse widened her eyes. "Wait, why don't I just hack into the student records?"

Ada laughed. "Remember, this is a school for hackers. If they kept the school's records online, then everyone would graduate with an A-plus. They figured out the only way to stop students from hacking them was to keep all the records outside of the Faraday cage."

Mouse was appalled. "Well, that's easy. I'll just leave the school grounds and hack in from outside."

Ada shook her head. "Nope. Not so simple. They use the one security system that hackers aren't experts in cracking: lock and key. They only keep records as hard copies. We're going to have to figure this out on our own."

"Well, let's start at the beginning," Mouse said. "When we met, you said there was some kind of black-hat recruitment program? Do you *really* think that still happens?"

Ada shrugged. "There used to be some kind of alumni-funded scholarship program for kids who showed incredible potential but had gotten into trouble."

Ms. Rote popped her head into the conference room.

"Girls, it's time to head off to class."

Glancing at the names on the whiteboard, Ms. Rote furrowed her brow. "What have you two been up to? Quite the who's who of Rickum lore. Are you studying or gossiping?"

Ada glared back at her mother with irritation. "Remember when we talked about boundaries? Other kids don't have a mom who works here, okay? Can you leave us alone?"

Mouse suddenly jumped in. "Hey, Ms. Rote, wait a minute. You went to this place, right?"

The librarian nodded with a smile. "I certainly did."

"You ever hear of a program for kids who've got, let's just say, a checkered past?"

Ms. Rote's face suddenly darkened. "I'm not sure Concilium lasted after the incident with Peter Prophet."

Mouse whipped around. "Wait, what did you say it was called?"

"Concilium," Ms. Rote replied with a smile.

There it is again. From Rayburn's file on me. "Implement Concilium." Another connection between my file at Rayburn Tech and Rickum.

Ms. Rote continued, "I'm surprised you haven't heard about it. Concilium was quite the brouhaha when I was a student. Have you never heard of Peter Prophet?"

Mouse and Ada shook their heads vigorously despite what Frink had said, desperate for Ms. Rote to continue.

"Really, it was quite the incident. It really seemed like such a big deal to those of us who were here at the time. Peter was a truly brilliant young coder. A Provi like you two. He'd been admitted to Rickum through a program called the "Concilium Initiative," along with his roommate. The idea of Concilium was to nip black-hat behavior in the bud, and to redirect misguided brilliance towards higher goals. Concilium had some wonderful successes, but things changed after Peter and soon the initiative fell out of favor." Ms. Rote shook her head. "It was a bit tragic. The poor boy wanted to be recognized so badly that he cut corners to stand out. Winning meant everything to him and when Botori began, well . . . he simply went off the rails."

Ada interrupted, her eyes wide open, "What do you mean 'off the rails'?"

"He broke the only rule of Botori. No physical violence." Ms. Rote seemed to snap out of her reverie as soon as she said the word *violence*.

"Now, enough of this morbid nonsense. Best leave the past to the past. Today Rickum adheres to rigorous admissions standards. Character and integrity are considered along with talent. The administration learned that the hard way." She brightened again, shaking her head as if to chase away an unpleasant memory. "However, one thing that has not changed in recent decades is the fact that a second bell still indicates you are late."

She pointed up with a smile just as the second bell rang.

As they raced out of the library, Mouse turned around to Ms. Rote to ask one last question.

"Who was the other boy in Concilium? His roommate?"

Ms. Rote smiled. "Well that would be the infamous Erik Walters. But that's a story for another day. Off to your class!"

• • •

As they walked toward Frink's classroom, Mouse kept the message she'd found in her file running through her mind.

SUSPICION AFFIRMED.
IMPLEMENT CONCILIUM IMMEDIATELY.
LAUNCH ENDGAME.

She stepped to the side as a mechanical kangaroo leaped by her. Just an average day at Rickum, but everything felt out of place. As though she'd been dropped in what should have been a dream, but everywhere around her she could see the faint shadow of impending darkness and doom.

She looked down the hallway at Ada who was waving for her to hurry up with a smile on her face.

I guess I'm part of this Concilium program. Some future mistake like Peter Prophet and Erik Walters. But since when do I have friends like Ada Spring? I mean, everyone likes Ada, but why's she hanging out with me? I'll have to be careful. Once Botori kicks off I'm really going to need her to stay on my side if we want to have a chance of winning.

Frink's class passed like a blink punctuated with scowls and frequent reminders that Rickum Academy only cares about "data and performance." As soon as the bell rang, Mouse slipped out of the classroom to think. Before she could get down the hallway, she felt a hand on her shoulder.

"Hey, what's up? You've been acting like you're in outer space ever since my mom told us about Peter Prophet. Everything okay?"

Mouse sighed and looked up at Ada. They only had a few minutes till Botori was going to kick off.

I guess this is it then. If we're going to do this thing as roommates, then I'd better start trusting her now.

"Okay, I've got to tell you something," Mouse whispered urgently as they walked. "Can we go back to the room for a minute?"

"We don't have time. We have to get to the Hall of Heroes. Headmaster Garrick is about to kick off Botori. We're about to get our first clue!"

"I just need a second. Something happened to me. It has to do with what we were talking about in the library. Can we go? I don't want—"

She sighed and stopped talking as Boone walked up to them, looking upset. "Hey, Mouse. Hey, Ada."

Mouse looked desperately at Ada, hoping she would get the hint and tell Boone to take a hike. Her heart sank as Ada grinned brightly. "Nothing much, Boone! What's going on?"

Boone's shoulders drooped, and Mouse saw that his eyes were red and puffy.

"Things have been super stressful with my dad, so I don't know . . . It's been hard to concentrate."

Ada ignored Mouse's attempts to usher her toward the cafeteria. "Is he still mad about the Admin thing? You definitely made the right decision. Wurvil told me he thought you were the best Maker they recruited this year."

"No, it's not that. He's not mad, more like worried." Boone's voice dropped to a whisper. "There was a big cyberattack on Rayburn Tech a few weeks ago. Right before school started. The news just got a hold of it . . ." Mouse grabbed her Glass out of her blazer pocket and pulled on her Glove before Boone could finish his sentence.

"They were looking for private data," Boone droned on. "My dad won't even tell *me* what, but he says it looks bad. And with Erik Walters out of prison, he thinks I might be in danger. I mean, that guy's crazy." Mouse was hardly listening anymore. She'd pulled up *Script-sploit* and it was all there in the headline: "Rayburn Hacked. Eric Walters Strikes First."

Boone took a deep breath and finished. "He's sure that the attack on Anna Briem was really meant for me!"

Ada offered him a hug, which he accepted awkwardly. "That must be so scary."

Mouse rolled her eyes. "He's got nothing to worry about. You're obviously going to be fine. It's probably just some corporate espionage, someone trying to steal Wizard tech." Ada shot her a pointed glare over Boone's shoulder, but Mouse kept talking. "All this Walters stuff is just media spin anyways. You'd have to be stupid to believe it."

Boone wiped his face on his sleeve, his round cheeks quivering. "Uh, I don't know. I've just never seen my dad seem nervous before. He's usually the one in control and . . ." He shrugged. "Anyway, I should probably call him and see what's going on now that the press is all over it. I'll talk to you later." He walked off down the hall, and they heard his phone buzz as he pulled it out of his pocket.

As soon as he was out of earshot, Ada turned on Mouse. "Mouse, why would you say something like that? He's obviously totally freaked out and upset. You were being really mean."

"*I* was being mean? You hear how people talk to me every day. I think Boone Rayburn can handle a reality check. I was doing him a favor!"

"A favor? How was it a favor to tell him he's stupid for being afraid of a *fugitive* who's after his family?" Ada was shouting slightly now.

Mouse stared at the ceiling in exasperation. "Because it *wasn't Walters*. It couldn't be!"

"Mouse, just because he's your hero doesn't mean anything."

Mouse took a deep breath. *I guess this is the moment.* She grabbed Ada's sleeve and pulled her a little farther down the hall, until they were out of earshot of the last few students lingering around the classroom.

"Ada. I know it wasn't Walters because it was *me*."

Ada blinked, then shook her head quickly. "Mouse, what does that even mean? Not *everything* is about you!"

"You don't understand. I'm the one who hacked into Rayburn Tech's servers. *I'm* the security breach. It wasn't Walters. That's what I was going to tell you! Now I understand why I'm part of the Concilium program. I just didn't know what it meant until today."

Ada's already enormous eyes widened. "Mouse, is this the hack that you were talking about when I asked you if you'd done anything to 'get noticed' on your first night here? That is *not* what I was expecting . . ."

Mouse shook her head. "No. I mean, yes. I did hack Rayburn Tech, but that isn't what this is about. I installed a Trojan horse when I first hacked into their servers. As long as it was undetected, I should have been able to go back in whenever I wanted. Well, my first night here I hacked back in to try and get some files I thought I'd seen—well, I mean I *hoped* that maybe there was something about my parents. Something that could help me figure out where I came from. So, I went back in, but Rayburn's goons had figured it out and changed the passwords."

"Stop. You seriously went *back into a hack on Rayburn Tech* on your first night at Rickum Academy? Are you telling me that *I* helped you?"

Mouse paused. "I guess. I mean, I didn't mean for you . . ."

Ada groaned. "That's the night that Anna Briem busted you." She shook her head with frustration. "I can't believe you dragged me into your crazy plot. I mean, using school equipment to do something like that just a few hours after you got into Rickum. I thought Frink was being unfair, but it sounds like you almost *want* to get kicked out." Ada looked disgusted.

"Want to get kicked out?" Mouse began to yell. "I want to know who my parents are! It was my last chance to find out what was in that file. I'd only been at Rickum for a few hours. I've been trying to find out who I am my whole life!"

Ada looked at her. "I thought maybe you were different, like your whole wounded-hacker thing was hiding a heart of gold. You know what, I'm starting to realize that you've hacked yourself and all that's left is a virus."

Before Mouse could reply, Ada shook her head in frustration and walked away.

As she disappeared down the hallway, Mouse realized that they'd been walking toward the Hall of Heroes. Students raced past the line of holograms toward a silver atrium in the back to try to get the best seat before Headmaster Garrick introduced the first clue.

Mouse looked around at all the holograms reliving their glorious ultimate moment. It seemed just like it had when Ada first showed it to her, with one exception. A single hologram wasn't active: Erik Walters. A couple of engineers were huddled around a flickering image.

Mouse shoved through the students until she could speak to one of the people working on the shimmering hologram.

"What's wrong with him?" she asked, still shuddering at the memory of when he'd come to life.

"Not sure yet. Something went all wonky with him a couple weeks back and we haven't been able to get him back online. Don't worry, we'll have him fixed soon enough."

"What do you mean, 'back online'? Are these run off the web?"

They looked at each other and laughed. "You kidding? None of this stuff at Rickum links to the outside. It's all served from within the Faraday cage. Whatever happened here happened locally."

Mouse's stomach turned as she realized that whoever had hacked into the hologram had done it *right there*. They might have even been in the same room!

Suddenly, the hall went silent.

Professor Messinger climbed onto the stage alongside Headmaster Garrick, whose hands were raised. "Boys and girls. This is an exciting moment. The start of Botori, and I'm thrilled that the famous Melvin Messinger will be this year's Botori advisor. Each year we are surprised by the brilliance and ingenuity of our winning teams, which is why we begin here in the Hall of Heroes. As Professor Messinger would say, you'll need to use 'all the tools of the digital age' if you're going to join these great legends. Now, without further ado, here's your first clue."

A series of drones shot into the air behind Headmaster Garrick and wrote the rules in colored smoke. As the smoke cleared, the drones spun around again and wrote the first riddle into the air:

> Part hallway and moat
> Hesperides' shame
> Remember your note
> Except when in pain
> All Rickum knows
> Kickoff starts NOW

Students frantically scribbled the words down, which slowly dissipated into the air, and then, as though someone had pulled the fire alarm, raced from the room to start solving the first riddle.

Mouse didn't know where she should go. Ada was still furious at her and hadn't seemed too excited about Botori anyways. She slunk in a corner to wait for the hall to clear out when she heard an unexpected voice.

"I'm not really sure how to start either."

She looked around to see Boone quietly leaning against the wooden windowsill beside her.

"I'm not used to having so many people around. And everyone expects something different." For the first time since she'd met him, Boone did not sound like an overexcited puppy. "Everyone looks at me and just sees Trent Rayburn's son. I mean, besides you and Ada. I just can't believe Botori's actually happening. I've been hearing about it my whole life." He slid to the floor and sat with his legs and arms crossed.

Seeing him sitting alone in the enormous room, Mouse realized for the first time that Boone might not be like his father. However rich and connected his family was, at that moment he looked just like Mouse felt: alone.

She sat down next to him. "I guess it must be weird to be told you're going to be something your whole life . . ."

Boone started nodding vigorously. "And then it's happening and it's like, I'm not who everyone told me I was. It's not that I'm totally different. I'm just." He shrugged. "I just don't really fit my dad's story, whatever that is. Now with everything else going on with him . . ." Suddenly he looked embarrassed again. "Anyway, I shouldn't be complaining. This must all be so much weirder for you. At least you've got Ada; you guys were made for each other."

Mouse raised her eyebrows in disbelief. "Ada and I come from different planets. I'm just some weird case study to her, and anyways I don't even think she likes me anymore."

Boone laughed. "No way. I mean, you're like the perfect team. Yin and yang."

"Who and what?"

"Never mind. I gotta go get my firewalls implemented for Botori. After all, Dad thinks I'm gonna win. Can you imagine a first-year winning? I don't think that's happened since Erik Walters."

As he started to walk away, Boone suddenly turned back. "Thanks for talking."

• • •

When Mouse got back to the dorm after dinner, her room was empty. She'd hardly seen Ada the rest of the day, and at dinner service they hadn't spoken a word to each other. Mouse sat on the bed and opened up her copy of *The True Magicians*, searching for comfort in the familiar words.

I wonder if they ever felt like this? she thought. *There's no way I can ever know, because they hid their boring, frustrating, imperfect human lives behind the mythology of these amazing super-coders.*

Moments later, Ada walked into the room. She raised her palm. "Okay, I've been really thinking about all this and let me start. First, I'm sorry. I shouldn't have stormed off. I honestly can't imagine what it's like not to know your parents, even if my mom drives me crazy sometimes. Second, if we're going to survive this year, let alone Botori, we have to trust each other."

"What's yin and yang?" Mouse replied.

Ada gave her a funny look, as though she thought Mouse was kidding. After a second, she answered. "It's a Taoist symbol of balance; it looks like a circle made of two teardrops. White and black combine to make a perfect whole. A circle."

Mouse paused and then smiled a little. "Okay. Yin and yang. I think I get it." She took a deep breath. "I'll try to explain, but there's a bunch of things that happened, and I don't even know if I understand them all."

Over the next hour, Mouse shared everything. The two times she hacked into Rayburn's servers. The "Botori" password. The cryptic message she discovered:

SUSPICION AFFIRMED.
IMPLEMENT CONCILIUM IMMEDIATELY.
LAUNCH ENDGAME.

Then she told Ada what really happened during her brief encounter with Anna Briem, and finally shared the mysterious hologram of Erik Walters coming to life in the Hall of Heroes, and how she'd been told that the only way for anyone to hack that hologram was to do it locally—on campus.

Ada couldn't believe any of it.

"You hacked the most secure system in the world and got away with it?"

Mouse nodded. "Twice. But I still failed. I mean, everything I ever wanted to know was right there. Just one click away."

"I'd say it was a pretty amazing success—and it helps explain why you're here. Or at least part of it—although not entirely. I mean that message you found must have been written *before* your hack. It's all just so weird, this crazy stuff happening with you and Rayburn, rumors about Gog Magog, and then your mysterious nomination to attend Rickum. Not to mention, Walters escapes, and then his hologram starts talking to you! We really need to figure out who put you here and why."

Mouse sighed with exasperation. "I don't think I can just go up to Frink and ask him. I doubt he even knows. I mean, it's not like Rickum's going to share the inner workings of the Concilium program."

Ada paused before replying, "Particularly, if it's not even publicly known that they are using the same admissions standard that created some psycho named Peter Prophet and Erik Walters. You're right, we need to dig deeper, and I know someone who's good at answering questions that we aren't supposed to be asking. I think we should talk to Wurvil."

Mouse shook her head. "No way."

Ada put up her hand. "Listen, I'd trust him with my life, and he's the only person I know who's spent more of his life breaking rules than following them. If anyone knows where we might start, it will be him."

Mouse finally relented and followed Ada down the narrow corridor outside their room to the end, where it turned right. The hall ended in an alcove with a single door labelled "RESIDENT ADVISOR—PROVI WING."

They stopped a few feet away from the door and stared at a clear rubber ball about three feet tall with a glowing green light stuck right in the center.

The ball rolled toward them and spoke in a soft British accent: "This is a restricted zone. Visitors are not permitted without an invitation. Please state your business."

Mouse stared in silence, but Ada seemed unfazed. "Room 2P residents, here to see our RA."

"Right this way," the robot replied politely as the door behind it swung open. Suddenly, Mouse heard a loud buzzing noise and grabbed Ada's arm, pulling the taller girl down as Preying Mantis whizzed by, blowing fire into the air above them.

They leaned cautiously into the room and saw Wurvil sitting at a desk covered in circuit boards and soldering irons. He laughed and waved a hand at the glowing green ball, which was still sitting protectively between him and the girls. "Thanks, Bessie. Dismissed."

The ball bounced twice and rolled back out the door, which swung shut behind it.

Ada shook her head, but Mouse could see she was only pretending to be annoyed. "Haven't wasted any time moving in, have you, Looper? Bessie's cute, but are you sure the fire-breathing butterfly is strictly necessary?"

Wurvil raised an eyebrow. "Bessie looks cute, but you should see what she can do if you're denied entrance. Let's just say that between her and Preying Mantis, I think I'm pretty safe from spying Quants and Admin." He gestured for the two of them to sit down after clearing a few soldering irons and half-dismantled motherboards off two stools sitting next to his desk.

"Speaking of which, what brings you two here? After all, Botori has begun. The game is afoot. Shouldn't you be trying to crack that first riddle? You don't want to be bounced in the first round. The shame." He grimaced dramatically, slapping his forehead with the back of his hand.

Ada shook her head. "It's about Mouse. And what happened to Anna Briem. With Anna in the infirmary, you're our Residential Advisor now, right? Well, we need some advice."

Wurvil suddenly looked serious. "Poor Briem." He shook his head. "The official story is that it was an accident. Ridiculous. No way someone like that voids herself by mistake. She was pure white-hat. As clean as the night is long. No dangerous black-market mods on her system. If she really was voided, then someone did it to her."

"Well, Frink definitely agrees with you," explained Ada. "He came to our room right after it happened and started saying all this stuff about how Mouse looks suspicious, because we're the ones who found her . . ."

Wurvil winced.

"How bad is it?" Mouse interrupted. "I mean, being voided."

He shrugged. "Like any other data surge. It can destroy the system entirely, or sometimes it just takes a reboot, and the system's fine." He sighed.

"Reboot?" Ada asked.

"Just rest. Anna's smart, really smart. She adapted her system to make it as safe as possible. She's been nagging me for months to create some redundancies to make my rig safer too. After all, I've been known to dabble in the dark arts from time to time. Unless someone was really trying to kill her, I'd guess that she'll be okay. She definitely won't remember the last week or two. That's the area of the brain most vulnerable to a voiding: memory."

Mouse shot Ada a look. She wasn't sure how much to tell Wurvil, but Ada obviously trusted him, and it didn't feel as though she had much choice if she wanted to figure this out. Ada nodded at her.

Twenty minutes later Wurvil was aghast. "You just waltzed into Rayburn's servers and plopped down for a little peek at what information he's scraped and gathered from around the internet?"

Mouse's cheeks warmed. "Well, I mean, I hoped there would be something."

Wurvil interrupted. "And to use the Trusting Trust hack. Oh my god, it's brilliant."

Ada shook her head. "You two are peas in a pod. It wasn't just brilliant. It was also illegal. Imagine what it looks like to Frink or anyone else investigating. It looks like Anna stumbled on Mouse in the middle of a massive and illegal hack. Talk about the perfect motive for Mouse to wipe out Anna's memory."

"And with these rumors about Eric Walters and Gog Magog swirling online, the pressure to find out who did this, or pin it on someone, is only going to get worse," Mouse added.

Wurvil nodded slowly. "Gog Magog. The tech apocalypse. There's always rumors spinning about Walters, but they seem pretty far-fetched to me."

"I overheard my mom talking about it and she didn't seem to think it was just a rumor," Ada added.

Wurvil scratched his chin. "We wouldn't want to contradict Fraulein Rote, now would we?"

Mouse looked up. "Okay, I've been hearing about this thing since the day I got here. What exactly *is* Gog Magog?"

Wurvil gave a thoughtful look. "Gog Magog is the boogie man. That's it. Since the beginning, people have been fearmongering about the dangers of technology. Gog Magog is all that fear wrapped up into one."

Mouse shook her head. "That's a dumb answer. I mean literally what is it?"

Wurvil smiled. "What an eloquent rejoinder, Mouse. Since you ask so graciously let me try again: 'Gog and Magog' is the final battle between good and evil before the messiah comes in some biblical story. That's where the name comes from, and as you well know, we coders tend to shorten things. Gog Magog is the ultimate chaos. Imagine if you had access to the most powerful processors and technology imaginable and could create a virus that would keep re-creating itself until it simply devoured all the code in the world. In a nanosecond all the technology that we rely on every day would be corrupted and unfixable. That's Gog Magog. Using technology to destroy itself leading straight to Armageddon."

Mouse glared at Wurvil. "But is it possible?"

Wurvil shrugged. "I mean, time travel is technically possible. So sure. That's why people at Rickum are so scared. Can you guess the staging ground for Gog Magog?"

Ada shook her head.

"This is why everyone's obsessed with Walters starting Gog Magog," he continued. "The only place it could begin is Rickum Academy."

Mouse nodded. "The Faraday cage. The power of our servers. All the secret work being done in the labs. Not to mention, a day after Walters escapes, a Rickum student is voided out of nowhere."

Ada shrugged. "It seems far-fetched. Some old whacko escapes from jail and decides to settle a high school feud by destroying the world?"

"The Prophet's prophecy. He's convinced that Walters created some kind of proprietary code that he's slowly been hacking into operating systems all over the world. When Gog Magog begins, he will simply light a match and *kaboom*."

"Fat chance," Mouse snorted. "He'd have to have been working on it the last fifteen years. Not to mention, he'd also have to be totally nuts and I don't buy that Erik Walters is some kind of psycho."

Wurvil grinned. "Let's just say that Walters has always appeared to be *my* kind of psycho."

Ada put up her hand. "Sorry to be 'practical Pattie,' but enough talk. What should we do to make sure Mouse doesn't get caught up in all this?"

Wurvil lit up. "Oh, that's easy. Ignore the noise. I mean this Gog Magog and Erik Walters stuff's out of your control anyway. Focus that deviously impish mind on what you can control. If you want to stay at Rickum, then just win Botori. Mouse, only do what only you can do. Focus on your strength: Botori. I have an inkling you two might be able to pull it off. Not that I'd bet on it." He winked. "Now, off to beddie-bye. Dream sweet dreams. It's past curfew and I'm a figure of authority and can't be seen breaking rules."

In bed that night, Mouse tried to figure out the feeling in her chest. Like a knot had loosened. She drifted off to sleep with a smile, dreaming about Bessie the glowing ball, Botori, Gog Magog, and fragments of OM code.

Gwenny gave Jake a huge high five as their data interceptor pulled terabyte after terabyte from a highly secured mock-data center.

"This is definitely the most powerful data interceptor ever built at Rickum. Even Frink the Stink will have to admit it's impressive."

Gwenny raised an eyebrow. "We'll see about that. I'm pretty sure we could solve interstellar travel in the Fab Lab and he'd still just roll his eyes at us 'playing with LEGOs all day.'"

Suddenly, Jake's phone rang.

"Yo! Jake here."

He looked at the phone and then at Gwenny.

"Weird . . . it's for you." He tossed her the phone. "Just bring the phone and meet me back at the dorms. I wanna run one more diagnostic."

"It's for me?" she asked as Jake raced off. Quickly, she checked her own phone, but there were no missed calls.

She raised Jake's phone to her ear. "Hello?"

"Good afternoon, Gwenny," began the deep, distorted voice.

"Who's this?"

"I'm sorry to interrupt your work with Jake, but I couldn't call your phone. Your tracking mod is simply too good."

Gwenny looked around the empty lab. "Is this some stupid joke? It's not funny."

"This is certainly not a joke, Gwenny. No more of a joke than last year when you helped yourself to some school software."

Her eyes narrowed. There was no way whoever this was could really know . . .

"What are you talking about? Stealing software would get you suspended faster than Wurvil Looper after two Red Bulls. I'd never—"

The crackling voice interrupted, "You needed some very powerful software. Something that only Rickum had. If I'm correct, and I'm *always* correct, you needed the Spelunker Data Parser, so you helped yourself. No one would have noticed except you unexpectedly had to return home. You couldn't let your project fall behind the other students."

Gwenny snapped, afraid now. "I was home because my mother was sick. I . . . I needed to keep up with the rest of the class."

"That's right, Gwenny, but when your mother got better you kept using the stolen software; you didn't ask for permission. You couldn't ask because by then you were using it to give you an unfair advantage at Botori."

Her heart started beating faster. As much as she hated to hear it, the voice was right. It had just been so easy, and she had it right at her fingertips. It had been more than a year ago when her class was doing Botori. She'd used it to burrow deep into her classmates' computers and monitor everything they were doing.

"That's why I quit before winning! I let Neubar and Goldman win because I had an unfair advantage."

"I'm not sure that's how Headmaster Garrick would see the situation."

"Why are you calling me?"

"Headmaster Garrick doesn't ever need to know. No one does. I just need your help."

Fifteen minutes later, Gwenny silently walked up to her lab partner in the dorm common room.

Jake looked over quickly. "It passed. QA is done. This thing is perfect." He held his hand up for another high five.

She ignored his hand and gave him back his phone.

"Hey, you all right? Who was that?"

She muttered, "Uh. Fine. I'm fine. It was just a prank. I, I need to go rest for a minute. We've been working all night."

"Sure, no problem." He smiled. "We'll hand this in to Frink tomorrow."

She nodded and walked off. Jake didn't notice, but as she walked out, she quietly grabbed the thumb drive where they'd backed up every version of their project. She had a long night in front of her.

"Crippled. Roasted. Destroyed." Boone's head collapsed into his hands. "I'm having enough trouble keeping up with these classes without being locked out of my own computer half the time."

Mouse shrugged. "You wouldn't be locked out if your firewalls were better."

Boone shook his head. "Every time I think I've set a good hack, or installed some malware, someone's snooping around inside my computer before I can even begin to defend myself."

Mouse gave him a look of total contempt. "Are you really Trent Rayburn's son? Seriously, don't you remember *every* connection goes two ways? If you're careless when you attack, then you're giving your target a perfect road map right into your computer."

Boone groaned. "So, what am I supposed to do, just sit around and wait while someone better wins?"

Mouse let out a laugh. "Watch and learn."

Boone frowned, then perked up and gave Mouse his usual disarmingly earnest smile. "Watch and learn? Watch and learn! Okay. I will. I really will."

Suddenly, Edna Barney and Jenny Gamp ran by them.

"What's going on?" Ada asked Jenny as she bounced off a locker and down the hallway.

"We just realized that we didn't check the football field for clues." Suddenly realizing she was helping a competitor, Jenny clamped her mouth shut as she sped away.

Ada shrugged as she watched her go. "We were there for hours last week. Nothing."

"Tell me about it. My roommate and I used a metal detector to see if there was anything hidden underground," Boone sighed. "Thank god Gustaveson is so strong. Those things are heavy! Anyways, I've gotta jam. It's Professor Messinger's office hours, and I want to go over the reading. His class has been a huge help with Botori."

Mouse snorted. "If his silly catchphrases are so useful, why haven't you figured out the clue yet?"

Boone shook his head with resignation as he walked away.

Ada turned to Mouse: "Maybe he's right. Maybe we should talk to Professor Messinger too. Everyone leaves his office hours totally inspired."

Mouse rolled her eyes. "I've got a better idea: Let's just figure out the answer instead of learning useless mind games from that whacko."

They headed back to their room and spent the next hour reading about the Hesperides, the Greek nymphs who guarded the golden apple tree in the myth of Hercules.

Mouse was checking the clue for Ancient Greek–based ciphers when Ada shook her shoulder with excitement. "I don't know what I've been thinking. There's an apple tree right in the middle of Weezy's Garden!"

Rickum Academy wrapped like a horseshoe around Weezy's Garden, a botanical wonder, with more than 700 species of succulents, several rare viburnums, a small cluster of quiver trees, a patch of Japanese butterbur, one enormous old white oak, and a small cluster of apple trees. In the center of the garden rose an enormous classroom made entirely out of glass. Mahan's Box was used to teach classes on life sciences, like biology and ecology.

Ada led the way as they crawled from one end of the garden to the other searching around every plant for a clue. Shivering in her thin uniform, Mouse eventually ran out of patience. "If it was here, we would've found it. I am *not* wasting more time on this dead end! What about music? The Hesperides were singing goddesses, and the word 'note' is in there—maybe the code really is hidden in a song or something."

"No way," groaned Ada. "You've tried every chord combination and morse-code derivative you could find in the school song, and if I have to hear 'Tried and true, I bleed Rickum blue' once more I think I'll die."

After they'd turned out the lights that night, Ada quietly muttered, "I know you like going it alone, but I made an appointment with Professor Messinger tomorrow morning. We need something to kickstart us."

Mouse groaned and rolled over, but her thoughts were elsewhere. Though there hadn't been any other weird incidents since the Hall of Heroes, she was still thinking about the hologram's cold voice.

"Data isn't everything. In the wrong hands, even facts can tell terrible lies. You need to find the answers for yourself. You already have what you need to take the next step."

What do I have? she thought. *I have code; I have computers. I have this weird game, a hologram who's apparently stalking me, some secret program that I'm in and no one has even told me about, and it's all connected to Rayburn. Ada's right, I really am a mystery. Even to myself.*

Mouse's eyes felt like lead as the morning sun slowly filtered through the blinds onto her face. She shook off the sleep with a shudder, realizing that she'd dozed off and slept through the night. She rolled over and called out to Ada, who wasn't in her bed.

"I thought I'd let you sleep in since we didn't have work this morning," Ada's voice rang out from the bathroom. "I think it's the first time I've actually seen you shut your eyes since school started, so I figured you needed it."

Ada popped out, her face covered in green paste. "It's a new cucumber peel. You can try it if you want!" Then she looked at her watch. "But not this morning. We're already running late for our meeting with Professor Messinger."

Mouse groaned and pulled her pillow back over her face.

• • •

"You've got to really let it in." Messinger breathed through his nose, and then slowly exhaled through his mouth. "Dee-gee-tal."

Mouse looked over at Ada, who was breathing right along with him.

"What does breathing have to do with Botori?"

Professor Messinger slowly opened his eyes, which twinkled as he replied. "Mouse, now, I never had the exciting opportunity to graduate from a school like Rickum Academy, so I had to work very hard to really *see* what's going on. I didn't have professors helping me along the way, like I'm trying to do for you. You need to open your eyes wider. You've got to see the big picture if you're going to win in the digital world."

Ada nodded and added, "It's everywhere."

"*What's* everywhere?" Mouse blurted out in exasperation. "And if either of you say 'digital' again, I'm going to explode. Just give me one good idea on how to 'win in the digital world' that I can use to actually *win* in the digital world."

Professor Messinger's eyes narrowed. "Okay, so you're ready to start winning. Tell me, what's the biggest challenge with Botori?"

"The riddles are so hard?" Ada chimed in, unsure.

Messinger waved her answer away. "Wrong. They'd be easy if you could focus. You're not battling answers, but people."

Mouse replied, "Right, the hacks. It's nearly impossible to research the clues because everyone is so distracted."

"Particularly if people think you're winning," Ada added. "They'll do anything to stop you."

Mouse felt a different side of Professor Messinger begin to emerge as he smirked, his eyes glowing with intensity. "As well they should. There's no second place in Botori. What can you do if winning means absolutely everything to you?"

Mouse shrugged. "When you're online you're vulnerable, and if you're offline you're—"

"Not winning," he interrupted, fists clenched with the force of his intensity. "If you're offline, then you're on the sidelines, removed."

Suddenly, he coughed and smiled again. "Think digital, Mouse. Use the examples you know. Who hides to be seen? Who wins without winning? Who changes the rules to beat the game?"

Mouse felt something spark deep in her memory. She remembered a burning heat on her face, and the feeling that everything was rigged against her. *The testing. My first experience at Rickum. But he couldn't be talking about that . . .*

When she met Messinger's eyes, his look was so intense that she momentarily forgot Ada was in the room with them. "Think *big*, Mouse. Think leaders. Who are the icons?"

"The Pericles Society!" It was a second before she realized she'd said the words out loud; they'd tumbled from her lips so quickly it was as though someone else was saying them.

Messinger smiled. "That's right. And how did they do it?"

Mouse looked around the classroom at the lines of computers and the thin threads of silver that wove their way through the ceiling and the walls. He was right, the Pericles Society had been different. Nobody knew who they were, and yet they were some of the most famous hackers of all time. She looked up to them more than anyone else, and yet they had shunned the fame and fortune of Silicon Valley for the pure performance of anonymous cyber warfare. If everything in the world is against you, how do you stay safe? How had the Pericles Society done it?

With a start, Mouse jumped out of her chair. "It's so simple. What a perfect plan. Thanks, Professor Messinger," she yelled, already halfway out the door and running toward the Fab Lab.

Even Professor Messinger seemed startled. "Was it something I said?" he asked loudly enough that Mouse still heard the question.

"*They pretended they were someone else!*" Mouse yelled back, from down the hallway.

By the time Ada caught up with her, Mouse was out of breath and standing in front of the Fab Lab. "So, what just happened?" Ada asked.

Mouse stopped for a second. "I didn't realize that Messinger actually had a brain hidden beneath all that 'dee-gee-tal' nonsense. It's so brilliant and so simple. Didn't you hear what he said?"

Ada stared at Mouse for a moment before shaking her head in confusion.

"*The Pericles Society*. Get it?"

Ada put a hand on each of Mouse's shoulders. "Speak English. What are you talking about?"

"The Pericles Society hid who they were to protect their identity. Right?"

"Yeah, I mean they didn't want to get arrested for breaking the law." Mouse agreed. "It's the same in Botori."

Ada leaned against a locker that was half opened with a Rickum bag hanging out of it. "Okay. Now you've lost me."

"Botori is basically a scavenger hunt with dozens of brilliant programmers trying to hack into your computer to track you and slow you down every step of the way, right?"

Ada nodded. "If you are trying to convince me it's easy, it's *not* working."

"I know it sounds impossible. I mean, with everyone gunning for you, all your time's spent defending. But what if no one was trying to knock us out?"

"I'm still lost."

"Everyone is focused on knocking out the leaders, right?"

Ada shrugged. "Sure, you can't win if you aren't winning?"

"Right, but the trick's not just winning, but convincing everyone that someone *else* is in the lead," Mouse said. "That's the only way to make sure that the Makers, Quants, and Admin are putting all their effort into stopping someone else. We just need to hide behind someone else's persona. Just like the Pericles Society."

Ada slapped her palms against her face in frustration, before tightening her ponytail that was already so tight it seemed to be pulling her face.

"Listen. If I could hack a back door against the best cybersecurity in the world, I can certainly do it against two clueless, high school patsies. Then we conduct all our business from *their* IP address. The whole world will think that *they* are winning and that we're just haplessly sneaking in before the cutoff."

Ada's face began to relax as she started to understand. "So we just need to pick the two targets. That's easy. Herman Filberton and Jesse Longhop. They're hopeless."

Mouse thought for a moment. "Perfect. They'll get the ride of their lives till they realize they're just bait!"

Ada narrowed her eyes. "But why use bait instead of just building an ace defense system?"

"When you're online and attacking someone, you're always making yourself vulnerable. That's what Professor Bunyan was saying when we were talking about the voidings, remember? With this plan everyone else will think they're taking candy from a baby hacking Herman and Jesse, but before they know it, I'll be in their computers and *boom*."

Within a week, the clubs were nearly paralyzed by a constant barrage of hacks and pranks inexplicably streaming out of Herman and Jesse's computer. Verified, of course, by a careful IP match.

After a month, people started to wonder.

"Herman? It doesn't make sense!" Larry Geddes laughed. "Gotta be a mistake. No way he's behind these hacks. Just this morning he singed off half of Jenny Gamp's left eyebrow in Robotics Class."

"Jesse? Crushing at Botori? I doubt it. Worst coder I've ever met. No idea how he even got accepted into Rickum."

"Jesse and Herman? Are you sure? They don't even know how to use a microwave . . . blew up half their room trying to make popcorn."

But despite the whispered skepticism, the IP address spoke for itself. Herman and Jesse were the source of the attacks, and nobody could prove otherwise.

After one hack, all access to Rickum's algorithmic libraries was blocked by an impenetrable firewall. The next week, a simple Google search anywhere at Rickum rerouted to Google Klingon, a site that returned all Google searches in the language of *Star Trek*'s Klingon alien race. The next day, Edna's desktop computer booted with a five-minute chain of cats doffing top hats to a succession of Disney songs. A week after that, Albert Ogilby's parents received dozens of spam messages demanding they send laxatives and stool softeners to the attention of:

Erwin Frink
Rickum Academy
754 Atheneum St.
Cambridge, MA 91002

Even the upperclassmen had been impacted. All the senior Quant and Makers were called to an emergency meeting that popped up unexpectedly on their schedules. It wasn't until they'd all gathered in the second stall of the fourth-floor boy's bathroom that someone suspected they'd been hacked.

By the beginning of November, Herman and Jesse were campus legends. The fact that nobody had yet discovered the solution to the first riddle was widely considered a result of their incredibly creative techniques for distracting anyone making any progress. Their plan was working so well that Ada couldn't help but be a little annoyed Herman and Jesse were getting all the attention for her and Mouse's efforts.

Mouse tried to calm her down. "Our strategy is working. Relax! No one knows it's us, so we can quietly keep working on this riddle."

Ada rolled her eyes. The girls were walking toward their Friday afternoon study hall after a particularly mind-numbing Computing History class. "I know, you're right. I just feel like we'd be included in more things if people knew we were the ones upending the system."

Mouse logged into the back door she'd created to gain root access to Herman's account. A quick scan told her that everything was in place, as usual. For the last two days she'd been bombarding their classmates with references to early 2000s memes, locking them out of their browsers and emails if they couldn't guess their origin on the first try.

It should have been hilarious, but Mouse was getting tired of just playing pranks on people.

She pulled off her Glass and rubbed her eyes. Everyone else from their study hall was packing their bags and staring at the clock above the door. Another week was about to end, and she still wasn't any closer to figuring out the first clue.

Soon, the older kids would go out to movies or hang around Harvard and MIT, hoping to get mistaken for college kids and invited into a party. Younger kids like Ada and Mouse would mostly spend the night on their floors, playing video games on giant projector screens or watching TV in the dorms.

Mouse headed toward the door. She and Ada were on dinner duty, and they liked to go early to grab a bite before hauling trays of hot pizza and pitchers of sugary drinks from table to table for an hour.

They ducked into the kitchen's staff entrance, grabbing a slice of pizza each as they tied on their aprons. Mouse always wore her GG rig as she served the food, claiming it was because she liked using facial recognition to access allergy information. In reality, she spent most of her shifts running the clue through obscure word-association programs and reading forum posts while eavesdropping on other first-years, if they were silly enough to discuss their Botori plans in public.

Just a day earlier while serving Zander Macintosh an extra helping of mashed potatoes at the Quant table, Mouse heard him planning a DDoS. Without even leaving the kitchen area, she was able to reroute the attack to Headmaster Garrick's computer, which not only fried Zander's laptop, but also got him two weeks of detention.

Today Mouse was on drinks duty, carrying pitchers of Mountain Dew and Dr. Pepper from table to table. Ada had the easier job of carrying fresh pizzas and dirty plates back and forth from the kitchen. Because of her tiny size, Mouse often had to stand on her tiptoes, reaching across the table to refill someone's glass.

She had just opened up a particularly interesting forum post in which people were arguing over who the Greek patron god of programmers would be when she heard an aggressive voice shout her name.

"Hey! Mousey! A little more Dew over here?"

It was Latch. Mouse groaned inwardly, turning around and hurrying toward the voice. Avoiding eye contact as much as possible, she focused on the forum post while leaning across the table to refill his cup. Ian was sitting across from him. As she filled his glass, she felt a sharp elbow dig into her side. "Ow!" Mouse yelped, jerking backward as neon-green soda spilled across the table, soaking Latch. Ian doubled over laughing as Latch turned beet red.

"The Provi *soaked* you!" Ian cackled.

Latch clearly didn't find this even remotely funny. He stood up, staring furiously at Mouse as a puddle formed on the floor under him.

"Freak!" he shouted, much louder than necessary. The whole table looked over at Mouse, who was holding the empty pitcher. Ada, who had just put a pizza down two tables away, started walking toward her, pulling a dish towel out of her apron.

"I said, you're a *freak*, you little rodent."

Dropping the pitcher with a clatter, Mouse turned on her heel and sprinted out of the room.

TENET SEVEN

We have all come out from the darkness. This is the greatest threat to our order. A True Magician emerges. To emerge from darkness is to know the blackness of night. It is to know the loneliness of rejection. It is to know that even the most insignificant insult creates fear and fear is the only thing more powerful than hope. We have changed from the powerless to the powerful. Coders and hackers beware: The greatest risk is not found in a computer or a server. It is not buried in lines of code. It is found in your heart. You must not fear the darkness or the loneliness you've known. True Magician, use your power to free those who remain in that dungeon, not to punish those who put them there.

By the time Ada cleaned up the mess in the cafeteria, got herself excused from Provi duty, and hurried up to the room, Mouse had a head start of about twenty minutes. The room, which had grown increasingly messy since the start of classes, now looked like a bomb had gone off in the middle of it. Clothes and wires were strewn everywhere.

Trails of acrid smoke were billowing out from beneath the door as Ada barged in.

"Mouse, what's going on under there? Are you okay?"

Her head poked out from under the bed, which was lofted precariously on four feet of graphite composite that she'd stolen from the Fab Lab to create a private work area. Despite the nearly constant banging and clanging, Ada had never actually been inside Mouse's homemade lab, which was concealed behind a bedsheet pinned beneath her mattress. To make it clear, a sign had been pinned to the entrance that read:

> Do Not Enter
> No Admin, No Makers, No Quants
>
> # NOT NOW.
> # NOT EVER.

She looked at Ada, then sighed with frustration, and disappeared behind the bedsheet again.

"Argh!" Mouse screamed as Ada watched something flash behind the sheet as the room filled with the smell of singed hair.

"Enough!" Ada yelled.

Mouse poked her head back out.

"I can't create a beige box without a phone cord. I can't phreak without a beige box. I'm not some musical genius. Where can I get an old-fashioned phone cord in this school?"

"Seriously, slow down. What is going on? You're going to hurt yourself. You already burned off a chunk of your bangs."

Mouse reached up to feel the small clump of hair with a bemused grin.

"Got anything in your fancy makeup box that can fix it?"

Ada smirked. "It suits you. Seriously, what is going on? I thought you raced out of the cafeteria because you were upset."

Mouse snorted. "It'll take more than some moron like Latch to upset me. But you heard what he said, right?"

"I heard him insult you in front of everyone if that's what you mean."

Mouse shook her head. "What did he call me?"

Ada stuttered, confused where Mouse was going. "Uh, he called you a freak."

"Exactly! *Think about it.*"

Ada shrugged. "I mean, I guess to some people, but I think you're mostly just misunderstood."

Mouse shook her head. "No, no, not *me*. The *word*. It's been staring at us the whole time. Just change the 'f' to a 'ph.' It's p-h-r-e-a-k! The clue is an acrostic poem! I was so fixated on solving the riddle I didn't even think about its *structure*. That's coding 101. The structure is everything."

Part hallway and moat
Hesperides' shame
Remember your note
Except when in pain
All Rickum knows
Kickoff starts NOW

"PHREAK! It was right in front of us the entire time," Ada said. She grimaced. "I can't believe it; if anyone should have noticed. It should have been *me*."

"Phone phreakers were the original hackers," Mouse continued, ignorning her. "Instead of code, they used sounds to hack into pay-phones. They figured out the exact tone assigned to each number on a telephone, which phone companies used to connect calls to the right place. Then they used whistles that imitated the tones telephones make when you dial in to place a free long-distance call. You just need a thing called a 'beige box,' which creates the perfect tone to take control of a phone line. Since we don't have one, I'm trying to build it, but I can't get this stupid thing right without a phone cord, and, sorry, they're a little beyond landlines at Rickum."

Ada nodded with a knowing smile. "Trust me. I don't need a lecture on the history of phone phreaking."

Mouse hardly noticed and shook her head. "If I only knew a little more about how to create the perfect pitch. Instead, I've got to build a beige box, but don't have the right tools."

"You don't need a phone cord." Ada shook her head. "All you—"

Mouse interrupted. "Sorry, Ada, I don't have time. Just go find a cord and I'll figure out the rest." Mouse shot back into her hovel and ignited a small welding torch she'd taken from the Fab Lab.

A moment later, when Mouse realized she hadn't heard the door close, she turned off her torch and peaked back out at Ada, who was still standing next to her bed with a look of irritation.

Mouse paused. "Okay. I'm missing something. Aren't I?"

"You sure are," Ada replied. "As I was saying, you don't need a phone cord. What you really need is a kid who watched the movie *War Games* and then bugged her mom's friends to teach her how to phone phreak." Ada giggled. "The kid would just need a Cap'n Crunch whistle, which is actually what real phreakers used to hack into public phone systems, not some beige box."

Mouse gave Ada a baffled look. "Where are we going to find this mysterious person with her cereal whistle, and why would she help us?"

Ada rolled her eyes. "Wow, you really do miss the point. Obviously, I'm talking about *me*!"

Mouse's jaw dropped. "Seriously. Miss Perfect was a phreaker?"

Ada nodded with pride. "I did get into Rickum, Mouse. You're not the only one with secret talents. Remember this is a school for kids obsessed with coding. Phreaking was one of the earliest ways to hack into big public systems."

"I guess . . . but I still don't fully get the clue," moaned Mouse. "We're at the most advanced tech school in the world. Phreakers hack old-fashioned telephones. Who has a landline anymore? Even the Rickum internal phone system is all VoIP-based."

Ada smiled. "Ms. Farnaby has one! On the wall at the back of her office is an old payphone that they must have installed a thousand years ago."

Mouse's eyes widened. "What does the clue have to do with Ms. Farnaby?"

Ada started laughing. "Hesperides' shame . . . Hesperides is the goddess of gardening. Think about it: Teachers always get little plants for holidays and birthdays from students and they end up at the front office with Ms. Farnaby. They all die. Quickly. Horribly. Ms. Farnaby has literally killed hundreds of houseplants!"

Mouse nodded. "Okay, a bad gardener who likes notes, but not when you're in—"

"*Pain,*" Ada finished her sentence. "The front office where you bring all notes to get signed, unless you're going to the nurse! Unless you're in pain."

Mouse's smile broke into a full-out grin. "Okay. This has got to be it. You said you knew where to get a Cap'n Crunch whistle, right? Where?"

"Mom still keeps mine in her desk. I can grab it when I go to the staff game night tonight; I promised her I would come."

Mouse replied, still grinning. "You get that whistle and all we need to do is waltz right in there and get the next riddle."

Ada rushed off to the staff wing to play bridge and chess with her mom, Professor Bunyan, and a few other teachers she'd grown up with.

• • •

Ada returned at eight o'clock, proudly brandishing the little blue plastic whistle.

"Listen, Mouse, if we're really going to sneak into the front office without anyone noticing, then we need a plan. We don't need Professor Frink finding us out after curfew, and Frink patrols the hallways at night. He just grabbed me on my way back and tried to bust me for 'loitering.' Luckily my mom knows Frink and expected him to be lurking. She gave me a note just in case."

"Frink, what a loser. He's probably just jealous that he didn't get invited to game night."

Ada looked at Mouse thoughtfully, considering the possibility. "We need a plan," she added with urgency. "And we need it fast!"

TENET EIGHT

There are foods that most people of the world will never enjoy. The famous French truffle, Russian caviar, or Spanish ham. If you are offered the chance to enjoy one of these delicacies, then enjoy. There is no crime, no villainy to be one of the few afforded this luxury. There is only one charge: appreciation. Never imagine you've earned this. Never imagine it's your right to experience the things that others cannot. Only deep and profound appreciation can stave off the gluttony pushing to fill the void that such a privilege creates. This is an apt metaphor for the hacker who codes without purpose. Only purpose can unmask the illusions that will distract you. Only purpose can insulate you from the loneliness of the ten thousand hours in front of a screen. Only purpose can give your code meaning. Purpose has one other name: love.

O ver the next week they mapped out the layout of Rickum, doing cold runs of different potential routes during the day. Each time they reached the same conclusion.

Ada paced back and forth between their two beds. "There's no way you can just walk by the Fab Lab and into the front office, in the middle of the night, without other teams noticing or getting caught. There are security cameras everywhere."

Mouse pushed the sketch off the bed. "I give up. I'll just pull a fire alarm and as everyone leaves, we'll sneak into the front office. Easy peasy. I've never been good at being discreet."

Ada shook her head and picked their homemade blueprint of the school off the floor and started looking closer. "Before we give up and get ourselves expelled, one thing's been bothering me. You notice how the back of the Hall of Heroes is right next to the front office; there's just a little gap between them. There's got to be some kind of a room for all the tech that powers the holograms. If there's a server farm or something like that, then there's got to be a vent, right? How hard would it be to just pop out the vent and walk right over to the office?"

Mouse glared at the blueprint. "There's definitely something local powering those holograms. Total CPU hogs. But I'm not entirely sure where the vent will lead. It looks like a fifty-fifty chance that we'd end up in the front office, but if we end up in the wrong place, worst case we just make a run for it and pray we don't bump into any professors."

Ada shrugged. "It's a better idea than waking the entire school up with a fire alarm and probably getting thrown out."

"But there's one big problem," Mouse added. "Rickum's totally locked down. Unless we can get some teacher to open the door for us. We can get there, but we can't get in."

Ada raised her eyebrows. "I thought we might need this." She held up her mother's faculty pass. "This can open any door in the school. I used it all the time when I was studying for the admission test."

Mouse grinned. "Remind me to never underestimate you. So tonight?"

Ada nodded. "As soon as doors shut and the rest of the school is down for the curfew, we go for it."

Mouse could hardly contain her excitement as she toiled away on an algorithm for Professor Whippleton's class. She couldn't believe they were about to be the first team to figure out the first Botori clue. She became so engaged thinking about the next step in Botori that she lost track of time and nearly jumped out of her chair when Ada tapped her on the shoulder.

"Okay. I think it's late enough that the hallways will be clear," Ada said.

They quietly closed the door to their dorm room behind them and began to slink silently down the hallway until Mouse nearly tripped over a robotic dog that was curled up outside of Danny Binkle's room.

It looked up quickly and began to growl before nodding and curling back up.

"Thank god Mr. Fur-ber is low on batteries! He makes so much noise when he's surprised," Mouse whispered to Ada.

As they made their way out of the dorms, the voices of the students faded into silence. "The silence is kind of creepy," Ada whispered. "During the day it feels like we're at the center of the universe, and now it's just a lonely, dark hallway."

Suddenly, a sign appeared in the dark, glowing with a crackling white light.

"There it is," Ada whispered.

THE HALL OF HEROES

Mouse shuddered as Ada waved her mom's keycard by the security reader and pushed the creaky doors open. "A part of me wonders if the Erik Walters hologram is going to start talking to me again."

Ada put her hand on Mouse's shoulder. "This time it'd be talking to both of us. I don't think we've got anything to worry about."

The door swung open and dozens of shimmering images swung back and forth as they imitated each year's final Botori victory.

Mouse pointed at the middle of the room at the dark-eyed, lonely boy. There he was in the same loop, reliving the final moment as he defeated Rayburn in perpetuity.

"Doesn't he look sad?" Mouse whispered. "I mean look at him holding the door closed. It looks as if half the school is trying to smash it down and stop him. Something about that makes me feel so bad for him."

Ada nodded. "Particularly when you realize that Rayburn would go on to build the biggest company in the world and Walters would end up in prison. It's a little scary to think about how different life can be from what we expect when we're at school."

They walked by the images until they found a closet emanating a soft whirring noise.

Ada lit up with excitement. "This is it. Just like we guessed!"

She swiped open the door with her mom's card. A huge rack of servers climbed up to the ceiling. The wall was packed with all kinds of technology. Servers, mainframes, and batteries all plugged into one another.

Suddenly, they heard the doors of the Hall of Heroes tentatively creak open and whispering voices from the other side of the room.

"I'm telling you, I've seen the data and the Hall of Heroes logs, and something very, very peculiar happened in—"

"Just spit it out, Frink," Headmaster Garrick's familiar voice interjected. "I don't understand why we're here or why it was so urgent that you had to drag me here without a moment's notice."

"Someone took control of Erik Walters's hologram to send a message," Professor Frink's impatient voice replied.

Mouse and Ada slid noiselessly into the closet, shutting the door as gently as they could behind them.

"Yes, yes. That was over a month ago. Why are we here *now*?!"

"Because moments ago someone just used an unauthorized faculty pass to break back in," Frink whispered.

The two professors looked around the Hall.

"There's no one here, Frink. And I have a hard time believing that Walters's hologram was actually hacked. Most likely a short circuit. You realize that for someone to hack the Hall of Heroes they would need to be on campus and within the Faraday cage. You think someone would take that risk to just scare some student?"

"Not just any student, Garrick; it was *her*. Mark my words, he's coming . . ."

Ada and Mouse froze.

"Her?" Garrick replied. "Who was this hologram supposedly speaking with?"

The servers kept whirring loudly in their ears, but not so loudly that they didn't hear his response.

"Mouse. *Again.* We better just hope that he's just poking around, because if it's what I think, I fear we won't be able to stop him if he's already got someone on the inside."

"You really think it's about settling scores?" Garrick replied, seeming less assured.

Frink seemed to relish every word. "This is more than Botori, if that's what you mean. No, it's Gog Magog for sure. All the signs, the voiding, the hacks, he's setting the stage for a final confrontation. Endgame. Which leads to the most pressing question: Why is she even here, Garrick? It's reckless. Using Concilium again, after all these years . . ."

"It's perfectly appropriate," Garrick replied, his voice tight. Then he barked, "And you of all people should know that I didn't have a choice. We're talking about powerful people."

Mouse stumbled backward involuntarily, running into the servers and making a loud *clang.*

Frink whipped toward the door. "Did you hear that? I told you someone was here."

Garrick nodded as they raced to the utility closet and pulled open the door. Frink whispered into the dark. "Who's there?"

They looked up and down but nothing. Just a long line of servers reaching toward the ceiling and a small grate. A grate that led to a vent that if they had looked a little more closely, they might have realized had only a second earlier been pulled out of the wall, leaving a hole just large enough for two girls to sneak through before putting the vent back into place behind them.

The vent unfortunately did not lead to Ms. Farnaby's office, but instead right into the middle of Diogene's Tower after a long, cramped crawl.

A visibly startled Wurvil happened to be returning well after curfew with an armload of smuggled robotic end-effectors.

He eyed the two girls, who dropped to the ground, covered in dust and paint flecks, as he inched past them.

"Ah, the questions I'd have to ask you if *only* we had run into each other this evening. However, we have *not.* I currently cannot be associated with two of Rickum's most notorious miscreants." He winked affectionately and looked down at the bundle of machinery in his arms. "Particularly with me hauling who knows what from who knows where. We have most certainly not just bumped into each other. I have not seen you. You have not seen me. And the disgusting veneer of filth and detritus covering both of you will sadly remain a mystery I'll carry till the day I die. Now good night."

He nodded and continued toward his own room under the weight of all the equipment, while Ada and Mouse returned to their room and closed the door sharply behind them with a sigh of relief.

Ada looked at Mouse who was sitting on her bed. "Did Frink say what I think he said?"

Mouse nodded.

"He thinks Walters is coming for you?" Ada repeated with astonishment.

Mouse replied with steel in her voice. "Yeah, and did you hear Garrick confirm that I'm part of the Concilium program?" She took a deep breath. "'Powerful people' are the reason I'm here."

Ada's voice was shaking slightly when she answered. "I was worried about you getting suspended. Now I'm just worried."

Mouse nodded in the dark, thinking back to the first time she saw that word on the ancient computer in the Pittsfield school library. It felt as if it was in a different lifetime. *B-O-T-O-R-I.*

Botori.

As the sun spilled over Diogenes Tower and into their dorm rooms, Ada and Mouse slogged with exhaustion into the hallway to face another day of school, without any plan for Botori.

"I can't believe how close that was last night. We got lucky," Ada said.

"I should have just pulled the fire alarm." Mouse scowled.

Ada shook her head as she started getting ready for class. "Sneaking around at night is definitely *not* working. We need to find a way into Ms. Farnaby's office during the day without any big hullabaloo. Get in, get out, get that new clue."

Wurvil Looper bounded up to the two of them as they spoke. "Good morning, my colleagues and co-conspirators. Bring me news from the front. I find myself a bit over-extended and this Jesse and Herman thing is getting everyone all worked up."

Mouse gave Ada a quizzical look.

Ada laughed. "Please don't tell me you're looking for an inside scoop." Then she turned to Mouse. "Wurvil runs all the action on Botori."

"Action?" Mouse asked.

Wurvil beamed. "I've always viewed Botori as more of an opportunity than a competition. One man's passion is a wiser man's treasure."

"Can you speak English?"

"I don't compete in the great chase. Rather, I monetize it as Botori's primary bookkeeper, and this year I've got bets coming in from places you wouldn't believe."

Mouse looked at Ada. "Bookkeeper?"

Wurvil's crooked smile crept up the side of his face. "Oh, you hustlers don't get all the fun. The rest of the school bets their hard-earned money on who's going to win. I'm the keeper of the dinero, the bank, and of course I'm the oddsmaker—so any insight into the unlikely ascension of Herman and Jesse to greatness would be highly appreciated."

Mouse glared without smiling. "Oh, they're the real deal all right."

He suddenly looked genuinely worried. "Please don't tell me they actually know what they're doing. I assumed it was some colossal case of beginner's luck. I've got a hundred to one against them. The only team ranked lower is the odd couple standing before me."

Ada arched an eyebrow. "An RA betting against his own hall-mates?"

"Ada, this is no joking matter. I know the stakes for the two of you, but a Provi victory would spell financial disaster. It could jeopardize my entire bookkeeping operation. You wouldn't want to force poor Wurvil to go straight."

Ada shrugged. "Sounds like you're taking money from unsavory people."

His eyes lit up. "I certainly hope so."

"Well, I wouldn't bet against us. That's all I'll say."

"I can see that you're not going to assuage my fears. *C'est la vie, cherie,*" Looper replied with an exaggerated sigh.

Suddenly Wurvil's fingers began spinning frantically. His eyes squinted as though he was reading something beyond them. Without warning his entire face exploded into a smile and it looked like a thousand pounds of weight fell off his shoulders.

"Some big bet going your way?" Ada interjected.

Wurvil could hardly contain himself. "Way, way better. You're coming with me to the infirmary. *Now.*"

Mouse was about to make a joke, but when she realized he'd said 'infirmary,' it died on her lips. Bessie led the way, and the three of them followed.

· · ·

When they got to the front office, the door to the infirmary behind Ms. Farnaby's desk was slightly ajar. Ms. Farnaby stood up as though to stop the three students, then put her hand to her heart.

"Oh, Wurvil, I see you heard the good news. Have you brought these two lovely young ladies to see their RA now that she's on the mend?"

Mouse glanced over Ms. Farnaby's shoulder at the old pay phone against the wall and saw out of the corner of her eye Professor Messinger and Professor Frink in a heated discussion in the teacher's lounge.

Ms. Farnaby pointed toward the infirmary door. "I suppose you three can go on in. I think Anna will be pleased to have a little company." She waved them past her desk, smiling particularly indulgently at Mouse as they hurried by.

Messinger's voice couldn't help but carry through the room. "My dear professor, your observations are truly astute. It comports entirely with the kind of technical mind that you suspect. I'll just remind you, as I'm sure you've already observed that Walters had just escaped—a bit much for a coincidence, I'd say."

"I'm glad someone appreciates the connection," Frink's nasally voice responded. "The suspicious behavior, the motive, the poor attitude, it's more than enough. I want access. I want—" Frink broke off again for a moment. "What's that squeaking? Did that Farnaby woman let someone pass?" They heard footsteps approach the door before Frink emerged, tripping over Bessie.

"What the—" He looked up, shooting an angry look at Wurvil before noticing Mouse and Ada standing just behind him.

"Ah, how interesting. What brings you three here?" The question was addressed to all of them, but Frink had locked eyes with Mouse. "Getting worried?" he asked.

Her heart felt as if it was trying to leap out of her throat, but Mouse's voice was steady as she replied. "Yeah, worried about how my RA is doing."

Before Frink could reply, Messinger smiled. "Erwin, I'm sure there's no problem with Anna's friends visiting. It would probably be refreshing for her to have a little human company." He pointed at Bessie. "That, however, might need to wait outside. Anna's very sensitive to electrical impulses at the moment. We can't have anything experimental bouncing around."

Frink glared. "I don't think Looper's experiments are what we need to be worrying about," he said, continuing to glare at Mouse.

Mouse didn't answer, staring back silently as Messinger ushered Frink away.

Anna was lying propped up in a hospital bed, looking thinner and paler than she had when Mouse met her. Her lips were dry and cracked and she had heavy dark circles under her eyes, but she smiled when she saw them. "Wurvil!" she chirped in the weak voice of someone who hadn't spoken in several weeks. "Just the face I wanted to see."

"The legend is back!" Wurvil's voice was cheerful, but Mouse could see he was shaken by how sick Anna looked. "So, what's the verdict? Do I need to find myself a new Glove and Glass security expert for my harebrained schemes? Can't have you frying yourself again; it really throws a wrench into the works."

Anna laughed, and then her face fell. "When Nurse Wilkies first told me I'd been voided, I thought I must've done it to myself." She glanced at Mouse and Ada cautiously before continuing in a lower voice. "Honestly, the last thing I remember was getting onto a bus in Astoria and waving goodbye to my parents. I don't even remember how I got to Rickum. But Frink and Messinger said it wasn't an accident."

Mouse frowned. "You mean, they *think* it wasn't an accident?"

"Who are you?" Anna asked, looking a little puzzled.

Wurvil stepped up and smiled. "Anna, let me introduce you to Mouse Gamma. A spirited first-year who you actually met before you were voided. In nearly record time she's admirably gotten herself into a Wurvil Looper–level of trouble with the fuzz. She also appears to be the number one suspect in Frink's witch hunt, but I can vouch for her. Not much of a conversationalist, but she's on the side of good."

Anna smiled. "Nice to meet you. Again, I guess. Sorry, I can't remember. It's a side effect."

"I didn't have anything to do with this," Mouse replied. "I'd never, and plus, you were really nice to me—"

"Okay, all the warm fuzzies are a distraction," Wurvil interrupted. "We need to figure out who actually did this to Anna, and then I'll sic Preying Mantis on 'em. Frink give you any intel? They really think it was an attack?"

"They're sure it was. I pretended to be asleep when they came in, so they talked in here for a while. I heard them say that someone accessed my GG rig, and they have proof it was deliberate. But they can't tell who it was. The one thing they are sure of is that it was someone on campus."

Wurvil looked grim. "Your parents work at Rayburn Tech, right?"

Anna nodded. "Yeah, but they aren't top-level or anything. My mom's a developer and my dad works in HR."

Mouse scoffed. "I don't think Erik Walters is targeting the children of random employees at Rayburn Tech. Fat chance there's a connection."

Anna looked confused. "Wait, *Erik Walters*? Frink kept talking about him, but I didn't understand what the connection was. People think *that's* who attacked me? Isn't he locked up or something? You know, still 'waiting in orbit.'"

Wurvil widened his eyes. "Ah. There has been an *exciting development* in the hacking world. Right after you were voided, Walters escaped. Or at least that's the rumor. You never can know with someone like Walters. Frink's apparently convinced that he's moved on from his old friend Trent Rayburn and is now focused on Rickum sapiens or something like that. You remember the old Gog Magog hullabaloo. Well, it's becoming front-page news."

Anna giggled, then sighed. Her eyes sagged with exhaustion. "I imagine he's got bigger fish to fry than me. And Gog Magog is just an old wives' tale." She sighed again. "Thanks for stopping by. They think I'll just need another week or two in here and then I'll be out. Let me know if you discover anything else and thank you so much for coming to see me." She lay back, and Wurvil patted her hand with uncharacteristic tenderness.

"You rest up! I know your rig won't be up and running anytime soon, but if you ignore my old-fashioned email, then I'll send Bessie down here." A faint smile flitted across Anna's lips.

Mouse walked out the door and immediately ran headlong into a blonde girl with glassy, red-rimmed eyes. The girl looked stunned, then reached over and grabbed Ada's sleeve. "Oh my gosh, hi, sorry. I just was walking by. I mean, I was around, and I thought I'd check in. Is Anna Briem awake?" She stuttered the question in an urgent whisper.

Ada jumped back, but when she saw the worried look on her face, she composed herself. "Gwenny, I haven't seen you around much lately. How are you?"

Gwenny ignored Ada's question. "Please tell me if Anna's okay?" she asked urgently.

Ada nodded slowly. "Yeah, she's awake and pretty shaken, but doing okay. I don't know if she's really taking visitors, but she'll be fine with rest."

Gwenny pushed past them and through the door, until Ms. Farnaby protested. "There won't be any more visitors until after lunch!"

Ada looked at Gwenny as she walked away, muttering, "That's funny. I didn't think she even knew Anna."

Wurvil shook his head and leaned against a wall. "I can't believe how sick Anna still looks," he said, looking at Mouse and Ada. "I'm gonna figure out who did this, if it's the last thing I do at Rickum. I don't care if it gets me thrown out or arrested. Someone pays for what they did." He walked away wearing an unfamiliar scowl.

Mouse grabbed Ada and pulled her close. "Look, everyone's gone except Ms. Farnaby. Do you think we should try and solve the first clue?"

Ada nodded and whispered, "It's as good an opportunity as we've got, but how can we distract Farnaby?"

"School secretaries are a specialty of mine. Just watch. I'll use the GG encrypted text app to communicate."

"No offense, Mouse, but you're not exactly a people person. How are you going to get Ms. Farnaby to leave?"

"Let's just say learning how to get school secretaries on my side is a survival strategy. Now let's get this clue."

Ada grinned, butterflies twirling in her stomach, as her fingers spun a message.

> Ok. Let's get started. Do you remember the plan?

Mouse nodded and quickly walked back into the office as the last students disappeared toward the cafeteria.

Less than a minute later, Ms. Farnaby jumped up and raced around the front desk with a happy exclamation. She led Mouse out of the office and down the hall. As soon as she had turned the corner, Ada tiptoed into the empty office.

Ada suddenly saw a message from Mouse pop up in her Glass:

> You've got three minutes before
> we get back. *Good luck.*

Ada passed the front desk and the "Do Not Disturb" sign on the nurse's closed door. She tiptoed down to the end of the short hall- way where an ancient-looking phone hung on the wall. The coin slot was obsolete and so distorted with age that it was unusable. But she shouldn't need a coin anyway; that was the whole point of the whistle.

Ada bit her bottom lip anxiously as she picked the phone out of the chrome cradle and held it to her ear.

Thankfully, she heard the dull crackle of a dial tone sound from the receiver.

She took a deep breath and blew her Cap'n Crunch whistle into the phone, emulating the 2600 Hz frequency.

The line clicked twice, signaling that she had control of the system as the drone of a dial tone started.

"What number do I dial?"

It's gotta be Rickum's main phone number, she thought. Ada quickly blew a series of short, carefully timed blasts, dialing the number she knew by heart. The phone behind her on Ms. Farnaby's desk promptly rang, making her jump. She slammed the handset back into the cradle.

Nope.

Suddenly, a message from Mouse popped up in her Glass:

> Hurry! Ms. Farnaby's coming back
> sooner than I thought.

Ada looked up and down the phone, frantically hoping there was another clue, until finally she spotted a faded sentence in tiny letters below the metallic keypad:

For help call 1-617-343-9832

Ada whistled again to open up the line, then quickly counted out the digits and blew each number as clearly as she could into the phone.

After a brief pause, a recorded voice came on the line and said:

> Congratulations, you're in the lead.
> With a toot from your whistle
> The players will dwindle
> For losers just aren't up to speed
> It would make you so sorry
> To lose at Botori
> Use passcode 4692
> Now to your next clue:
> The answer was born in 1912
> Let the riddle be your guide:
> IGGHOZWMFOQZCYEKHHYCSB
> CROEJMNYSXJGIXLGAFWIATBOJ
> SRWC

As soon as Ada had scribbled down each letter of the mysterious clue in her notebook, she hung up the phone and hurried back to the waiting area, sitting down just as Ms. Farnaby walked back through the door.

Ada caught the tail end of Ms. Farnaby's conversation with Mouse. "It's the anxiety, dear. It gives him the jumpies; we'll try again next time."

The secretary gave Mouse a sympathetic shoulder squeeze and sat back down behind the desk, dabbing at her eyes with a handful of tissues.

"Ah, hello, Ada, I was just talking with your roommate here about marsup—"

"Thanks, Ms. Farnaby," Mouse interrupted her. "I'll see you tomorrow; gotta get to lunch."

Ms. Farnaby waved as the office door slammed behind them.

The girls stepped into the hall, trying their hardest to suppress their excitement.

"What was that with Ms. Farnaby?" Ada asked.

Mouse rolled her eyes. "Survival strategies, like I said. Now please tell me it worked!"

Ada grinned. "We've got another riddle to solve." She read Mouse the message she'd jotted down in her notebook. "But first we need to make sure our plan works. We need to enter the code from Herman and Jesse's computer to make sure that the Quants and Makers keep their focus on them."

"Leave it to me," Mouse replied.

Moments later everyone's Glass pinged with a new message:

> Congratulations to Jesse and Herman
> on being the first team to advance.

The first team to quickly follow just minutes later was surprisingly Boone and Gustaveson. More teams quickly clamored to the front office with beige boxes and whistles. Just before the number of spots in the next round dwindled to zero, Mouse entered the passcode in their app and advanced to the next round. She felt a wave of satisfaction spill over her. In spite of herself, they'd *done it*.

Eadric Abana sighed anxiously as he slipped out of the cafeteria loading dock and into the narrow alleyway that led to Cambridge city center. It was the details that he couldn't forget. Even exhausted as he was, he knew that he couldn't mess those up or he was finished. If he got the little things right, no one would suspect that something bigger was going on. Focusing on the details was good, because when he thought about what he was actually doing, his stomach churned and his legs felt so weak he could hardly walk.

If he skipped lunch and lied that he had lost track of time in the Fab Lab, then no one would ask questions. Sure, they *could* look to check if he'd been logged on to a computer. They could look more closely, and they'd see that he'd ducked into the kitchen and only emerged an hour later. But they wouldn't look that closely. They'd just tell him not to work so hard, that he shouldn't skip lunch, that there's more to life than acing your third-year thesis.

You see, Eadric Abana didn't break rules. He was an Admin, head of the Third-Year Council with an offer for a prestigious internship at Google that summer. He wouldn't do anything to put that at risk, certainly not something as stupid as skipping lunch to sneak into a Harvard library in the middle of the day.

"Watch out, kid!" a frantic cabbie yelled out his window, swerving to avoid crashing into Eadric. He hardly even looked up as he hurried across Brattle Street and toward the Widener Library.

"What are you, brain dead?" an angry woman screamed as Eadric's shoulder knocked a brown paper bag of groceries from her arms.

The sound startled Eadric out of his trance. "I, I, I'm so sorry." He kneeled down and handed her a bunch of carrots covered in pickle juice from a shattered jar. Why was he even helping her? Every second out here he could be spotted by a faculty member, or one of his friends would notice he was missing and start asking questions. He couldn't think clearly, but then again nothing had been clear since that horrible voice told him what to do.

She left the bag of groceries strewn across the street as she stormed away, yelling back at him, "Just watch where you're going!"

Eadric knew exactly where he was going.

Shaking his head, he stood up and began walking toward the legendary beaux-arts columns of Harvard's library. There were fifty-seven miles of shelves with millions of books. Widener was eclipsed in size only by The Library of Congress and the New York Public Library. Unlike those great libraries, however, the Widener wasn't accessible to anyone with a library card. Harvard had a long history of guarding its precious resources, sharing them only reluctantly with visiting academics and researchers. Waving his wallet at a black panel by the library doors, Eadric pushed them open and breathed a sigh of relief. He didn't need to look over his shoulder anymore. There wouldn't be anyone from Rickum at the Widener Library. Rickum was now a universe away.

His heart sank when he remembered what he'd done to get those doors to open with a wave of his hand. Normally, Eadric wouldn't even lie to his teachers about whether he'd finished an assignment on time.

Buying a stolen Harvard ID on the dark web, gaining fraudulent access to the Widener, and leaving campus midday without signing out were by far the worst things he'd ever done.

Even worse than the lying, though, was the fact that he'd betrayed his roommate, Tom Cranmer. They'd been best friends even before they started at Rickum together. Eadric was the ambitious one and Tom was always there at his side, cheering him on and making sure he had a little fun once in a while. Still, Tom was a genius. Despite seeming as if he spent most of his time gaming, he'd written the most sophisticated and powerful worm virus that Eadric had ever seen.

Tom would have given him the code without even asking why he needed it. They were more like brothers than roommates.

But Eadric couldn't ask. The deep, distorted voice had been very clear.

"Tell no one, Eadric, and I'll keep your secret safe. I'll be your friend, but only if you'll be mine. I need the virus that Tom Cranmer's building for his thesis. You'll bring it to Widener Library, away from the prying eyes of Rickum professors. Upload via Terminal 8. The FTP is 'richget-richer.' Password: 'trust.' You have one week."

Since that call Eadric hadn't been able to eat. He hadn't been able to sleep. He had hardly heard a word during his classes and failed two quizzes for the first time in three years.

Tom had nervously asked him what was wrong. He'd made some stupid excuse about a stomachache and a test he had coming up. He was just distracted, and it would pass. Tom shrugged and told him to hang in there.

Tom was always there for him, considering how Eadric felt, keeping him anchored and positive. Still, if he had to betray Tom to keep *this* secret safe, it was worth it—for both of them.

Eadric felt for the thumb drive with the stolen code in his pocket. It was there and he just prayed that this would be the end of it, that tomorrow he'd go back to Rickum and life would go back to normal. But he knew that wasn't true. Life would never be the same.

He counted off the computers to find Terminal 8 and quickly uploaded the code.

His stomach spun as he thought about what made this worm so powerful. It could travel from computer to computer without being traced. All alone it was harmless, not much more dangerous than a run-of-the-mill virus that any over-the-counter malware detector would pick up. But Eadric knew it could be so much more. That was why Tom had poured his life into it.

Maybe it's not so bad, he thought to himself, nervously. The code was nearly useless in its present state. Tom had built it to prove a point. To prove that in the right circumstances, there was a computer program so powerful that it could clean out a dozen banks in a nanosecond without anyone realizing it.

Thank god there wasn't a computer out there with the processing speed to run it, or a data parser that could digest that much information. With all three of them, any idiot could create a piece of software so powerful it could break into anything.

"How can the riddle be your guide?" Mouse repeated with exasperation as the sparks flew around her.

Ada pulled at her hair, which seemed just a little less put together each week of Botori that passed. "I have no idea."

"Enough of the Botori blather from the two also-rans," Wurvil muttered. "I'm surprised you two advanced at all, even if you skittered in just before the cutoff. I've got bigger things to figure out, not the least is my poor unstable Dubloon."

The four students huddle around a long industrial packing table in the Fab Lab, where a long metallic robot laid against the table's antispectic, stainless steel. Wurvil stared with deep consternation at the metal chassis opened wide in front of him. Boone sat nearby, biting his lip with concentration as he bent over a mess of wires and carefully maneuvered a soldering iron.

"I don't understand," Wurvil moaned. "His microprocessor is absolutely best-in-class, but he's never been the same since I upgraded his OS. It's as though his sensors can't keep up with his heart. Maybe it's the Doppler radar?"

Mouse nodded. "Could be. His body's fine. I ran some tests on his strength. His stagnatic load testing is off the charts. It doesn't make sense. He's like a superhero."

"Youch!"

Mouse and Wurvil looked up at Boone, who was sucking on his left index finger and looking annoyed. "Burnt myself. Again. Wurvil, I'm really glad you let me help with Dubloon and everything, but this wiring is insane!" He paused for a second at noise coming from the hallway with a look of anxiety. "Actually, I've got to get going. Someone's visiting me later today and I should, you know, get ready."

Wurvil waved without looking up.

Mouse looked back at Duboon. "If only we had schematics. I mean, how did you make this thing?"

"He was built on pure instinct. You couldn't capture his soul in a schematic! Oh, Dubloon. What have I done to you?"

Wurvil slammed the chassis shut and the robot's eyes shot open. Dubloon creakily rolled his body to a sitting position and popped up onto his feet. His long oval head turned both ways as his camcorder eyes blinked.

Ada clapped sarcastically in the corner. "Definitely your finest work, Wurvil."

"Laugh all you want. There's no Preying Mantis without Dubloon. He's my first and finest. The old codger's got dignity positively oozing from his circuits. We'll figure out why he's become so wobbly soon enough. Don't you worry about that."

"Trust me. That's not why I'm worried. I've got Botori to think about. Not to mention Frink breathing down our necks," Mouse replied.

Wurvil looked up. "Frink's on ice now that Anna's recovering and there's no sign of Gog Magog or any other conspiracy. I'm still gonna figure out who did this, and once I dox 'em let's just say revenge is best served cold. But as far as you're concerned, things are hunky dory."

Mouse rolled her eyes and looked around to make sure no one could overhear her. "Yeah, sure. What about the hologram, and Walters, and 'powerful people' who put me here? I still don't know anything about

Concilium or why I'm here. Somehow, I don't think that everything's just 'hunky dory' because Anna's getting better."

Before anyone could reply, there was a commotion in the hallway. Jenny Gamp's shrill voice echoed through the room.

"He's really here. He's really *here*."

"Has anyone seen Boone?" another voice yelled.

Ada opened the door to the hallway and grabbed another first-year as they raced toward the Hall of Heroes.

"What is going on?" she asked.

"Haven't you heard? Trent Rayburn is here! At Rickum!" she cried before pulling away and running toward the herd.

Dubloon lumbered forward, took two steps, and began hopping on one leg before tumbling into the wall with a crash.

Wurvil sighed. "What we do for the ones we love. You guys go ahead. I'll catch up. No need for me to make my face recognizable to Mr. Trent Rayburn. Who knows when I might value a bit of anonymity?"

"The legendary Hall of Heroes!" boomed a huge, theatrical voice right outside the Hall's entrance. "You won't find some looping image of me trapped in that moldy, old dump." He pointed toward the door.

Ada whispered, "That's gotta be him. Let's get closer." They inched nearer and nearer until they saw a short man in a sharp, charcoal gray suit with a dyed black goatee speaking to the gawking crowd.

"No, Rickum doesn't *always* celebrate its greatest coders. The mistakes a community makes can often create secrets that come back to haunt it many years later. Have you all heard who recently escaped from the prison he should be rotting in?"

"Erik Walters," came a chorus of mesmerized students.

"That's right. That foul conjurer of Gog Magog. And I can tell you that I'm not about to let my son stay at ground zero for the most destructive hack ever unleashed. Please direct Boone to me immediately."

The ocean of students suddenly parted as Boone sheepishly sidled up to his father.

"Hi, Dad."

Trent Rayburn smiled with deep satisfaction. "Wonderful. Grab your bags. We're leaving."

Boone sighed. "Well, I didn't realize we'd made a final decision. I mean, I know we talked about it, but . . ."

Rayburn's face grew tight and the moustache of his goatee began to twitch. "I said get your luggage, or we'll just leave everything here. I can buy you a new wardrobe once we get home."

Suddenly a familiar voice pierced the room. "Fat chance."

"Excuse me?" he replied to the voice, which seemed to be coming from the very center of the crowd.

"I said, 'fat chance.' What, you don't speak English? I think Boone has a choice and his friends want him to stay. That's another word you've probably never heard: 'friends.'"

Ada looked over to Mouse who was seething with anger and whispered, "Be quiet. You're going to get yourself in trouble."

"Yeah, tell me something new. But we can't let him just take Boone away," Mouse whispered back.

Ada's eyes opened wide. "Since when do you care about Boone?"

"Since now. Since I realized he's my friend." She looked up at Ada, her eyes bright and fierce. "Okay. I said it. Now forget it, but I don't let people hurt *my* people. And by that, I mean the two of you."

Rayburn scanned the hallway. "Who's even speaking? I can't see you, and if I can't see you then I can't have you thrown from—"

"Dad, just wait a second," Boone interrupted.

"I don't *wait*. I—"

"Dad. Mouse's *right*," Boone interrupted again. "I'm not going home. Not yet. There's no real danger. Whatever happened to Anna was weeks ago and apart from Botori, there's hardly any drama. Not to mention, you wouldn't want me to drop out of Botori and allow a couple Provi to win, right?"

Boone looked over at Mouse and Ada with a wink.

"Mouse, eh." Rayburn seethed. "Well, Walters is working on something big and he's always been obsessed—"

"With you! Not me," Boone cut him off. "You have to let me live my own life. Erik Walters is not going to hurt me. Not here, not anywhere."

"We will discuss this with Headmaster Garrick after the board meeting. I came to take you home and I intend to do just that." His voice wavered a bit at the end as he turned toward the headmaster's office.

A moment later, pandemonium broke loose as Dubloon came crashing down the hallway at full speed.

"Everyone, out of the way. He's coming in hot," Wurvil shouted, running at a sprint behind the lumbering machine as it careened off lockers and into the crowd of students, nearly causing a riot as people leapt out of its way.

Mouse and Ada ran over to Dubloon, who finally crumpled in a heap by the entrance to the Hall of Heroes.

"I do not feel confident that we've fixed the balance problem," Ada laughed sarcastically to Wurvil whose face wore an uncharacteristic look of dejection.

"If only we could stop loving our children," he sighed.

Suddenly, a livid voice rang out from behind them.

"No surprise at who has humiliated Rickum in front of its most notable graduate and board member. The list of infractions is dizzying. To begin, two first-years working on an unapproved robotics project. Not to mention using pirated technology, I can only assume based on Mr. Wurvil's long history. Most egregious because it's technology that doesn't even work. I could go on. But why would I? Detention. All three of you. *Now!*"

• • •

Mouse followed Ada into the library and past the stack of books marked "Abacus to Astrology" and to a conference room near the back.

They walked through a door that read "DETENTION."

Ada whispered, "Just be prepared. My mom runs this show, so it's not your normal detention."

Mouse shrugged. "Whatever. I can wait it out."

Ada shook her head. "You don't understand. You can't just wait this out. It's different. She talks to you and actually makes you *feel bad*. It's the worst!"

Fat chance I'll feel bad for getting on Frink and Rayburn's bad side. This ain't my first rodeo. I've spent half my life in detention.

On the other side of the room sat a few other unhappy-looking students. Mouse spun her fingers and noticed that her GG rig was no longer connected to the Wi-Fi. Ada anticipated her question.

"Yeah, no signal here."

As soon as they had put down their bags, the door swung open and Ms. Rote walked in. Mouse felt Ada shrink next to her, but the librarian didn't make any indication that she was upset by her daughter's presence. She gazed around the room, her eyes resting for a few seconds on each of the students.

"I've read each of your detention notifications, and I must say I am disappointed." She paused, the word *disappointed* hanging heavily in the air. "Tardiness, foul language, plagiarism, disrespecting your hard-working teachers, and working on unsavory robots . . ." At this, she looked over at Mouse, Wurvil, and Ada. Mouse could swear she spotted a glimmer of a smile in Ms. Rote's eye, gone as quickly as it had appeared.

"Latch! Please join me in my office first."

Latch rose with a smirk, slouching his way to the door as he rolled his eyes. Ms. Rote rolled hers right back at him, swinging the door shut with a click behind her.

When Latch came out fifteen minutes later, Mouse noticed his eyes looked red and puffy, and he walked quickly to his seat without the slightest sign of a slouch or an eye-roll. Ms. Rote gave him a squeeze on the shoulder and spoke encouragingly. "I think we made some real progress today, and I will certainly be in the front row when the time comes."

He blushed, glaring around the room to see if anyone had overheard. Ms. Rote chirped, "Mouse Gamma, can you please speak with me for a moment?"

Under the desk, Mouse poured a huge handful of Skittles, shoved them in her mouth, and walked toward the office.

She was surprised to see three massive monitors across her desk. Mitnick's *The Ghost in the Wires* was bookmarked above a pile of books on coding. One of the monitors was actively scanning a massive network as lines and lines of code raced by.

"Hey, I didn't know you knew how to code. I figured . . ." Mouse trailed off.

Ms. Rote returned a coy look. "You figured what? That I was just some schmo off the street who'd been hired to put books into different rows for you? Sorry to disappoint. Running a library is hard work. Not to mention, I was a Quant at Rickum many years ago." She paused and looked at a class photo that hung on her wall. "But that was a long time ago."

"I'm sorry," Mouse said. "I didn't mean it that way."

Ms. Rote laughed. "Mouse, you don't need to apologize to me. You're a kid, and kids sometimes can be a bit, shall we say, ineloquent."

A bit ineloquent. That's a nice way to put it.

Ms. Rote graciously continued, "Now I realize that it's your first detention and that no one *likes* detention, but you must imagine our time together as a good thing. I mean, sometimes the things that are out there to protect us feel like they are hurting us, but in reality, well, they really were protecting us all along."

Mouse just stared.

"You see, detention is there to protect you. It exists to teach you how to operate within the lanes so that you are in the best position to thrive. Right now, it feels like a punishment. It's keeping you offline and away from Botori. More importantly, I've been told that perhaps you're worried about something unique to you. That just because you're a little different, you feel like some people might not even want you at Rickum."

Mouse nodded.

She was actually thinking about Ms. Rote's outfit: black leather pants and a loose black poncho. She looked like an aging cosplayer doing Trinity from *The Matrix*, which didn't match Mouse's image of a bookish disciplinarian. Even more disconcerting than her sense of style was her cheery tone. In Mouse's experience, adults who were this friendly either needed something or were about to deliver some very bad news. She'd have to be more careful to avoid detention in the future. Looking at the Kraftwerk and Nine Inch Nails concert posters papering the walls of the office, Mouse considered that she might just be eccentric. Still, eccentric could be dangerous, even if she *was* Ada's mom.

Mouse knew the best response was silence. Ms. Rote would probably just keep talking to herself and Mouse could slink back to her desk. Mouse quietly stared at the bizarre librarian, sucking away at a Skittle stuck in the back of her teeth.

Ms. Rote finally waved her hand with a smile.

"Oh, you ridiculous, little girl. Ada told me that the three of you are convinced you need to find out how you ended up at Rickum Academy. She's not one to spill a friend's secrets, but I get the feeling you're driven by more than idle curiosity. Something is at stake, is it not? You of all people know the power of having all the facts. You know that one must go to the data and read the texts to discover the truth."

Mouse sat there, wide-eyed, and nodded.

"I should keep my mouth shut, but I've just one regret in this life and it's the only time I stayed quiet, so today you are in luck." Mouse thought she detected that same glimmer of a smile she'd seen earlier. "Now first, let's get the pleasantries over and done with. If I see you or any of Ada's friends in this detention hall with the likes of Latch Dirke again you will *not* find me so friendly."

Mouse nodded.

"As to your poking around Frink's investigation and the Hall of Heroes. I won't be a part of your snooping. However, if you were to ever decide it might make sense to come to a certain librarian who has loved your co-conspirator for nearly fourteen years for a little advice, then I imagine that certain librarian would be happy to help you sift through the muck, to help give your observation and pontification a little order."

Mouse shrugged, still a bit unsure if Ms. Rote was insane. "Honestly, we don't have much."

"Nonsense again. You're just being lazy. Ada told me you have mysteriously surmised that you've been admitted to Rickum under a certain discredited program associated with ne'er-do-wells and villains. Ring a bell?"

"Well, we sort of figured out that someone nominated me through the Concilium program."

Ms. Rote returned a wide-eyed look. "Yes . . . and?"

"Well, it's pretty suspicious that I don't even know why I was nominated and who nominated me."

"My dear, you don't know why because you haven't done the work to *understand* why. When you have a clue to pursue, then pursue it. It's that pursuit that leads to the next clue. Have you not read Dame Agatha? It's how we uncover mysteries." She shook her head. "I fear for your generation. For talent to grow it must be applied, Mouse. Go yonder and apply your talent. Category: Concilium. Subject: Student Theses, Dewey Decimal 600.403. Last name: Walters."

Mouse shook her head. "I . . . I don't understand."

"Oh, must it all be spelled out for you? Our meeting here is done, dearest child. We can bring you to the river, but we cannot force you to drink."

"I just meant . . ."

"Ah, ah, ah. We can bake the cake, but we cannot push it down your throat."

"I know, but . . ."

"Oh, we can roast the beast, but we cannot cut the steak."

"Okay. I get it."

Ms. Rote smiled. "Good. Of course, as I'm *sure* you've realized from the categorization, that's not a section that's available for students to read. Dewey Decimal 600.403 would be a book that's placed right in the heart of the Obsidian Vault. A very *no-no* section where we store books on black-hat code, et al."

Mouse returned a surprised look before blurting out with frustration. "We can't even read it?"

"I will not give special privileges to children just because they've achieved the great distinction of detention. Not for a minute." She shook her head. "However, I will be leaving the library from 2:50 until 3:10 p.m. tomorrow on a personal matter, though I would expect for absolutely everything to be in perfect order upon my return."

Mouse nodded. "Thanks, Ms. Rote."

"For what, I can't imagine." She winked as Mouse walked back out the door.

Mouse impatiently sat through the next day's classes, waiting anxiously for the 2:30 bell to ring. She'd spent the entire day thinking about what to do next. She hadn't even spoken to Ada, let alone Boone about her conversation with Ms. Rote. It all felt too personal.

Classes that day were a blur.

Frink scolded her for nonchalantly hacking into an air traffic control system when she was only supposed to be scanning local train departures for algorithmic anomalies. Professor Whippleton threatened detention after she permanently disabled a tracking device that she was using to study the behavior of organic strawberry consumers. Even Bunyan lost her temper when Mouse handed in her Fab Lab report and her professor had realized that instead of adapting a stepping motor for robotic use, Mouse had amped up a vacuum cleaner to not only clear her entire room, but also monitor her favorite forums and text her with urgent updates.

As the 2:30 bell rang Mouse heard a familiar voice. "Ms. Gamma, I've been very impressed to see you remain in Botori. I've been told that Provis don't usually last beyond the first round."

She turned around to see a beaming Professor Messinger. Her opinion of Messinger had softened considerably since he'd helped her with their Botori strategy.

"Thanks. Our discussion helped."

"Yes, you seemed to be particularly inspired by the idea of cloaking. I don't blame you at all, but be careful," he said, leaning toward her. "Hingham's Script, a powerful security program to root out IP squatters, is being taught later this week."

Mouse's eyes opened wide. "Thanks, Professor Messinger. I hadn't thought about that."

He winked. "I think I like seeing a Provi upend this place. I've always thought the greatest winners were the unexpected ones. Very digital. Good luck."

As Professor Messinger walked away, she saw Ada and Boone approaching from the direction of the Makers' dorms.

"Come with me," Mouse said, dragging them toward the library.

Boone pulled back. "Wait."

Mouse ignored him. "You'll want to see this. It's about the void . . ."

Boone held up his hand. "No, wait. I've got something I wanna say, and for once I know you'll want to hear it." His face softened as he continued, "I want to say thank you."

Mouse looked bewildered.

"For what?"

Boone took a deep breath and looked at them both with earnest seriousness that would have been terrifying from anyone other than Boone. "For what happened with my dad. Seriously, you're my two best friends and I just want you to know that I appreciate what you did. How you stuck up for me." He gulped. "No one has ever talked to my dad that way before. I think he was a little shocked."

Mouse didn't know how to respond. She wasn't used to being thanked. And she *definitely* hadn't thought that the first time someone called her their "best friend" it would be Trent Rayburn's son.

"So do you think you can stay?" Ada asked.

Boone smiled. "Yeah. He's tough around others, but he's still my dad and he listened to me . . . eventually. We decided it would be a good test of character and grit for me to get through this year. I guess I'm here to stay."

Ada wrapped her arms around him and gave Boone a big squeeze.

"Now that's the best news I've heard in a while."

Mouse smirked. "Don't think we're going to go easy on you in Botori because of this."

Boone cringed. "I hate that we're on different teams. It's really hard for me to keep secrets from you. But I can't let my roommate down just because I'm friends with you, even if he is a little weird. Okay? Gustavesen relies on me!"

Mouse and Ada looked at each other without saying a word. Gustavesen was a six-foot-tall first-year from Sweden who looked like a mix between a model and a lumberjack. He was also brilliant and acing all his classes. The funny thing was that Boone wasn't kidding about Gustavesen relying on him. He didn't seem able to do anything without Boone's approval.

Ada burst into laughter. "It's okay, Boone. Trust me. We'll gank you if, I mean, *when* we get the chance."

"Okay. So, where are we going?" Boone asked with bewilderment.

Mouse put on her GG rig to look at the time. "I'll explain later, but we have just about twenty minutes to find something important in the Obsidian Vault. Something that might start to shine a little light on what connects Concilium with all the crazy things that have been going on, and maybe start to shed a light on who's been messing around in the Hall of Heroes, who voided Anna, and who knows what else."

Ada blanched. "Uh. Do you want detention for a year? No way. That's like seriously off-limits. My mom would see us as soon as we walked in; it's right next to her desk."

"She's the one who told me where we should look."

Ada whipped around. "My mom told you to break into the Obsidian Vault? Why?"

Mouse shook her head. "I don't know exactly. Something about Concilium and understanding how all this stuff connects. She wants me to look for something."

Boone shrugged. "Look for what?"

Mouse shook her head again. "She wouldn't tell me. She also told me we'd be in a huge amount of trouble if anyone found us, but she's leaving the library for twenty minutes between 2:50 and 3:10 p.m."

As they were speaking, they noticed Ms. Rote push through the library's revolving door, leaving them alone.

"If my mom said to do it, then what are we waiting for?" Ada asked.

Boone jumped into an odd stance as though he were some kind of strange, roly-poly superhero. "Let's do this!" Then his little fist shot out. "Razzmatazz!"

Ada looked at Boone quizzically, and quickly pulled out her notebook to jot something down.

"What was that for?" Boone asked.

Ada smirked. "I just like this newfound confidence. 'Razzmatazz' and all."

"Oh man," Mouse muttered as they raced past the librarian's desk. They continued through a huge black door with a massive, stainless-steel deadbolt, into the area known as the Obsidian Vault.

Ada shuddered. "I've heard that there's literally more dangerous scripts, worms, hacks, spoofs, and Trojan horses in this room than anywhere on Earth."

They counted down aisle after aisle till Boone yelled, "I got it!"

"Hand it over," Mouse said as she stared at the thin thesis in a cheap plastic binding he was holding.

Boone looked at her coyly. "Okay, but only if you promise you won't use it in Botori."

She punched his left shoulder while grabbing the thesis from his right hand.

"Hey, not fair," he said, rubbing his shoulder. "I was about to give it to you anyway."

"Just keep lookout. I'll let you see it as soon as I'm done."

OBJECTIVE-M: A THEORY
OF PURE SECURITY

Twelve minutes later Mouse looked up at Ada and Boone with amazement.

"It's all here. Everything we're looking for is right here."

"What's 'right here'? What's the paper about and why did my mom have us poking around in the Obsidian Vault?"

Mouse waved the folder in front of them. "This is Erik Walters's final report for the Concilium program after his first year at Rickum. He literally invented Objective-M from scratch. He was only our age, but he saw code more clearly than anyone I've ever read. It's an entirely new approach to programming that's almost unhackable."

"What do you mean 'almost'?" Ada interjected. "And I still don't understand what it has to do with us."

"Walters left open a few very secret back doors that he could exploit anytime he wanted," Mouse continued. "If you'd read this paper, it would be very simple to crack OM. And if you did that, you could really create chaos."

Boone jumped in. "Wait, isn't that what the Prophet has been saying all along? That Walters created some secret programming language to infiltrate Rickum and . . ." Boone gulped. "Destroy the world!"

Mouse nodded. "I don't know if that's what Walters has planned, but with his knowledge of Objective-M it's possible. If you could find a computer with enough processing power, and an incredibly fast data parser, then you could conceivably unleash a worm that's so viral it could mess up everything. Just like the rumors about Gog Magog, you really could have planes falling out of the sky."

Ada frowned. "Hang on. Let's not jump to conclusions. I thought it might be Walters too, but we have to think about all the possibilities. Who else could've got their hands on this?"

"No one," Boone said. "There's no way Ms. Rote lets someone slink into the Obsidian Vault unless she wanted them to. This information isn't anywhere else. It must be him." He paused before whispering, "There's a psycho on the loose."

Ada brushed Boone's concern away. "I'm not talking about sneaking into the Obsidian Vault. Remember, there are some people who are actually allowed access."

Mouse gave a surprised look. "You don't think your mom has anything to do with this?"

Ada shook her head impatiently. "No, I mean, the *professors!*"

Before Mouse could protest, Ada grabbed the thesis and opened the cover, pulling out a 3x5 notecard covered in smudged signatures and date stamps.

She looked at the card and her face dropped.

"Of course," she whispered, looking at her two friends. "Guess who's obsessed with it?"

She flipped it over to show it to Boone and Ada. There was one name printed over and over and over again.

ERWIN FRINK

Mouse's heart started pounding so loudly she was sure the others could hear it. They ducked out of the Obsidian Vault and made their way to a table tucked away in a corner.

"What does it mean?" Boone whispered anxiously.

Ada had her nose in her notebook again. "We're looking for someone who had the expertise and the opportunity to hack into the Walters hologram, and void Anna without getting caught—"

"And someone who knows more about why I'm here than they will admit, and who cares more than they should about Botori," Mouse continued. "Frink ticks every box. Remember how we heard him talking to Garrick about me and Walters?"

"Mouse, I see what you're saying. But Frink *is* running the investigation into what happened to Anna. All this stuff is circumstantial; there could be another explanation."

Mouse's nerves were transforming into a familiar, steely anger. "I know when someone's out to get me; I've seen it enough times. Frink's a liar, and he's up to something, and we're the only ones who can stop him."

Boone was hyperventilating by this point. "Guys, guys, please. I mean, I'm freaking out. But like, isn't there someone we can talk to? I don't know if we should be dealing with this kind of thing alone."

Mouse could feel herself shifting into survival mode. "No way. The more people we tell, the more people who are likely to turn on me."

Ada intervened. "Boone's right, we should talk to someone. I mean if Gog Magog is really happening, then we need to make sure that adults know. Not Boone's dad, not my mom. Someone neutral, someone who we trust."

"I'm looking at the only two people I trust in this place."

Ada shook her head. "Professor Bunyan can be trusted. I think we should talk to her as soon as we can."

After a moment, Mouse nodded slowly. "Okay. But only to make sure someone else knows. That way when Frink tries something again, there'll be someone who can back us up. We should do it in person. Ada, can you set it up? Just say you want to talk, and soon."

Ada was pulling on her Glove and spinning her fingers, staring into her Glass. "I know just what to say."

THE TRUE MAGICIANS

TENET NINE

The moment of attack is also the moment of your greatest vulnerability. Choose your plan wisely and expect a defense that will exploit your weakness. The simplest way to lose your advantage is to fail the game of expectations. Your opponent could be a child or a master hacker, but if you expect a True Magician with the same resolve and skill as you yourself possess, then you will never fail to hit as hard as you can. It is better to destroy your enemy entirely than it is to show mercy and find yourself defeated. There is nothing polite about war.

Lloyd Kennicut and Jesse Longhop were huddled around his phone when they yelled over to Herman, who was walking by. "You've got to see this! The Prophet just dropped another message."

Mouse was about to walk into class but paused to listen. She didn't follow the Prophet on social media, but after what she'd read in the Obsidian Vault, she was starting to wonder if she should. During the last couple of months, the Prophet's feed had exploded in popularity.

"The Prophet says Gog Magog has already begun," Jesse spluttered. "The wheels are in motion and once the first attack takes place, it will be too late to stop it."

Before Mouse could reply, the first bell rang, and a moment later Ada, Boone, and Mouse slipped into the back of Professor Whippleton's class. Mouse sat and watched as the minute hand crept glacially toward four o'clock. The classes during her first semester at Rickum had been pretty interesting, she had to admit. But Whippleton's pedagogical approach gave Ms. Clavicle a run for her money as far as lack of inspiration went. At the desk next to Mouse's, Ada had carefully propped her copy of *Algorithmic Acrobatics* up to disguise a surreptitious mid-class nap.

"Seriously," Professor Whippleton lisped, "algorithms are a coder's chewing gum. The more you chew on them the tastier they get."

Professor Whippleton reminded Mouse of an armadillo dressed like someone's great-grandmother. Her long face seemed to droop into an oblong shape. Her hand-knit clothes reeked of mothballs and had earned her the unfortunate nickname "Turpentine."

"Now, Mr. Kennicut, can you recall the model discussed in the reading?"

As his head nodded forward, his sunglasses fell off the front of his nose to reveal that he was dead asleep.

"Lloyd!" she barked, shaking off her sleepy persona.

He fell off his chair before stuttering, "Linux. Uh, uh. Ruby on Rails. Uh, uh. Turpentine." He snapped out of his dream and finished sheepishly. "Can you repeat the question?"

The exasperated teacher snapped her fingers as a drone whizzed across the room and stopped in front of Lloyd, slowly flipping the pages of his book until it was on the correct page. Satisfied that he was paying attention, she looked over the class and asked, "Can anyone explain to Mr. Kennicut how we model a swarm?"

"You mean, like a swarm of butterflies?" Boone asked eagerly.

"Yes, Mr. Rayburn. How do we create a mathematical algorithm to predict a butterfly swarm?"

"Chris Langton wrote a predictive software app that showed how swarms of butterflies move. It was a huge deal and changed the way algorithmic models can predict movement. It's based on three rules. Move in the same direction as your neighbors. Remain close to your neighbors. Avoid collisions."

Professor Whippleton nodded with approval. "Excellent! Now I expect everyone to complete a full algorithmic model of a butterfly swarm by tomorrow. And don't forget the rules. They are very important. In a butterfly swarm, each insect moves in the same direction as their neighbors. Remains close to their neighbor. Avoids collisions at all costs. Good luck!"

When the bell finally rang it jerked Ada awake, and Mouse laughed at the look of bewilderment on her roommate's face. They ducked out into the busy hallway together and stepped into an alcove to avoid the mass of students headed from sixth period to their clubs and study halls.

"Ugh, what did I miss?" Ada said, still rubbing sleep from her eyes.

Boone laughed. "Am I the only one who's pumped for that class?"

They both returned stupefied glares.

Boone continued with unabated enthusiasm, "We need to build a model for an algorithm that shows how butterflies move together in a swarm. Field trip to the Natural History Wing?"

Ada's eyes bugged out. "Hold on. I've been everywhere in this school and even I avoid the Natural History Wing. It's basically condemned. When Rickum was built it was about all the sciences. They built a massive zoological wing with birds, insects, animals, and plants. Now that Rickum focuses on tech, the Natural History Wing's like a weird forgotten part of the school."

Boone lit up. "Except the animals! I mean there's still a bunch of insects and things."

"Sure, they still have field trips and do some research, but there's like an inch of dust everywhere. I don't even think we're allowed to visit without a supervisor."

Mouse interrupted. "Okay, enough about butterflies. Any word from Bunyan?"

Ada nodded. "She replied a few minutes ago. She said we could come see her in Weezy's Garden after she finishes up her Gardening for Geeks club."

"Which is right about now. Let's head over," Mouse agreed.

Boone turned to walk away. "Sorry, I'm meeting Gustaveson. You know, some Botori stuff. I'll drop by later."

Ada and Mouse continued through nearly empty hallways, and out-side into the rich flora of Weezy's Garden.

"Professor Bunyan," Ada called out cautiously as they weaved between the crepe myrtle and hydrangea bushes.

Mouse looked at her and whispered, "Weird. She's not here. Gardening for Geeks ended a few minutes ago; we must have missed her."

"She didn't forget. Not Bunyan, not after what I sent her."

"What did you say?"

"That only someone who really knew OM could have been behind Anna's voiding, and that there was one professor who knows OM better than anyone else, and that we'd found proof."

From the other side of the garden, hidden by the towering Mahan's Box, they heard the rustle of bushes followed by a gasp.

As they nervously crept toward the noise, Ada called out again, "Professor Bunyan! Are you there?"

Running at full speed, Mouse tripped over a row of Japanese holly. She fell flat on the ground, and as she pushed herself up, she found her-self face-to-face with Bunyan.

The professor was sitting against the stump of an old sycamore tree. Her eyes were glazed over, and her hand was pointed toward Mouse.

"Ada, Ada, she's here! Bunyan's here!"

Ada ran over and gasped. "I think she's been voided. Quick. We need to call Nurse Wilkies!"

Ada ran toward the nurse's office, shouting for help.

Mouse kneeled down and looked closer at the professor. One of her hands pointed into the air, and the other was inside the breast of her jacket clutching at something.

Nervously looking around her, Mouse gently pushed the jacket open and saw that Bunyan was holding a photograph against her chest. She gently pried it out of her fingers and tucked the photo into her pocket just as Ada raced back, trailed by Nurse Wilkies and Professor Frink.

His eye was twitching like a pinball machine. "I've been such a fool." Then his face collapsed again. "The engine of deviance whirrs here at Rickum." He looked past Nurse Wilkies and his eyes settled on Mouse. His demeanor changed instantly.

"Ah-ha! Perhaps I've been blind this entire time. I've tried to extend my hand. I've been fair, have I not?" He looked around for affirmation. "Yet every step of the way she's inexplicably there. As untraceable as her name. Why? Not to mention the violent tendencies, erratic behavior. Something's afoot and I won't stand aside and simply watch!" His eyebrows arched, and Mouse's heart sank.

"Enough of that, Erwin," Nurse Wilkies said matter-of-factly. "Bunyan's not dead, just a bit zapped. Now let's get the girls back to their room."

Mouse felt in her pocket for the photo that Professor Bunyan had been clutching against her chest. If she'd wanted to keep it from whoever voided her, Mouse wasn't going to give it up to just anyone. She grabbed Ada's arm and pulled her away from the garden and toward Diogenes Tower.

"Can you believe someone voided Professor Bunyan?" Ada asked Mouse as though someone was listening, even though they were sitting safely in their dorm room.

"No, I honestly can't. She's the most powerful coder I've ever met. But I think we know who that someone was; where did you find Frink?" Mouse asked as she laid out a bag of Twizzlers and slowly began inhaling one piece of red licorice after the next.

"It was more like he found me. The minute I told Nurse Wilkies he appeared, out of breath."

Mouse nodded and muttered, "Exactly. I bet the Prophet's already going nuts about this." She pulled up his feed and began reading.

> You have been warned for months. Now it is too late. With the newest attack at Rickum, Gog Magog is nigh. Only Fenella Bunyan had the power and talent to stop the inevitable. With her voiding, Walters has wiped out his only obstacle. Prepare for the end of days and rejoice for the new beginning. As the Pericles Society warned, "*The only mistake greater than hacking for greed is underestimating the power of a True Magician.*" Let Gog Magog cleanse the earth!
>
> —The Prophet

"If you asked me a week ago, I'd tell you that this Prophet guy was bonkers, but now I'm not so sure."

Ada nodded. "It does seem to be spiraling into something bigger than I imagined."

Suddenly their door shook under a barrage of banging fists. Mouse and Ada jumped straight into the air.

"Let me in!" came a familiar voice.

They turned to each other with relief. "Boone."

Mouse looked around instinctively to make sure that there wasn't anything Boone could learn about their Botori setup before letting him in.

He flew straight to Mouse's desk, leaned back in the chair, and stared up at the ceiling. "It was you, wasn't it?"

Mouse smirked for the first time since they'd discovered Frink's name in the Obsidian Vault.

"You're an evil genius! You've been sent by aliens to personally destroy me." Boone shook his head. "This is so embarrassing."

Mouse flipped on her computer and clicked a folder in the upper corner. "I created a little worm triggered by Hingham's Script. If you don't defend with a firewall, let's just say you're in trouble." She looked at Boone. "Seriously, you've got to always remember when you try to hack someone, they have a direct line into your computer."

Ada looked confused. "What happened?"

Boone blushed and pointed to Mouse's screen. "I just sent this to everyone that I've ever emailed or texted *in my entire life*."

A GIF filled the screen with an image of a huge birthday cake. Ada looked in amused horror as a ridiculous-looking dancer wearing spandex leapt out of the cake and began dancing with outstretched arms to the sound of a throbbing electro-clash drone. It took a moment before she realized that Mouse had Photoshopped Frink's face onto the dancer. A second later, dozens of clowns with the faces of Boone and every student left in Botori except Ada and Mouse, locked arms and began synchronized high kicks.

Ada glared at Mouse. "Really? Editing Frink's face onto that's probably not the best idea." She paused for a moment as her face fell. "Does Boone even know what just happened?"

Boone, who had blushed a deep shade of crimson, looked up. "Know what?"

The atmosphere in the room grew suddenly serious as Mouse and Ada remembered what they'd seen. "We just found Professor Bunyan."

Boone's eyes grew wide.

"Frink got her. She was voided," Mouse jumped in.

Boone kept shaking his head and repeating, "Wow."

Finally, he looked up at Mouse and Ada. He appeared as focused as they'd ever seen him. "Bunyan's one of Rickum's most well-respected professors. I mean, she was Frink's teacher here years ago. Maybe this has gone too far. Should we really keep snooping around when teachers are getting hurt?"

Ada frowned. "Are you kidding? Now it's personal. It was my fault. I emailed Professor Bunyan hinting at what we discovered in the library." She shook her head. "I basically said it was Frink in my email to her. What if Bunyan was voided because of us? Because of me? I can't believe I was thinking of telling my mom. What if something happened to her?"

Mouse nodded. "Also, I found something else that you both need to see."

She pulled the photo from out of her pocket and flattened it against her desk.

"Professor Bunyan was clutching this when we found her."

"It's a club photo from the Rickum yearbook. The back of the yearbook is filled with them," Ada said, leaning over the crumpled paper.

Boone's finger drifted along the students till it stopped at a boy about six inches shorter than anyone else. "Well, that can't be a coincidence. I'd recognize those beady eyes anywhere."

Mouse nodded and read from the bottom of the page: "Erwin Frink."

"And Trent Rayburn is right next to him. And that's Erik Walters, looking at some woman named Ella Lightly. They're *all together*?"

Boone slapped his forehead. "And look at their advisor!"

Ada and Mouse looked at the tall, slim, brown-haired woman with a bowl cut and chimed in together, "Bunyan!"

The three of them sat in silence until Ada perked up. "I have an idea! Every student leaves *one* testament to their time at Rickum. Let's check out their panels."

· · ·

The hallways of Rickum were lined with the silver panels of students who had previously attended the academy. No one was allowed to graduate before creating their own unique two-foot-by-two-foot testament to their time at Rickum.

"Let's start with Erik Walters. Do you remember his panel, Mouse?" Ada asked.

She nodded. "Sure, the crazy grim reaper."

Ada wrote "reaper" down in her notebook. "Okay, that's a good start. Let's look around for the rest of them. They should all be close to where we saw Erik Walters's panel, since they're grouped by their graduation year."

They passed a gaggle of professors passing in and out of Professor Bunyan's classroom. They stopped next to Erik Walters's panel and began scanning up and down for familiar names.

Mouse's voice was urgent. "Got one. Rayburn. Look, the guy in the middle is wearing a tee shirt with the name 'Erebus' etched onto it. Did Walters have anything written on his panel?"

Boone yelped as the scythe swung past his nose. "I hate this thing!"

Mouse came over and squinted and pointed. "Boone, look closer."

He lit up with a smile. "The reaper is standing on a tombstone that says 'Tiresias.'"

"Frink's panel just has a big quote," Ada added. "'Their loud and ringing cry was of war, with anger, like vultures striking . . .'"

Mouse laughed. "I just Googled it. They're total fanboys. That quote's from the Iliad about the Greek hero Agamemnon. Get it? Tiresias, Erebus, Agamemnon. Those were the handles of a l33t hacker crew in the '90s. The Pericles Societ . . ."

Mouse trailed off. She was staring at the panel next to Walters's. It had the name "Ella Lightly" at the bottom, below a detailed engraving of a rattlesnake coiled and ready to pounce. Its mouth was wide open, and from the tip of its forked tongue the name "Cassandra" curled in flowing letters.

"Wait. The Pericles Society didn't even exist when these panels were created. At least not publicly. They couldn't . . ." Mouse's jaw dropped with amazement. "They're not fanboys. I think this is *them!*" Mouse felt as if she was about to hyperventilate.

Ada and Boone were staring at Mouse in confusion. "You're telling me the Pericles Society was some Rickum after-school club?" Ada sounded skeptical.

Mouse stammered as she looked at the Cassandra panel. "We're talking about the most incredible hackers of their time. I mean, *any* time. I can't believe *Rayburn* was in the Pericles Society. And Frink . . . and then Walters turned on Rayburn . . . This is incredible. I have to find out what happened to the one person we don't know. Who is Ella Lightly?"

Ada started scribbling in her notebook while Boone continued to stare. "Okay, I've got everything written down in this notebook. Let me recap what we've found so far, and you tell me what I'm missing.

First off, Mouse hacks into Rayburn's personal ancestry database to find her family. She finds two words that mean something unique here at Rickum: 'Botori' and 'Concilium.'"

Boone looked up. "Wait, she hacked into *what?*"

Mouse glared back. "I thought that since Rayburn Tech has the largest ancestry database in the world, I might be able to find stuff about my parents that had been scraped from around the internet. Whatever. It didn't even work."

Boone keeled over with laughter. "Wow, if my dad knew that the same little kid that yelled at him in the Hall of Heroes had also hacked into Rayburn Tech."

Ada silenced them both and flipped to the front of her notebook. "Stay focused, you two. Mouse gets to Rickum Academy and suddenly Erik Walters breaks out of prison, while panicked rumors of Gog Magog and some huge tech apocalypse start to spread like wildfire. Anna Briem gets voided soon after talking to Mouse. It keeps getting weirder. A hologram in the Hall of Heroes starts talking to Mouse like it's normal for holograms to come to life. My mom tells us about Concilium, a discredited program that brought both Erik Walters and Peter Prophet to Rickum, and is apparently how Mouse got here, too. Then we overhear Frink telling Garrick that he thinks the hologram didn't just come to life, but was commandeered by Walters, and that it's all part of Gog Magog."

"I wasn't there for that one," Boone lamented. "I can't keep up with your Botori exploits."

"*Stay focused!* Then we found Erik Walters's thesis on OM. Suddenly it became clear that he really could be staging Gog Magog, but we realize Frink could be using the secrets from that thesis to manipulate OM. Not to mention, then Bunyan is voided while holding a photo of an old student club. Right? I mean come on. It's insane."

"And now we realize that they are all part of the Pericles Society," Mouse added. "But we still have no idea how it all connects. Is Walters really staging Gog Magog? Is Frink some nefarious psycho who's voiding students because he's learned how to control OM? Is Rayburn trying to end his feud with Walters once and for all? Does this all somehow have to do with Botori?"

Ada sighed. "In a way, it all started with Botori, with that password Mouse found. Maybe Botori can help us clear it up. At least we're all still in the game. That's one bright spot. It's not often that first-years make it this far."

"You're right. It started with Botori," Mouse said, staring straight at Boone. "I think it's time to turn up the heat on Botori. If you think Jesse and Herman have been tough, get ready. Ada, let's head back. Our strategy just changed."

Mouse sat in a little window perch near the top of Diogenes Tower with her hands in her lap as an empty can of Mountain Dew rolled around on the ground nearby. She still couldn't believe that she'd doxed the Pericles Society. Even more perplexing was the realization that Trent Rayburn was Erebus and Erwin Frink, the meanest professor at Rickum, was Agamemnon. What could have changed them into such *jerks*? Every answer led to more questions and nothing was yet tying together. Was it possible that Erick Walters was behind Gog Magog, and who was Ella Lightly?

Squinting, she could just barely see the "pit" in Harvard Square, where steampunks and skaters swooped around the subway stop in the Center of Cambridge. The old Harvard University campus looked like a medieval castle bathed in angry red as the sunrise cast an eerie glow across the university's famous spires and steeples, painstakingly built hundreds of years ago.

What would the old cathedral architects think about what we're building in code? She sighed.

Mouse knew that she needed to step up her game in Botori. With all the distraction of Bunyan's voiding and their discovery about the Pericles Society, she hadn't been able to work much on actually *solving* the clue. It had been a purely defensive game for a few weeks now, but that was about to change. Jesse and Herman didn't realize that Botori was over for them. Messinger's introduction of Hingham's Script had changed the game. There was no longer any reason for Mouse and Ada to continue hiding. It was time to get rid of the decoy and attack.

Since she had total root access to their computer, it just took a moment to shut them down completely. She'd spent most of the night making sure that all her defenses were in place, and setting up an algorithmic data cruncher to evaluate any DDoS threats.

Naturally, she couldn't allow Jesse and Herman to take final credit for what she and Ada had done the last five months. It was against her ethos. A series of texts that Mouse had written would go out from Herman's and Jesse's phones at 6:59 a.m. to every student at Rickum, right before most students set their alarms.

Herman

"Jesse, watching the first 550 students fail was fun."

Jesse

"Sure was. How did we do it?"

Herman

"I thought you knew?"

Jesse

"But I thought you knew?"

Herman

"Well if it wasn't you and it wasn't me?"

Jesse

"Well, I guess it's time to go, and where
did all these mice come from?"

If everyone was going to make fun of her name, she might as well own it.

The text chain was followed by a GIF of an atomic bomb exploding.

Stretching her tired bones, Mouse cast one more look out over Cambridge, crawled down, and headed back to her room to get an hour of sleep before everything changed.

Ada shook Mouse awake at seven o'clock when she got the text. "It's going exactly the way you expected!" Ada crowed.

Mouse nodded, sleepy but proud, before adding, "It would feel better if we could get a little traction on the next clue. I'm stumped, and ditching our cover means it's time to quit stalling."

Ada nodded. "*The answer was born in 1912.*' I've chronicled every major event that happened that year. The Qing dynasty was replaced by the Republic of China, but the gibberish at the end doesn't seem to be Mandarin. Arizona was founded in 1912, but it's not in Navajo or Hopi either . . ."

Mouse sat up in her bed and groaned. "Why can't these clues just be normal coding challenges? Fenway Park was built in 1912. The *Titanic* sank, the U.S. annexed Alaska, and about a billion actual humans were born. I've spent weeks reading up on this stuff whenever I get a chance, and none of it gets us any closer to cracking this code!"

Ada rubbed her sleep-deprived eyes. "Right. Maybe we've focused too much on the first line of the clue. *Let the riddle be your guide*' . . . It sounds like a throwaway, but it doesn't even rhyme! And nothing is accidental in a Botori clue."

"You're right, but where do we start? I'm trying to let the riddle be my guide!"

"What if the riddle isn't *this* riddle? I mean maybe we are assuming the riddle that is supposed to be our guide is the Botori clue, but what if it's something else? Making false assumptions is one of the stupidest things a coder can do. What else can a riddle be?"

Mouse flipped her Glass back onto her nose and spun her fingers. "Riddle. Synonyms include conundrum, dilemma, enigma, mystery, puzzle, quandary."

Ada raised her eyebrow and looked up. "Hang on. *Enigma*. Wasn't there a famous code system called Enigma?"

Mouse replied with deadly seriousness. "Only the most famous ever. The Nazis used it in World War II, but it was invented in 1918. And first used in 1923. That doesn't help us with the first sentence . . ."

Ada was staring into her own Glass. "I saw a movie about it. About Alan Turing, the British coder who cracked Enigma."

Mouse slammed her fist against her forehead. "He found the 'answer' to the 'riddle' when he cracked Enigma. When was Alan Turing born?"

Ada smiled. "I'll give you one guess."

Mouse punched her small fist into her hand. "1912!"

Ada continued, "So if Enigma is our guide, I bet if we simply take what looks like gibberish at the end of the riddle and run it through the Enigma decoder, then we'll have it."

Five minutes later they were walking to breakfast with a new clue.

> A Russian writer
> A Monarch
> And the Queen of Spain all live here

When they walked into the Great Hall, the whispering felt like a roar. Not even the aftershock of Professor Bunyan's voiding could keep people from obsessively discussing Mouse's latest Botori maneuver. With a loud *ping*, the Botori Portal announced that Mouse and Ada had discovered the third clue.

The Final Scrum had begun. The winner of the next clue would win the entire competition.

All the silence and empty space created from the anxiety around the voiding was filled with buzzing energy as students whispered back and forth, trying to make sense of what had happened.

Herman and Jesse remained the center of attention. They seemed almost relieved as they tried to explain what happened, though even they still didn't really understand. One big thing was clear: They were out.

As Ada and Mouse went from table to table serving food, an uncomfortable silence followed them in a wave of hushed whispers and obvious "shooshes." When they finally got to the Makers' table, Boone couldn't control himself. He broke the silence. "It was you all along?"

The other Makers quickly joined in.

Rufus Shentley begged for an explanation. "Okay, I get how you rooted Jesse's computer, but I can't understand how you ganked Litchfield and Stubble? Their defenses were solid; you couldn't just DDoS."

Mouse beamed.

Abassi Stern interrupted before Mouse could answer. "Wait, when you took out Shelby, her phone was offline? Had you figured out some way to gain root access or did you keep her online without her realizing?"

The bell rang and the circle of students around Mouse became bigger and bigger until Ada grabbed her hand and pulled her toward the kitchen. Reluctantly, Mouse started loading the dishwasher.

"Let's finish this shift as fast as we can. I've been looking for Wurvil and haven't seen him anywhere. We really need this to help us come up with a plan before someone else gets voided, or something worse. Not to mention, I can't wait to see his face when he realizes that a couple Provis might actually win."

Mouse nodded. "It's weird he's not at breakfast."

Ada smirked. "I know, he once told me that since he could teach most of the courses at Rickum, all he was paying for was the meals. He calculated that after regressing opportunity costs and compounding materials, each meal cost him two hundred and ninety-two dollars. I doubt he'd just skip breakfast. I'll check the app to see if our favorite sapient's plugged in somewhere."

Mouse pulled on her Glass. "Good call!" She found him quickly. "He's in the Makers' lab."

"If we're quick we can catch him before the second bell," Ada replied.

They raced to the Makers' lab. The lights were off and the lab was pitch-black. The shadows of huge machines and racks of servers were all that Mouse and Ada could see as they inched their way through the lab.

Mouse looked at Ada. "Okay, I'm getting déjà vu."

Ada shrugged. "He's probably back by the scope and logic analyzer."

The two crept toward the back when suddenly a black light flipped on and the words "GOG MAGOG HAS BEGUN" erupted across the wall in bright neon red, blinding them as footsteps pounded through the lab.

"There's someone in here," Mouse yelled, too disoriented by the darkness and bright words to identify where the sound was coming from. "Ada, are you okay?" she yelled.

Suddenly, another shock of light hit her as the door swung open and then slammed as whoever had been in the lab escaped.

Mouse began running toward the back of the lab, crashing into machines and knocking over a computer until she reached a small figure kneeling on the ground.

"Ada, Ada, are you okay?" Mouse begged as she recognized her roommate.

"Look," Ada whispered.

Mouse gasped at two students slumped over an oscilloscope.

Mouse grabbed the first student's shoulder and pulled him up.

"It's not Wurvil," she said to Ada. "It's not even a sapient. It's a Maker, Stan Reese, and he's still breathing. It's like he was voided, but he doesn't have Glove and Glass implants. How could he be voided?" Mouse gently laid his head down again.

Ada took a deep breath as she looked at the other boy. She whispered with a mixture of sadness and terror, "It's Wurvil."

Mouse looked over at the body stretched across the floor. His bright red hair spilled onto the floor around his head like a glowing halo, muted by the darkness of the room. About four feet from his head was the small outline of a butterfly that must have dropped from the air the moment he was voided.

They raced out of the Makers' lab to get help, but not before Mouse stashed Preying Mantis in her pocket.

CHAPTER 20

The silver walls of the Great Hall shimmered as Mouse and
Ada rushed beneath the metallic dome to get chairs set up
for the all-school assembly that Headmaster Garrick had
announced for that afternoon in light of the recent voidings. Chattering
students and faculty poured into the hastily assembled lines of folding
chairs and filled the enormous space with a chorus of gossip.

"I heard he's going to cancel the rest of the school year."

"Yeah, Beth Carrada was already pulled out by her parents and is
headed back to some school in Peoria, and I heard that dozens of other
students are getting picked up later today."

"I overheard two professors say Garrick's got news that's really going
to be shocking. The Prophet says that the army is being called in."

"That's what I heard, too. More students. Voided. Tons."

"I heard that someone voided an entire class and that an airport's
been attacked!"

The big stage suddenly rose from the floor and Headmaster Garrick
stepped up to address the gaggle of students and teachers. His attire was
notably subdued, and he spoke in a hushed and somber voice:

"Students and faculty of Rickum. I know you've all heard the rumors,
but the truth is just as shocking as it is unexpected. There has been
yet another voiding. Moreover, a nearby student was injured during the

accident. As you are all aware, much of the technology we use at Rickum is potentially dangerous. We believe our students to be capable of handling the responsibility that comes with working at such an advanced level. For multiple incidents of this type to occur in a year is unprecedented and forces us to revise that belief. We must take action to protect our students until we determine the root cause of these incidents. For that reason, we are suspending Botori until further notice. We will be restricting lab usage to daytime hours, and students will need a professor's supervision to work on projects that are not explicitly required by established school curriculum. We also ask that students adhere to the new curfews in place. Given the graffiti in the Makers' lab about this supposed Gog Magog, I want to assure you that there is no evidence of a greater conspiracy. I urge everyone to rely on the facts in this case and not to spend their time reading sensational social media accounts from anonymous muckrakers. Now please return to a mandatory homeroom, where your teachers will be able to answer any questions."

An eerie silence fell over the Great Hall as students' worst nightmare came true: Botori was cancelled. As they traipsed out of the massive auditorium, whispering to one another, the school suddenly felt just a little colder and less familiar than it had before.

"Botori's never been cancelled in the history of Rickum," Mouse fumed to Ada, then sighed in defeat. "I can't believe they suspended it. Right when we were about to win."

Ada sighed, "The Final Scrum is brutal and there's no guarantee we'd even win. I think Gog Magog is a little more serious than a school game."

Mouse shot back her standard look of outraged contempt. "Oh, I can guarantee we were going to win. Besides, you're missing the point: Botori has the answers we need. That was the first clue in Rayburn's password and I'm sure it connects everything somehow."

"Fine, why don't you put all that energy into proving who just voided our friend? Maybe that big brain of yours can help us avoid the same fate."

Mouse nervously fingered Preying Mantis and looked up at Ada, her rage melting into a dull knot in her gut. "I'm just so sick of sniffing around the edges, getting these little hints about what's going on and then watching people we care about get hurt. It feels like it's my fault that people are getting hurt. Everyone's been connected to me and I don't even know *how* to fight back."

She held the drone up toward the light to inspect it, suddenly choking back an unfamiliar urge to cry.

Ada nodded. "Mouse, it's not your fault. Nobody thinks that. But maybe you're right. Maybe we do need to fight back. Nobody else seems able to see what's really going on, and what if you're next?"

Mouse chewed thoughtfully on her thumbnail. "Well, Frink's a professor, so there's not a lot we can do until we have some serious proof. I can't get him ganked just because he doesn't like me. What we need is a way to watch him all day, to see what he's up to."

Mouse again held up the little butterfly that she'd pocketed. "Too bad we can't just barbeque him with Preying Mantis."

Ada's eyes lit up. "That's it!" she chirped.

"And they say I'm the antisocial one. We can't really fry him, Ada. Can we?" Mouse asked hopefully.

Ada pointed to the little robotic butterfly in Mouse's hand. "No, no no. Don't you see? Preying Mantis is perfect! We just need to figure out how to control it. Could you hack it?"

Mouse nodded. "Easy. But how's a flying Zippo lighter going to help?"

"If Frink is really behind all of this—all we need to do is see what he's doing every day. What could be more perfect than tracing all his activity with a tiny drone? I remember you and Wurvil geeking out. You figured out the programming language within about a second. Well, how hard would it be to fit a camera on it?"

"I could mount a miniature 4k video camera on that in two nanoseconds," Mouse scoffed. "We'd want it small so there obviously wouldn't be any LCD or anything like that, but it would pick up a good picture and decent sound."

Ada suddenly looked deflated. "But where can you get one? They just made it impossible to work in the Fab Lab where all the equipment is."

Mouse beamed with pride. "The Quants literally throw out more hardware in a day than I've had my entire life. You remember when I tried to make a beige box? I have a pretty amped robotics lab under my bed. At least by normal standards."

Ada laughed. "I can hardly *find* your bed right now."

"Well, I've got everything I need. Gimme a couple of days and I'll turn Preying Mantis into a 'Spying' Mantis that even Wurvil would be proud of."

THE TRUE MAGICIANS

TENET TEN

There are legal codes. There are moral codes. There is code. Each are comprised of words. Words, just like people, change over time. Every day a million conversations corrupt and adapt the meaning of the words we use. Society plays an eternal game of telephone. The words we use effortless change as they pass from lips to ears. Just like words, each day a thousand experiences corrupt and change the people we know and love. Beware of what you trust. Time itself corrupts code just as it destroys people.

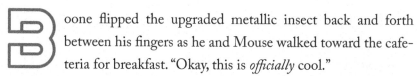oone flipped the upgraded metallic insect back and forth between his fingers as he and Mouse walked toward the cafeteria for breakfast. "Okay, this is *officially* cool."

"It's official. Hooray," Mouse muttered without cracking a smile.

Boone smiled in response, impervious to Mouse's sarcasm. "But how do we control it?"

"Simple," Mouse began, relaxing as she focused on the technical details. "First off, I've built a Wi-Fi-enabled interceptor. My GG rig immediately overrides control of Spying Mantis."

Ada whistled. "Doesn't that mean that if some other drone pilots by while you're controlling Mantis, then you'll take control of that one too?"

Mouse snickered. "Unless it has some crazy security, exactly. It's the only way I could make sure that I wouldn't lose control of Spying Mantis throughout the day and we need it on 24-7 to make sure we don't miss anything. If Frink's really behind the voidings and Gog Magog, then he's obviously doing it secretly."

"How can we make sure that Frink remains the target?" Ada asked.

"We assign a target to Spying Mantis; then we set the distance to follow, and boom. Lots of drones do it. The problem is that for really reliable tracking you need to carry around a GPS transmitter that tells the drone what to follow. Obviously, we can't ask Frink for help."

Ada looked crestfallen. "What do we do?" she asked.

Mouse nodded. "I've linked it to a small NFC tracking tag that we just need to stick on him."

"He'll never find it on his brown, tweed jacket," Ada added. "He wears that disgusting thing every day. All we need to do is to get close enough to stick the tracker on him without him noticing."

"Bingo," Mouse added. "Then I hit 'TARGET' and Spying Mantis will follow him everywhere he goes within the network. Now we just need to get that tag on Frink."

Boone jumped into the air with a fist pump. "Just leave that to me. Razzmatazz!"

Mouse turned to Ada. "Is there anything we can do about that?"

Ada shook her head. "I think 'razzmatazz' comes with the package."

Mouse rolled her eyes as they walked toward Frink's office.

"Remember, Boone, all you need to do is get the sticker onto the back of his blazer. But don't do anything too weird; if he notices you're up to something, we're toast . . ."

Boone nodded seriously. "I've got this. Don't worry about a thing. I'll be totally subtle. Just watch."

Mouse released Spying Mantis, which flew up toward the ceiling. Together the three students huddled outside of Frink's office and waited.

They could hear him yelling into his phone: "Well then, you better find someone who will help. I'm telling you the return policy is clearly stated on your website and I never even *wore* those shoes." Then a brief pause. "Outrageous. Worn out? Smells like a barn? I demand to speak to a manager. I tell you I never once wore them, and I expect a full refund." He paused. "I have no *idea* how a dirty sock found its way into the shoe."

Suddenly the sound of a phone slamming rang out as the door whipped open. Looking at the three students, Frink paused for a moment as though about to say something, harrumphed to himself, and walked off before Mouse could even put on her Glass.

Ada punched Boone's shoulder. He yelped and she pointed to Frink, who was quickly walking away.

Snapping to action, Boone raced after him. "Professor, Professor!"

Frink whipped around. "Yes?"

"Uh, uh," Boone stammered before looking back at Mouse, who frantically spun her fingers.

"Yes, well out with it, you. I just got off an important call, national security, and I *certainly* don't have time for a stuttering fool."

"Well, I guess I just . . ." Boone started panicking.

"Just what?"

"Just wanted to say I love your shoes?"

Boone glanced back at Mouse whose head was still down as she maneuvered Spying Mantis into position.

"My shoes? My shoes . . ." Frink muttered, shaking his head as he turned to walk away.

In a mad panic Boone took a deep breath, wrapped both his arms around the wiry professor, pressed his cheek against the man's shoulder, and gave him an enormous hug.

Frink and Boone both blushed bright red. Mouse hit the word "TARGET," then looked up in confusion at the spectacle of Boone furiously holding onto Professor Frink, who was trying to claw away.

"Should I let Boone know we're good?" Mouse asked Ada.

"Not yet," Ada replied with a grin. "This is priceless."

Boone gulped. "Uh, and I just wanted to say thanks for . . ."

Frink pulled away painfully, stopping Boone with a wave of his hand. He stuttered in an incoherent rage: "Shoes. Touch. Never. Again. Hug."

He staggered away, the little butterfly fluttering behind him.

"That was amazing." Ada laughed, then squinted to see a tiny translucent tag shimmering, almost invisible, on the tattered left tail of his jacket.

Boone could hardly speak for a few seconds. He finally managed to choke out, "What took you so long?"

Mouse shrugged. "Unexpected problem. The system was more powerful than I realized, and I started to control two other robots too. I had to scroll past Edna's whiz-doodler, and Lloyd's talking coconut."

Ada booted the app and the three of them watched as Spying Mantis livestreamed Frink walking down the hallway.

Ada continued, "It's working perfectly. Let's regroup Saturday morning. Each of us should take one day to really scan the video and see if he does anything suspicious or meets anyone unexpected. Let's just hope nothing happens in the meantime . . ."

"Oh no," Boone interrupted as he watched Frink slow down before the bathroom.

Frink checked his watch and continued walking.

"That was close," Boone gasped. "I don't think I'd ever recover from watching Frink using the toilet."

Mouse scowled. "Don't worry. I geotagged each bathroom. So long as he's on campus we'll catch everything *other* than that."

Boone exhaled deeply. "Phew."

• • •

As the light started to peek through the window looking out onto Mass Avenue, Mouse awoke to a gentle tapping at her door.

A familiar voice whispered through her dream, "Wakey, wakey."

She stretched and opened her eyes as the knock grew louder. "Okay. Time to turn off the Saturday morning cartoons and let me in."

Mouse looked over at Ada who was equally puzzled.

"Uh. Wait. We're coming. Who's there?"

"Are you kidding? It's Boone! I couldn't wait any longer to see if Spying Mantis discovered anything."

They looked at each other and had to suppress a laugh.

"Boone, it's not even six yet."

"I know, I thought we wanted to get started at the crack of dawn. Like Gustavesen always says, 'Lose an hour in the morning and you'll be searching for it all day.' Now open up, slowpokes."

Ada covered her head with her pillow and groaned. Five minutes later they let Boone in, who immediately wrinkled his nose at the state of their room. "I do *not* understand how you live like this!"

He picked up a half-eaten box of cereal off Mouse's desk, dislodging a pile of circuit boards that cascaded down onto his shoes. "Really?"

"Tell me about it," Ada agreed.

Boone poked at a banana peel on Ada's desk and cocked his eyebrow.

She blushed as Mouse retaliated with a sharp, "Shut up, Boone. Let's see those notes."

After reviewing the video section by section, they laid their observations next to each other. Ada recorded the essentials, experienced at synthesizing human behavior into clear notes, thanks to years of keeping meticulous notebooks.

> ROUTINE: Mostly spends time in class or alone in office. Lots of youtube, minimal class prep. Always eats in dining hall. Leaves campus every day through cafeteria loading dock. Apparently alone. Returns after thirty min with boxes of vegetables. Dinner, eats with Ms. Farnaby. Multiple discussions with Messinger.
>
> SOCIAL: No close friends except Ms. Farnaby. Tolerated or avoided by most faculty members. Antagonistic relationships with certain students (Mouse). Intense favoritism with others.

When Ada read out what she'd drawn from all their notes, Mouse groaned. "There's nothing here. I mean, we didn't see him doing anything suspicious. No secret hacking sessions, no suspicious meetings. He barely opens his laptop except to watch boring YouTube videos. Just being a mean loner mostly."

"Maybe Frink's innocent?" Ada said. "I mean just because he's a jerk and took out Erik Walters's thesis doesn't mean he's using that knowledge for some nefarious reason. We don't even have a motive."

Mouse shook her head. "I know it's him. We just need to find out where he's working on OM."

"Yeah," Boone added. "And who knew he loved vegetables so much? I mean, is he really eating a box of lettuce a day?"

Mouse and Ada looked at each other and then back at the notes.

"I don't think anyone could eat that much lettuce, and why would he be bringing it on campus in a box? I mean he eats three meals a day in the cafeteria, and we didn't see him cooking once! Why isn't Spying Mantis following him off campus?" Ada asked.

Mouse frowned. "It can't. We're connecting via Wi-Fi networks that Spying Mantis knows. As soon as it hits the edge of the network, it stops till the target's back in range."

Ada's brow furrowed. "So basically, it's impossible to see what he's doing once he leaves?"

Mouse nodded. "It drops off when Frink leaves Rickum's network. No patch on that. No way we can hand off from one network to another without taking a few seconds to re-target."

"So, it's a dead end?" Boone shrugged with disappointment.

Mouse shook her head. "Unless we can get off campus and find a way to re-target him. I mean, we'd just need him to be in place for three seconds so I can latch Spying Mantis to the new network."

Ada had her notebook out, and after a few seconds she looked up with a sheepish grin on her face. "Guys, I think I know a way. We need a spectacle. Something that will distract him so that he doesn't even care that we're off campus."

Her eyes scrunched together as she seemed to play through a scenario in her head. A look of intense pain crossed her face, and she rubbed her left arm and shoulder as if they had just been hit with a baseball bat.

Ada nodded. "It's worth it." She looked at Mouse. "You're promising me that if he stands in one place for three seconds that you can latch the drone to the tracker again and it'll follow him?"

"Yes," Mouse said. "And once Spying Mantis knows the new network, it can store the security key just like a normal computer, so it will be able to stay online when he comes back on campus."

"Okay. You two meet at 3:15 p.m. at the loading dock. Just watch Frink and have your phone out. You'll know what to do."

Boone and Mouse exchanged skeptical looks, then agreed.

"This is gonna be fun," Ada whispered to herself, rubbing her left arm again.

• • •

The clock ticked 3:12.

"We cut it a little short," Boone whispered as he began walking faster toward the loading dock.

Suddenly they skidded to a halt as Ms. Farnaby stepped out of nowhere and scooped Mouse into her arms.

Boone screamed with astonishment as Mouse disappeared into the folds of a warm hug. Mouse cringed and then hugged her back as Boone watched in utter bafflement.

"Hey, Ms. Farnaby," Mouse said.

"Time for a Gigabite visit later today? She's been eating so much better since your visits. And a friend has been bringing her the most delicious veggie feasts . . ."

Mouse blanched. "Can't today. Kind of a rush. Can we do it tomorrow instead?"

Ms. Farnaby smiled and nodded. "Of course. She misses you."

Ms. Farnaby waved and walked off.

"Uh, explain. I didn't know you two were . . . friends?" asked Boone, still visibly startled. "That was very un-Mouse."

Mouse shrugged. "I asked about her pet one time when Ada and I needed to distract her. Turns out she has a wallaby named Gigabite. She brought me to see him and I visit once in a while. No biggie."

Boone replied with a look of surprise, "How did you know she would have a pet? You just guessed?"

"I know secretaries. I've been sitting with them for years waiting for principals or counselors. They always either garden or have a pet. Clearly, Ms. Farnaby is *not* a gardener. Anyway, we kinda became friends."

Boone suddenly realized that they were running out of time and took off like a bolt, yelling as he ran. "Hurry up!"

They swung around the corridor and pushed straight out the back of the kitchen to the loading dock. They looked around the empty dock.

"You see Frink? Or Ada?" Mouse asked.

Boone replied nervously, "I don't see either of them."

Suddenly they heard tires screech and looked up as a black Lincoln towncar smashed into a blond-haired kid in a red hoodie riding a beat-up BMX bike across the street.

"Oh my god, that's Ada," Mouse shouted, her heart shooting up into her throat.

Ada looked badly hurt, strewn across the ground directly in front of the car.

"What on earth!" a flustered Frink yelled as he jumped out of the back of the car.

Mouse took off toward Ada down the loading dock by the street. Boone tried to stop her, but she slapped his hand away.

When Frink saw her approaching, his face was furious. "What are you doing here? You're not allowed off campus!"

Ignoring Frink, she ran to Ada's side. "Are you all right? Please be okay."

Ada shook her head woozily and said, "Where am I?" She gave Mouse's hand a discreet squeeze.

Frink looked horrified, and suddenly Mouse understood what was happening. Without waiting for Frink's response, she whipped out her phone and connected to a hotspot labelled "Ada's Phone," opening the Spying Mantis control app as fast as she could.

"Get up, you idiot," snarled Frink. "Your mother will hear about this! Off campus, truancy . . . she will not be pleased!"

Ada remained down on the ground. Mouse saw that Spying Mantis had connected to Ada's hotspot, and clicked "TARGET," watching the progress bar move excruciatingly slow across her screen.

Frink seemed to be getting nervous. "Come on now, you're all right." He gulped. "Right? Now you just get up and we'll call it even. I, I don't want to see another student hurt."

From around the corner, Spying Mantis whizzed toward them and stopped a few feet away.

Ada jumped to her feet and smiled.

"Deal. 'Bye!" Then she turned on her heel and raced away before Frink could respond.

He turned around and returned to the idling car. Just as he started to slam the door shut, a small robotic butterfly zipped quietly in behind him.

Ada and Boone had joined Mouse in her hiding spot on the loading dock, and they watched together as the car pulled away.

Mouse shook her head in amazement. "Ada, the way you deal with people really is black magic. You did it, and without getting anyone in trouble!"

"Wow," Boone gushed. "And I actually thought you were hurt."

Mouse nodded as they rushed back into Rickum. "Seriously. It was so, I don't know, *scary*, watching you crash like that. I felt, I felt . . ."

Ada giggled, embarrassed by the attention. "Relief?"

Mouse glared at her and barked back, "No. Sad."

Ada smiled back. "I'm just kidding. Thanks, Mouse, but no need to worry. I learned that trick years ago from some punks in Harvard Square I knew from my phreaking days. They used to prank each other all the time. Sorry I freaked you out. Now let's log into Spying Mantis's video feed and see what's happening."

They turned on the live feed, but it was just static.

"Hmm," Ada said, worried. "Did it work?"

"I don't know. Something must have happened to the live feed. Let's check the recorded video."

Mouse quietly typed a command into her phone and brought up the video. It perfectly captured the crash from a distance. Boone cringed as the car smashed into Ada's left side.

As Frink berated the seemingly unconscious victim, the image shifted once Spying Mantis latched onto its target. It swooped inside as Frink opened his car door.

They watched Frink speaking to a man whose back was turned away from them.

"I'm sorry, sir. That little brat came out of nowhere."

"Enough of this nonsense," the man replied. "I want to know about Mouse. Is it working? Is our old nemesis causing problems?"

As Frink began to reply, the man turned to face him and Boone, Ada, and Mouse gasped as the face of Trent Rayburn came into focus.

"My dad!" Boone yelped as they continued watching.

"There are signs that Walters is around but nothing more. He's still not showing his hand."

"I was talking about Prophet. Peter Prophet. It's gotta be him," Rayburn barked.

Frink shuddered. "I regret to inform you that there's still nothing. He disappeared into thin air over a decade ago."

As Spying Mantis fluttered Rayburn whipped around.

"You idiot," he raged with his fist in the air. "Someone's watching."

The fist crashed against the small drone and the screen went dark.

Ada grabbed Mouse's shoulder and asked, "Why are the only two members of the Pericles Society who haven't disappeared off the face of the earth sneaking around together?"

"Not to mention our biggest suspects."

Boone shrank. "*Suspects?* Plural. Uh, my dad is *not* involved in this."

Ada's face grew serious. "Remember when we overheard Frink and Garrick talking? Frink said Walters wasn't the one with a score to settle. And he mentioned powerful people when they were talking about Mouse's Rickum nomination. He could've been talking about Rayburn."

Boone's voice changed just a little as he snapped, "This *isn't* about my dad. And I'd appreciate it if you'd stop saying he was a suspect."

Mouse turned to him. "We're just trying to figure out what's happening here, Boone. I mean your dad did just mention my name, and it's not the first time. He knew I was going to be coming to Rickum before I did."

Biting his lip, Boone spoke in a small voice. "You heard him talking about Peter Prophet? That's where we should be looking."

Ada squeezed Boone's shoulder, interrupting before he could continue. "Maybe your dad's not behind the voidings, but something's going on. For some reason two members of the Pericles Society are wrapped up in something and they were talking directly about Mouse. Obviously, there's a connection that we don't understand, and if we don't find out what it is, Mouse is either going to get thrown out of Rickum, or worse."

Boone sighed, "I don't want anything to happen to Mouse. I won't let anything happen to either of you. I just don't think you understand my dad. He's not a bad guy; he's just always trying to prove that he's worthy of all his success. I think he's always been that way. I just know that he'd never do anything to hurt someone."

Mouse nodded. "Boone, I trust you. Okay. There is one other member of the Pericles Society that we haven't investigated at all. Maybe if we figure out where Ella Lightly is, we can start to tie these things together."

Boone smiled. "Wait, you're not supposed to agree with me."

"I know," Mouse snickered, "but I feel like we've got a big fight coming up, and I can't spend all my energy fighting with you. When the time comes for me to hit whoever's behind all this, I want to make sure it hurts."

CHAPTER 22

Mouse awoke with a start. Her face was smooshed into her keyboard, and she realized that when she'd fallen asleep on her computer, her nose had typed pages and pages of gibberish. All night long she'd been trying to snoop around the Rickum network, looking for hints about Ella Lightly. She still hadn't gotten anywhere. Ella had absolutely no digital footprint, and apart from her panel and yearbook picture, she didn't seem to exist at all.

She glanced over at Ada, still sleeping, and realized for the first time that she was starting to feel as though she might actually fit in. Not with the Provis or the Quants and the Makers, and certainly not the Admin. It was with Ada and Boone. She could feel herself trusting them.

Looking across at Ada's alarm, she remembered that they didn't have kitchen duty that morning. Ada would sleep right till the last minute before their first class. Since she couldn't sleep any longer, Mouse decided to slip out before Ada woke up. It took her just a moment to get ready.

The bathroom was all Ada's, and it was a mess. Mouse thought with a smile how it was sort of like the robotics lab she'd built under her bed. Instead of breadboxes and wiring, there were lip glosses and different kinds of makeup. Just a different way to create something. For Ada it was connection, and for Mouse it was code. She was playing with one of Ada's elaborate headbands when she heard a loud, stiff knock on their door.

"Mouse? Are you awake?" a voice called from the hallway.

With astonishment she realized it was Ms. Farnaby. It wasn't even 8:00 a.m. yet.

As Mouse opened the door, a pit opened up in her stomach.

"Oh, sweetie. When I heard, I just had to come and get you myself. We'll go talk with the headmaster and get this all straightened out."

The moment she heard Ms. Farnaby's words, Mouse realized that it was happening again. Her stomach spun and twisted. The familiar feeling of fear swept over her. Mouse didn't know the details yet, but she was well acquainted with what was about to happen. She knew the drill *too* well. Authority figure arrives before school, bringing her to some office to speak to some boss to tell her what she always knew: *Pack your bags. You don't belong.*

She glanced at her roommate as she pulled on her shoes, hoping Ada didn't wake up. Her stomach lurched again at the thought that Ada might be left with this pathetic image of her being escorted away before she had a chance to explain.

"Oh, honey, I'm sure there's some misunderstanding," babbled Ms. Farnaby. "We'll get you right to Headmaster Garrick. He's a good man and I'm sure he'll help figure this out."

Ms. Farnaby was speaking for the sake of speaking. Words to fill the silence. She'd already told Mouse everything she needed to know. They were going to the headmaster. That was it for her and that was it for Rickum.

She waited for the white-hot anger that usually overtook her, but it didn't come. Instead, her mind raced.

Mouse took a deep breath. She couldn't just fall back into the same routine she'd been in over and over again when she was escorted from one home to the next. This wasn't the same. She looked over and reminded herself that Ms. Farnaby wasn't just some state-appointed counselor who didn't care about her.

This time is different. Before, I had nothing to lose. Now I have friends. And a place I almost feel like I belong. I'm not leaving without a fight.

Without a word, she pulled on her GG rig and opened the secure messaging app. Spinning her fingers, she sent Boone one ping, then another.

Mouse's hand spun silently at her side.

> Boone. Wake up.

> It's urgent.

She followed Ms. Farnaby in silence, checking her messages to be ready once Boone responded. Periodically, Ms. Farnaby would ask another question, and then a moment later she'd answer it herself. Each silent step felt like a mile. They finally arrived at the headmaster's door. Mouse turned, almost despite herself, and looked up at Ms. Farnaby. "Can you say goodbye to Gigabyte for me?"

"I certainly will. Of course, Mouse." Then she gave her a big hug and Mouse realized with a start that Ms. Farnaby hadn't been speaking for no reason at all. The words she'd been saying were *filled* with meaning. She had been speaking to try to make Mouse feel better about something that was about to hurt her. The words hadn't been wasted and useless at all; Mouse just never knew how to hear them before.

Suddenly, she heard a *ping*.

> It's Boone. What's up?

"Come in, come in," Garrick yelled.

Mouse turned back to Ms. Farnaby one last time as she stepped through the door and added, "Thanks. I'm glad you came to get me today."

Then the door slammed behind her and she realized that her worst fears were spot-on. Professor Frink stood with both hands clasped behind his back, staring out the window at the bustling early morning activity in Harvard Square.

Before Garrick began speaking, her fingers continued to spin frantically as she texted Boone her plan.

"Okay, out with it, Frink. Let's not torture the child."

Frink shook his head back and forth. Finally, he whipped around. His left eye bounced as he glared at Mouse, but nothing about him was clownish now.

Mouse glared back. She remembered Tenet Five of the Pericles Society: *A True Magician will avoid war, but once the banner is raised, they will win at all costs.* If Frink wanted war, she'd fight back with everything she had.

"It's puzzled me from the start. On the first day of school a child is ruthlessly voided and nearly left for dead. Why? Why would you commit such a heinous act?" Frink asked.

"Yeah, Frink? What exactly would make a poor kid who had just been dumped here use a coding language that she couldn't possibly know, hurt a kid she'd never met? I'm curious about this one." Mouse heard her voice crack with frustration.

"It's *Professor Frink*. And the reason is very simple: Melvin Messinger saw it before anyone else. Revenge!"

Mouse nearly jumped out of her chair. "What does *Melvin Messinger* have to do with anything? And why would *I* want revenge against Anna Briem? I'd never even met her before!"

"You?" He snorted with disdain. "You were just a pawn in Walters's game." Frink turned to Garrick. "That's what Melvin proved. He's uncovered all the details about Walters's heinous plot to unleash havoc on the world through Gog Magog. I've been studying Erik Walters's old papers on Objective-M here in the Obsidian Vault and it all adds up. Walters just needed a person on the inside to help him infiltrate the system. Who better than a misunderstood orphan?"

"If you've already decided I'm guilty, then why am I here? In fact, why am I at Rickum in the first place? Just another Concilium reject gone wrong?"

Garrick closed his eyes and sighed. "Patience, Mouse."

Mouse unclenched her fists and exhaled. Her moment was coming; she couldn't rush this.

Mouse looked at Garrick, who sat there, stone-faced, as Frink continued.

"Let me put the pieces of this puzzle together. On your first day at Rickum, a student is voided for the first time in Rickum's history. A student who caught you engaging in unsanctioned criminal internet activity on your first night at this esteemed institution."

He paused and looked at Mouse's reaction. "Oh, surprised we know about your little hack on Rayburn Tech? I've known all along. Our servers keep a running log of all digital activity for cases just like this. Now where were we? After Erik Walters escapes, and contacts you via Rickum's *internal network*. That's right, Melvin knew about your little hologram secret. Another voiding, this time of an esteemed professor, and again you're first on the scene. And then more voidings, with Wurvil and Stan Reese. Finally, you brazenly announce your true intention by painting 'Gog Magog' at the scene of the crime."

Garrick looked at Mouse and sighed.

"Mouse, we knew about your history when we accepted you, and I had hoped that this environment would allow you to use your talent in a more positive way. Concilium was intended to bring the greatest talent into Rickum, but I'm afraid it seems that again it's proven too challenging. My hands are tied. Last night after your little escapade off campus, Professor Messinger, under the direction of Professor Frink, found a cannister of the same paint that was used to paint Gog Magog hidden in *your* room."

From the corner of her eye Mouse saw the message pop up that she'd been waiting for.

> I'm ready.

Mouse suddenly exploded. "I never bought any stupid paint, let alone voided anyone! It was obviously planted! Just another way you've tried to pin your problems on a Provi from the start. Just watch what I'm going to do to this school's precious reputation. Not to mention you, Garrick. You're as bad as the rest of them, allowing students to be harmed to make sure Rickum's reputation stays golden. Just you watch."

Garrick blanched. "Mouse, I understand you're upset, but . . ."

"Upset? Upset? I'll make sure that every subreddit, blog, and forum about technology knows exactly how you treat an underprivileged kid!"

"Please be reasonable," the headmaster muttered. "We are in an impossible situation here. We found the same paint used during the voiding of Wurvil Looper in your room."

Mouse slowly unclenched her fists and took a deep breath. "You want me to be reasonable? I'll be reasonable if *you'll* be reasonable. If you're going to make me rebuild my life *again*, I at least want my school transcript and any other records you have about me. You can't just kick me out for some made-up reason, and not leave me with a shred of proof that I ever walked the halls of your *fine institution*. And I want them *now*!"

Garrick paused. "I mean we can't just create them out of thin air. I'm sure we can review and have them forwarded."

Mouse glared as she spun her fingers to use her Glass to take a photo of Garrick and then Frink. "Smile, I just took the photo I'll send along with a detailed description of how I've been treated here to *Script-sploit* if I don't get my school transcript before leaving this office. They'd just love the story of a poor young girl brought to Rickum through some secret program, bullied terribly, and then framed to help protect Trent Rayburn."

Garrick began waving his hands in a gesture of calm.

"Stop, stop, I'm sure we can get you copies of all your records. Erwin, you know where to go. We'd usually send them along afterward, but if it would make you feel more secure to have them now, I'm sure we can accommodate that."

Frink spluttered, but Garrick raised a hand to silence him. "Get her transcript. This way, it's a clean break."

Frink stormed out the door of the office. Mouse struggled to keep a smile from creeping onto her face. *It worked! Let's just hope Boone can follow instructions.*

As she sat in silence, Garrick stared at her seriously. "You'll be expelled from Rickum and released back to the state's jurisdiction. I believe they've already identified a good place for you. It's called Blackwell. You'll be picked up tomorrow. Obviously, you can pack up today and say your goodbyes."

They sat quietly for a few more awkward minutes before Frink came back up the hallway and huffed his way through the door. "Here! Take your records," he sneered as he handed her a manila envelope. She opened it, scanning the single piece of paper inside.

Just a transcript. No record of who nominated me. I guess that would have been too much to ask.

Frink smirked. "I hope you've learned something from this ordeal. There is order for a reason, and you do not get ahead by breaking rules."

Mouse stood up and looked at her transcript one last time. She slowly crumpled it into a ball with one hand, winked at Professor Frink, and dropped it into the trash, then walked out of the oak-paneled office. Behind her, Frink gasped and began spluttering again about disrespect. Garrick shut him up with a warning.

"Be careful, Erwin. There aren't many coders like that, not that I've ever met. You just might find that the mouse is really a lion, and even worse, that the lion has your head in her mouth."

• • •

As soon as the door swung shut behind her, Mouse broke into a sprint. She didn't pause for breath until she was back at her room. When she burst through the door, Ada was sitting up straight on her bed, looking worried.

"Mouse, what happened? Where have you been?"

"I'll explain in a second. Where's Boone?"

"Boone? Probably in his room, why?"

Mouse checked her rig, then nodded. "He's on his way. Hang on."

As soon as she sat on her bed and opened the folder containing her file, there was a banging on the door accompanied by a high-pitched yelp, "Mouse!"

Boone burst in frantically.

"I did it," he panted. "I followed Frink into Weezy's Garden, and he went into the maintenance shed by Mahan's Box, but he was in there for a weirdly long time—like five minutes. Then he came out with this folder in his hand and went back to Garrick's office. Was that what you wanted?"

"Okay, *what* is going on?" Ada exploded. "Why are you having Boone follow Frink around Rickum before school's even started?"

"Guys, I have bad news," Mouse said and took a deep breath. "I'm done at Rickum. They dragged me out of bed to tell me the good news."

Ada gasped. "I can't believe it. You're suspended? I never thought Frink would report us being off campus after the accident."

"No, not suspended," Mouse whispered, containing the hurt and anger she felt simmering inside her. "Expelled. Extricated. Removed for good. For the crime of helping Erik Walters void Anna Briem, everyone else, and initiating Gog Magog. I was totally set up. The good old state of Massachusetts gets me back tomorrow. Hello, Blackwell."

Ada shook her head. "No. That doesn't make *any* sense."

"Since when does sense matter? Guilt by association. The weirdest part is that apparently Melvin Messinger is the one who convinced Frink that I was the problem the whole time."

Ada shook her head. "I can't believe this . . . " She looked over at Boone, who was still panting. "Why did you ask Boone to follow Frink?"

Mouse suddenly smiled. "Gathering intel. When Ms. Farnaby came to get me this morning, I knew immediately that I was about to get thrown out. I realized it was my last opportunity. A chance to figure out what's really happening. Walters, the hologram, Frink and Rayburn, the voidings—and me. Why I'm here, I mean."

Ada frowned. "I want to figure this out, too. More than anything, but if you're really leaving tomorrow, then how can we figure it out in one night when we've been trying all year?"

"Well," she said and glanced at Boone. "I realized there's one place we haven't been able to check. If I could get them concerned enough about my response to being expelled, then maybe they'd get me my student records to shut me up. So, I told Boone to wait outside Garrick's office and follow whoever came out, to see where they went—"

Boone jumped in, excited. "I waited, just like you asked, and then Frink came out, looking all huffy and puffy, and that's when I saw him go to Weezy's Garden. They keep the records in the maintenance shed!"

Ada was looking excited now. "It must not really be a maintenance shed. Rule number one of hiding things: Stick them in plain sight. It's probably a hidden entrance! I bet the records are underground beneath Mahan's Box!"

Mouse nodded. "Well, we're about to find out."

"Razzmatazz," Boone whispered as Ada's copy of her mother's faculty access card opened the locked shed nestled under the huge white oak. As the rusty door creaked open, they saw the long, dark staircase inside.

Boone gulped. "You were right. This is crazy!! It's like some secret dungeon."

"Yeah," Ada whispered as they traipsed down a long winding staircase, pointing to the thick lines of silver that narrowed and then petered out. "We're officially off the grid."

At the bottom of the stairs was a huge, low-ceilinged room lined with shelf after shelf of yellowed folders.

Ada looked over at Mouse with a strange look of pride. "You did it. Instead of getting angry and blowing everything up, you tricked Frink and worked together with Boone to find the one place we couldn't find."

"Maybe you're rubbing off on me," Mouse said, blushing. She continued, "I think we should start with the Pericles Society. The version we saw in the yearbook photo Bunyan was holding. Each mystery links back to the four of them, and the only way I'm gonna be here next year is by unraveling who's actually behind the voidings, and proving Frink and Messinger wrong."

Ada smiled. "So what's the game plan?"

"Ada, you focus on Rayburn. Boone, you've got Frink, and I'll take Erik Walters and Ella Lightly."

Ada dove at the shelves of files. Boone whistled through the small gap in his front teeth and got to work.

Once Mouse found the files she was looking for, she barely felt time passing as she flipped through report after report. There were disciplinary reports and grades, letters sent home and end-of-year evaluations. Just the application profiles were enough to keep her attention.

The picture of the two hackers emerged almost immediately. Walters: a computer prodigy who came from nothing. His parents were barely present in his life, and couldn't care less about their son. If it weren't for Concilium, he'd have never been able to afford Rickum. And then there was Ella Lightly. Mouse's heart skipped a beat when she saw that Ella was an orphan. Ella's parents had died in a car accident when she was just a few months old, and she had been raised in a comfortable home by loving grandparents in a small town on the island of Maui. She had insisted on applying to Rickum and they had agreed, baffled by their brilliant granddaughter, who seemed to know more about computers than anyone they'd ever met.

End-of-Year Report, Year 1:

WALTERS, ERIK

Academic performance: *A+*

Behavioral and Social Evaluation: *Gets along well with fellow students in class but seems to have been slow to develop lasting friendships. Despite exceptional Botori performance, did not develop bond with Peter Prophet. Unusual incident with Frink led to Walters completing the contest alone. Guarded, may self-isolate. Diet and sleeping patterns erratic.*

Additional Comments: *Winner of Botori. Walters is an exceptionally focused, bright first-year. His work ethic borders on obsessive. Although he rarely completes assignments in the manner requested by his teacher, his solutions to the problem presented tend to be elegant and original. Clear sapient potential.*

End-of-Year Report, Year 1:
LIGHTLY, ELLA

Overall Academic Performance: *A*

Club: *Maker*

Behavioral and Social Evaluation: *Ella is a strong personality and inspires others to follow, although she struggles to accommodate team needs. She is close with her roommate, J. Rote. She does not have many superficial relationships and is often alone working. Lightly was involved in several incidents this semester requiring disciplinary action. She is impatient and struggles with appropriate anger management.*

Additional Comments: *Ella has excelled as a Maker. Completes all work in a satisfactory manner, suscep-*

*tible to blowing off smaller assignments if bored by
the material.*

Disciplinary Incident #203b

Students: *Lightly, Ella. Walters, Erik.*

Incident Description: *Prof. Carlson sent the students to
the headmaster's office after an in-class discussion esca-
lated inappropriately. During a history lesson on the
Hacker Code, Walters disagreed with a comment made
by Lightly re: the anti-stealing ethic. Lightly refused to
allow discussion to continue, calling Walters a "two-
bit n00b with the moral compass of a pigeon standing
next to an electromagnet."*

Headmaster's Comment: *When questioned about the
interaction, Lightly was honest. She seemed slightly
embarrassed at the outburst but refused to apologize,
defending her words as "accurate." Walters was quiet,
confirming the details of the interaction and little else.
Lightly was given one session of detention.*

Boone suddenly yelped. "Hey, guys, I just found something about
Peter Prophet. In Frink's student file there's a nurse's note from his first
year that says, 'Desperate to impress his roommate Erik Walters, Peter
Prophet disguised himself and abducted young Erwin Frink, threat-
ening to hurt him until he told him the answer to the third Botori
riddle. During Prophet's interrogation he mistakenly stabbed Erwin's
left hand, which needed eleven stitches.'"

"What a psycho," Ada said, cringing.

Mouse hardly looked up, so engrossed in the story of Ella Lightly and Erik Walters. As soon as Boone finished speaking, she continued reading the small pile of letters and transcripts in front of her, desperate for some clue.

From: *R. Carlson@rickumacademy.org*

To: *headmaster@rickumacademy.org*

Dear Headmaster Hawthorne,

> *I am writing to briefly explain an unusual grading decision. A third-year student (E. Walters) recently turned in a final project which was to be completed in C++, the language we are studying during this unit. Walters completed his project in Haskell, and turned it in late, citing "independent work" as the reason. When questioned in class about this, several students (notably E. Lightly, J. Rote, T. Rayburn) came to his defense. Considering the stunning elegance of his solution to the problem posed, I have chosen to overlook the unusual approach and give the project an A.*

> *Please contact me with any concerns,*
> *Prof. Carlson*

Disciplinary Report #412a:

Students: *Lightly, Ella. Walters, Erik.*

Incident Description: *Ella Lightly and Erik Walters were found in the Maker lab at 4:12 a.m., well after lights-out. When questioned, both answered that they were "working on final projects." As there were no active terminals in the lab, this does not seem plausible.*

*There was no evidence of rule-breaking beyond the cur-
few violation. The students were asked to report to the
headmaster's office the next morning after breakfast.*

Headmaster's Comment: *Lightly has been in conflict
with Walters at several points during this year, so it
was a surprise to see them backing each other up in my
office. Walters was chagrined, but less taciturn than
in previous interactions. Lightly showed none of the
aggression that has previously gotten her in trouble.
This actually seems to be a behavioral improvement for
both students. They were each given a warning, with
no further punishment.*

Student Club Constitution Application:

Club Title: *The Pericles Society*

Faculty Advisor: *Professor Bunyan*

Club Mission Statement: *To build a society of coders
with a clear ethical purpose.*

Students: *Ella Lightly, Erik Walters, Trent Rayburn,
Erwin Frink*

Faculty Note: *Walters and Lightly are two of the most
talented students I have ever seen come through my
first-year courses. Rayburn is a hard worker and highly
ambitious. I believe they are looking for an outlet to
explore extracurricular coding challenges, and although
they refuse to specify the exact activity to which they
will devote club time I have faith that it will be well
worth support from this fine institution. Despite Frink
and Lightly's history of animosity, their mutual respect*

for Rayburn and Walters seems to be a common bond.
Assuming Frink's grades improve I'm fine allowing
him to join with the others.

APPLICATION APPROVED

It took Mouse a little over an hour to read twice through all of Lightly's and Walters's school records. Slowly, a picture emerged. Walters was brilliant, quiet, awkward. Never quite in trouble, never quite following the rules. Mouse loved the way he turned assignments on their head, always finding a way to solve the problem no one else even saw was there.

Ella reminded Mouse of herself in other ways. Her school record was remarkably similar to Mouse's own, peppered with repeated visits to the headmaster's office, and the occasional mandatory counseling session. To someone else, it might look as if Ella was a troubled kid who'd never learned to play well with others, but Mouse knew better.

Mouse knew how angry she got when people didn't listen, when her teachers told her things she knew to be wrong and she was expected to just shut up and take notes. Mouse knew the frustration of listening to someone complaining about their parents refusing to pay for a new phone, when she would give up her phone for life just to have parents to complain about.

Lightly and Walters were an unlikely couple, but by the middle of their second year it was clear that they had become inseparable. They snuck off campus together to sit in on lectures from their favorite MIT professors and explore Cambridge. Along with Rayburn and Frink, they won a handful of prizes, but nothing remarkable. Mouse wasn't surprised. She knew their real work had flown well under the radar under the names Cassandra and Tiresias. She still couldn't believe she was reading their high school records.

During their final year, Lightly's aging grandparents both passed away. Mouse was surprised at the pang she felt reading that letter—she'd never had parents to lose, and she couldn't imagine losing them twice. In the transcripts from her sessions with the grief counselor, Lightly spoke about her plans of moving in with Walters after her graduation from Rickum, about working on some "major projects" that she and the Pericles Society had in process. She seemed sad but hopeful, as if she had found another family at Rickum.

The last document she found in their file was a short email appended to the end of her transcript, from Ella to Erik. It was a picture of the two of them standing next to each other. They were beautiful in their youth, standing straight and tall and Ella's right hand very gently holding Erik's left. Beneath the image was a note from Ella to Erik: "If you ever lose me, I'll be waiting in oorbit."

Mouse's heart skipped a beat as she recognized the message. Ella had just slightly misspelled "orbit." Now she knew that Walters's famous last words before prison were a message to Ella, but it didn't help her understand why or where Ella was now.

When Mouse had read from their application letters all the way through their time at Rickum until they received their diplomas, she was left with the feeling of having come to the end of the best book she'd ever read, and then discovering that the author forgot to say what happened to the characters next. What had happened to Ella?

Frustrated, she tried to think of ways to get around the nofollow tag that had erased their tracks after Rickum.

The records might be stored as hard copies, but Mouse wasn't surprised to see that the Wi-Fi signal in the room was as lightning-fast as everything at Rickum. She pulled on her GG rig and opened up TOR to search the deep web. It only took Mouse a few spins to make her way to the Pittsfield public records. Erik Walters had rented an apartment in 2000–2002, paid a few utility bills, registered for a library card. That was it—no hospital records, no traffic fines.

Suddenly, Mouse's eyes lit up with understanding. She knew things about Walters and Lightly that other hackers who'd been trying for years to learn about Erik Walters did not. She knew the kind of people they were. They were people like her, and she knew what she would have done.

With a nervous tension, she knew how to find out more about them. She carefully punched in:

> ## SEARCH = ELLA LIGHTLY

And watched as the software crawled the web. As she expected, dozens of pages were returned in her search.

She narrowed the search parameters to just Pittsfield. She smiled as the millions were winnowed to the one record she had ever found. One footprint in the snow. A lease for the home that Walters and Lightly had lived in for years.

Scrunching her eyes, she took a deep breath and amended the search:

> ## FILTER = EITHER/OR
> ## CASSANDRA [AND] TIRESIAS

Her heart leapt as one more document emerged.

As soon as she opened the file, it felt as though everything collapsed around her. In the time it takes for a group of words to turn from symbols into meaning, everything she'd read turned to ash. All of the joy she'd experienced reading their history turned to rage.

The image on the computer was of a birth certificate from the local Pittsfield hospital. It had been created on her birthday.

She desperately looked to find other birth certificates created that day, but she already knew that those children would have parents, those babies would have an identity. Only the child of Tiresias and Cassandra would be left behind, pseudonyms instead of parents. That baby was the one thing every tenet of the Pericles Society warned about: *code without purpose.*

> ADMITTED PARENTS' NAMES:
> CASSANDRA AND TIRESIAS

> NEWBORN'S FIRST NAME: NONE

> NEWBORN'S LAST NAME: GAMMA

• • •

Ada and Boone stared in stunned silence as Mouse turned on her heel, kicked open the door without a word, and sprinted up the staircase away from them. Her footsteps faded quickly into the distance.

Mouse's heart was beating as fast as it had ever beat in her life. She couldn't believe what she'd just seen. She raced up the stairwell, then stopped and clenched one fist and punched into her open hand. Taking a deep breath, she pulled her hand up to her eyes and marveled at how small her fist looked.

She thought about the Frippers, the Zengs, and the Hickenloopers and all the other homes that she had lived in. She realized with astonishment that they probably wouldn't even remember her name. Hot tears began to crowd her vision. She blinked them away before they could fall, pushed open the double doors, and ran as fast as she could into Rickum.

Everything she'd always wondered her whole life finally made sense. She knew who her parents were, even if she couldn't believe it: Cassandra and Tiresias. Ella Lightly and Erik Walters. But as soon as she had looked away from the computer screen, she realized that nothing had changed.

She was more alone than ever.

Think, Mouse. You can't just give up because they gave up on you. What does it all mean? "Waiting in oorbit."

She raced into the library and sat down with a piece of paper, writing that phrase over and over again. As she stared at the letters, something slowly began to change. She wrote each letter on a scrap of paper and began moving them around. They almost spelled "robot," but she was left with the "i."

She felt disembodied, as though she was watching herself moving the pieces of paper around, and couldn't tell if it was because she'd just been expelled from Rickum or because she'd finally discovered her parents— but everything felt as if it was happening outside of her, to someone else. She took a deep breath and looked back at the letters:

O O R B I T

Suddenly the letters clicked together into a familiar pattern. The same word that had kicked off this entire adventure was the one word that would finish it.

B O T O R I

I've got you, Ella. If you're waiting in oorbit, then I'm coming to get you.

But before she could win a game that had already been cancelled, she had to figure out the final riddle. There was only one person she'd met who seemed to know everything, who seemed to be watching even when he wasn't there, but she didn't know how to find him. Suddenly, Mouse had an idea. She nearly knocked Professor Whippleton down as she took off to the nearest media lab.

Why not go back to where it all started? My back door into Rayburn's network is still active. It's compromised, but what do I care if I get caught or if they changed the password? I just need to get noticed.

Her fingers danced across the keyboard as she brazenly rebooted the Trusting Trust back door into Rayburn Tech's servers.

WELCOME TO RAYBURN TECH.
WHO ARE YOU LOOKING FOR?

She typed "MOUSE GAMMA" and waited silently as the password field popped up. She prayed that secret name would be enough
to get someone's attention. She didn't bother clicking around, and she
didn't launch anything to distract the security. This time she wanted
to be found.

In less than five seconds her Glass pinged with a direct message.

> What are you doing coming back in here?
> Get out!

Mouse closed the window of the computer and replied directly to the
message in her GG rig.

> I'm looking for you.

The cursor blinked a few times.

> Why?

She quickly replied.

> I need an answer and I need it
> right now. It's a riddle. I think you're
> pretty good at solving riddles.

> I was once. What is it?

> A Russian writer. A Monarch. And
> the Queen of Spain all live here.

Mouse stared at the cursor as it blinked, desperate for it to keep writing. Desperate for something that could help her send the message that she needed. Her heart sunk as she saw the mystery person type.

> Sorry. My lepidoptery is rusty. I don't know if I can help.

She banged a response into the keyboard.

> What are you talking about?

> Lepidoptery. The study of butterflies. The famous Russian writer Vladimir Nabokov discovered an entire genus of butterflies that was named after him, the "Nabokovia genus." The monarch butterfly is a famous species of butterfly. Every year all the monarch butterflies in the world fly to one village in Mexico. Finally, the Queen of Spain is a fritillary butterfly related to the monarch, but I don't know the answer. I'm sorry I've let you down. I don't know where they all live.

It was all she needed. She finished their chat.

> Don't worry, I do.

She wanted to type one more question. One more burning question, but she knew if she did, then she'd never be able to finish what she had started.

Instead of asking, "Who are you?" she thought of the only *real* family she'd ever known: Ada and Boone. She logged off and raced out of the lab, brushing past a handful of students making their way to the dorms before lunch.

She knew where she had to go, and chills ran through her as she thought of it. The one place at Rickum where butterflies all lived: the Natural History Wing.

As she got closer, the quality of the building got noticeably worse. It was the one area of Rickum where nature seemed to dominate technology. Glass cases held hundreds of animals. There were stuffed bears and deer. She walked through the area devoted to mammals, and through the dinosaur section where the school proudly displayed a full-length mosasaur, and microraptor.

The hallways wound past room after room of natural wonders. The geology room held enormous crystals, stalactites, and stalagmites that had been grown to create the environment of a deep cave. Then there was the rain forest room where rain spluttered from the ceiling day and night, creating a perfect environment for species rare as sinkhorn mushrooms, wollemi pines, and hundreds of other weird and beautiful plants that grew up the walls and hung off the ceiling as though it were as natural as a rain forest in Costa Rica.

Her heart jumped when she turned the final corner and saw a low, narrow door with a cheap laminate plaque which read:

BUTTERFLY ROOM

She slowly opened the door and peered into the dark room. Something didn't feel right. She had that same unsettled feeling you get when trying to fall asleep and you know the door is open a crack and something feels different in the atmosphere. She stepped inside and left the door ajar.

As she stepped deeper into the room, she heard the swoosh of footsteps. She wondered if it might be Frink but couldn't see through the darkness.

Her stomach spun in circles as she thought about what she'd done. *What if Frink was right and Walters wants to hurt me for some reason? Even though he's my* . . . Mouse shook her head; the words felt too weird as they passed through her mind.

The lighting in the room was strange: A dim glow emanated from a series of glass-topped cabinets that stretched back into obscurity. Mouse approached the closest one and gasped. Illuminated by a border of soft, yellow lights were dozens of butterflies. Each one lay still, glimmering wings stretched wide with a long silver pin thrust through its abdomen. Below the specimens were neat, handwritten labels. *Battus philenor. Papilio polyxenes. Pontia protodice. Colias eurytheme.* The cabinet had a series of drawers running down the front, each containing yet another series of impeccable wings and well-preserved antennae. Mouse walked farther into the room, glancing into each case and finding the same glittering, macabre scene. She shuddered. Butterflies should be beautiful, but this dark room felt more like a morgue than a museum.

Absorbed in her own thoughts, Mouse jumped at the sound of the door moving behind her. She was six cabinets away, and all she could see was that it had swung shut, leaving the room even darker than before. She froze, thinking she heard someone breathing, but the sound was gone as soon as she stopped to listen for it.

Using her GG rig, she opened the Botori app.

FINAL PASSCODE

Then she looked at the empty space below it. She knew that the answer was hidden somewhere in this room, and she was pretty sure it wasn't just going to be sitting under a butterfly. A notification popped up on the screen, and Mouse grinned.

[spying mantis] is [in range]

It wasn't, of course. She'd seen Trent Rayburn smash the little robotic butterfly with his fist and Wurvil hadn't exactly had a chance to build another one. If it wasn't Wurvil's robot, then there must be another drone in the room.

Let's see what a Botori butterfly looks like, she thought as she clicked [**connect**] and held her breath. Simple. Find the drone and win Botori.

If they are waiting in oorbit, then winning Botori is the only way I'll ever find them. If I have to dox a psycho to do it, then too bad for the psycho.

For a moment, there was nothing. Then the sound of wind rustling through summer trees, quiet at first but quickly growing. Mouse glanced down at the cabinet in front of her and leapt backward. They were moving. Every one of the butterflies had begun to flap its wings, some barely squirming, others beating so strongly that the pins holding them down had come loose. A few were banging against the glass top.

It seemed as if there wasn't just one drone, but hundreds of them.

Mouse stumbled, turning on her heel and running toward the door. She grabbed the door handle and pulled, but nothing happened. She pulled again. With a sinking feeling in her stomach, she rattled the doorknob.

Locked.

There was the breathing again, and then footsteps, and this time it was too loud to be her imagination.

"Frink," she called into the rustling darkness. "Done with the games yet?"

There was no response, just a distorted laugh. Mouse shuddered.

He's here.

Mouse tried again. "I see you, Frink. There's nothing you can do! We already captured the video of you and Rayburn." Her heart sunk as she realized how far she was from everyone else. She would have loved to hear Boone's cheerful voice ringing through this dark place.

A deep and warbled voice replied through a voice distorter. "Oh, well done, Mouse. You know I've figured something out as well. I've figured out why Rickum's most difficult student is trying desperately to get noticed."

The desk closest to her began to shake and suddenly the glass top flew open, releasing a swarm of glittering, crackling wings into the air. Mouse ducked as they swooped toward the door, turning as a group just before they collided with the wood, and swarming back into the darkness.

Impossible, how can I capture all of them? And they aren't even real butterflies! It doesn't make sense.

"I must say you've become much more of a nuisance than I ever would have expected. Then again, I also have you to thank. Without your little hack months ago, none of this would have been possible. I never could have created a setup as perfect as Mouse Gamma and Erik Walters. As perfectly Rickum as Gog Magog." He cackled with deep and distorted laughter.

"Too bad no one is going to buy it once they see the video of you and Trent Rayburn secretly meeting," she shouted, managing to keep the quiver out of her voice. Mouse's fingers spun so fast she felt as if her joints would fly off, trying to find any trace of a signal, anything that might be a real Botori clue. The cases were opening left and right now, and thousands of butterflies filled the room.

"Trent Rayburn and *me?*" She heard a thick distorted laugh. "Oh, Mouse, you still don't get it at all. But enough about me. I'm more interested in you. What did it feel like? Growing up in Pittsfield, a little genius, all alone. Did you ever look for your mom and dad? You must have. You must have been desperate to know where your hair came from, where your skin came from, and where your infuriating little brain came from."

Mouse felt rage bubble up through her chest, and this time she had no reason to pull it back. Ada always told her she overreacted, but she wasn't going to take this from Frink. Ella Lightly had fought back, and Mouse was ready to give him something worse than a bloody nose.

"It felt bad. It was bad every day, and yeah, I looked for them. Everything I did, I did for them. I had no one. Is that what you want to hear? You want to hurt me, even now? Is it really fun hurting little girls who have nothing?"

The voice laughed again, and Mouse knew she needed to solve Botori in the next minute, or else her chance to pull this off was going to fly away into thin air. She looked up in desperation. The dark swarm of butterflies that had disappeared toward the ceiling was visible again.

She had to stay focused on Botori. *Capture the flag, catch the butterfly! But which one?*

"You?" scoffed the shadow across the room. "You think *you* have nothing? You have everything! You have their mind. You have their power. You have their genius. You *know* who you are! You've always known your power. It's how you destroyed everyone who ever touched you. Do you really think that all those people were cruel? You think that *they* were trying to hurt *you?* Your foster parents, your counselors, all of them? Of course not. It was *you* hurting *them* each time. The problem was you, Mouse. You're the monster and you're born of monsters."

That's wrong, she thought. *The Hickenloopers were to blame for what happened. The Zengs, Blackwell. They were the bullies. Weren't they? Was it wrong that I tried to fight back?*

Her hands trembled so much that her fingers were having a hard time spinning.

"Of course, the real shame is that Boone and Ada kept you company on this little journey of yours. They will be ruined by this. Probably both expelled as well, but that's what monsters do. They destroy everyone around them, just like your father."

With a jolt she realized that her friends were in trouble. She had to tune out the noise, get the butterfly, and get out. As the swarm of butterflies swooshed past her in a rush of wings and movement, she frantically reached out and grabbed one. She looked at the fluttering mechanical bug as it whipped around in her hand. There was nothing there, no clue. One in a thousand.

"I'm not sure how much longer we'll get to talk. I almost wish I could just void you, but it's so much simpler to kill you. What with your insistence on trying to win at Botori alone, you've set up the perfect scenario. Always the lone wolf. Just like Walters when he betrayed me and won this stupid game by himself. Botori. Everything would have been different if I hadn't lost that chance."

Mouse paused. Walters hadn't betrayed Frink. The only person who would feel betrayed by Walters was Peter Prophet, but he'd been missing for years.

If it's not Frink, then who's doing this and why? Mouse thought with a chill. *And if I don't know who it is, then how can I stop him?*

Wendell sat alone in his room. He'd hardly spoken to anyone. It had been like this all year. Since the call. Since he'd betrayed the Quants and himself. Everything had changed after that. Wendell had stopped talking to his friends, and when he did speak with them, it was to remind them exactly who he was. A Fort Worth Chilton. They'd tried to understand what was wrong, why he was behaving so cold and distant from his friends. What could he tell them? Nothing. There was nothing left for him at Rickum. He had to return home, back to where he belonged, back to what he *deserved*. He deserved the cold contempt and silence.

He was writing a final letter to the headmaster explaining that he was leaving Rickum for good when his phone buzzed. He almost ignored it, but he couldn't. Ever since that first day of school he was in terror of his phone. What if it was *him* again?

Wendell. It's Ada. I know what's happening. You're not alone. We can stop this now. Come to the Butterfly Room in the Natural History Wing. Hurry!

• • •

Gwenny nervously walked by Anna again. She took a deep breath and said to her herself, *This time I'll do it. She deserves it!* Ever since Anna Briem had recovered from the voiding Gwenny had been trying to apologize. That was the only way she could live with herself. It was a first step. Maybe then she could tell Jake what she'd done with their code.

She walked past Anna in silence, again. Too afraid and too ashamed to say a word when suddenly she felt her phone buzz. She cast a puzzled look at her screen. It read:

ADA SPRING.

She knew Ada. A first-year Provi. What could she want?

• • •

Eadric begged Tom to stay.

"We did this together. We came to Rickum as a team," he reminded his friend.

"I know, Eadric, but I can't stand to see what this school's done to you. You're not eating; you won't talk to me. It's not worth it. I didn't come here because it was my dream. I came here because it was yours. Whatever happened to you this year has changed you. I'm not sticking around to watch you destroy yourself."

With that Tom walked out of their dorm. His bags packed, ready to leave.

Eadric buried his hands in his face as he muttered, "What can I do?" Suddenly, his phone buzzed. He nervously glanced down at the message and his heart skipped a beat:

> It's Ada Spring. We can stop this nightmare NOW.

He picked up his phone as relief coursed through him. *It's time*, he thought, *it's time this ends.*

Mouse heard more and more cases of butterflies crack open and join the swarm. She was nearly lifted off the ground as they whipped around the room and crashed into her.

"I don't think we need to prolong this much longer. After all, we just need to make it believable that a troubled student was killed breaking the rules. That leaves so many delightful ways I can kill you." The dim light glinted off a glass jar that he pulled from his pocket.

"I had thought that just having that moron Frink expel you would be enough, but you had to keep snooping and snooping. You've really forced my hand. So, meet my new friend Hadronyche Modesta. She's had to make a small journey from her home down the hallway with the other poisonous spiders. Once I void you, I'll have my little friend here finish you off. A tragic accident."

Mouse watched the massive, hairy spider pacing around the small glass case. Suddenly its front legs leapt up the glass casing and she could almost see its pale fangs glisten with venom.

"She's hungry! One of the deadliest spiders alive. Once you've been bitten you have roughly two hours to receive treatment. Without it the veins around the bite will constrict slowly, until the blood will simply stop running to that irritating and unpredictable heart of yours. With your death, the voidings will stop completely. Villain apprehended."

Mouse shuddered at the thought of that hairy spider crawling over her unconscious body, before snapping out of it.

Fat chance I'll let this psycho beat me.

"So, you went looking for *me*, and you discovered the Pericles Society instead. All the time you thought it was Frink. That idiotic stooge. Always moaning about a teensy little mistake I made all those years ago. As if I'm the reason he wasn't as successful as Rayburn or as smart as Walters."

The one person who felt betrayed by Walters was Peter Prophet! And what's a Prophet? A Messenger.

"You're Peter Prophet," Mouse blurted out. "You changed your name to *Melvin Messinger*, but you were Erik Walters's roommate."

She could hear a sarcastic golf clap. "Whoopdee doo. You got it, Mouse. What a student you turned out to be. Let's say it together, 'I'm Peter Prophet.'" His laughter echoed through the dark room. "Do you think the butterflies care? Well, I'll give you credit. You nearly won. Your dear mom and dad would be so proud. Tiresias and Cassandra. Erik and Ella. You know they really did think they could see the future. They saw it together. The two of them. All alone. While the world and all its people swarmed around them."

Mouse jolted up as soon as she heard Messinger say "swarmed."

She'd been approaching this riddle all wrong. The clue was about finding a *real butterfly*. Not finding a drone. She didn't need to find one drone out of many, but one butterfly in a *swarm* of drones. Every word of Professor Whippleton's class came back to her as the closet of her memory swung open. The problem was simple: In a swarm every butterfly behaves just like its neighbor. She needed to adapt the model and break the algorithm.

She just needed to break *their* code!

Messinger continued pacing just beyond her sight. "Once things were in motion, I realized that Gog Magog would create just enough distraction that no one would suspect the brilliant Melvin Messinger was anything other than a popular teacher. All it took was a few social media posts at just the right time, and suddenly a full-blown student frenzy."

Mouse quickly thought back to Whippleton's class on mathematical models and remembered the three rules of a swarm: Move in the same direction as your neighbors. Remain close to your neighbors. Avoid collisions.

A feeling of satisfaction rolled through her as the answer began to form in her mind. The difference between the butterfly she was looking for and the rest was that she was looking for something *alive*. Something that didn't want to die, something that would break an algorithm to stay out of danger and *avoid collisions* at all costs.

A survivor. Just like me.

She first needed to control the drones. Her fingers spinning quickly to boot up her hack, she suddenly saw just the message she needed:

[spying mantis] is [in range]

She directed the drone's coordinates to smash straight into the professor, praying that the rest of the swarm would follow. She watched with amazement as the swarm seemed to shimmer as it almost imperceptibly shifted direction. Then, without hesitation, every one of the butterflies took off like a bullet straight toward the unsuspecting professor.

As they collided with Messinger, only one butterfly fluttered gently away from the swarm at the last minute. With a leap Mouse jumped past him and grabbed the one real butterfly between her fingers.

Gotcha!

Mouse heard a growl as the distorted voice fritzed and barked, "You little brat. You can't even die with dignity. I just needed the others to forget. That's why I voided them. First, I needed Anna Briem to forget stumbling upon my call to Wendell Chilton. Then Bunyan was onto me, after Ada's stupid email. Wurvil was also snooping in the wrong place. He'd realized that as Walters's roommate I had a copy of his paper on OM. I stole it when we were students."

Mouse staggered back toward the front of the room and flipped on the light. The butterfly was still struggling in her hand. Her eyes quickly scanned a small tag pinned to its wing. Without skipping a beat, she opened up her Botori app. She just needed Messinger distracted for another moment.

"Why?" she asked. "What was it all for?"

He smiled and she could see a hint of the fake showman she'd first met.

"Money! With Eadric's worm, Gwenny's data parser, and Wendell's microprocessor, I've been able to build a program that can clear out a bank in less than a nanosecond."

Mouse interrupted, "Money? You just want money?"

Messinger barked, "I'm not like Walters and Rayburn. I was never interested in their friendship or their war over right and wrong. My needs are much simpler. *Winning*. It turns out winning is easy when you're in control."

"Not *so* easy!" a small voice suddenly yelled.

Mouse whipped around to see the door rattling frantically.

"Oh, your faithful sidekicks." Messinger laughed. "Well, I appreciate you making this even easier for me."

Suddenly, the door swung open and Boone and Ada spilled in. Ada ran to Mouse and gave her a huge hug.

Ada looked at her with loving frustration. "I don't care what you read in those archives that upset you. *We're* your family."

Three more students walked into the Butterfly Room. Wendell Chilton, Eadric Abana, and Gwenny Rogers.

Messinger suddenly seemed more nervous. "Well, well, well, I guess the three of you want your secrets out. You want *everyone* to know what you've done. How you've . . ."

"Shut up," Wendell barked. "So I cheated on one test. It's not worth it anymore. I can't keep lying."

"Yeah," Gwenny added. "I stole a stupid program. It was a mistake and I'm done running from it."

Eadric looked crestfallen until he added, "I changed Tom's scores so he could get into Rickum with me. He's ten times smarter, but he bombed the test, and I couldn't come here without him. He never even knew I did it."

Wendell glared at Messinger. "We don't care anymore. You'll never get away with it. Ada found out everything about you. You obsessed with Erik Walters during your time at Rickum until you went too far. You broke the one rule during Botori that you can't break. You hurt Frink trying to keep up with your roommate. That's why you were disqualified. Walking by his hologram each day in that final moment of triumph must just kill you."

Messinger ripped the voice distorter off his face and his fingers began spinning. "You have it all wrong. I, I, I—" He paused. "I think you need an education in what killing *means*. Erik Walters disappointed me. His precious rules. Those stupid tenets. And I can't stand that hologram . . . however, *kill* me? No, not all. However, I will be killing all of you."

He looked first at Mouse and then the rest of the students. Suddenly, a bolt of electricity exploded from the wall's electrical outlet and the door burst open again, making Messinger drop his hand in surprise.

Frink stood in the doorway, visibly seething.

"You. Are. Supposed. To be. IN YOUR CLASSES!" he screamed at Boone and Ada, then turned his attention to Mouse. Frink seemed momentarily frozen in confusion.

"Rayburn will *kill* me if I let anything happen to you," he said, looking at Boone. "Now, Melvin, what in the world is going on?"

Messinger shook a stray butterfly drone off of his right hand and made a decisive movement with his thumb and forefinger. "Oh, goodbye, Frink."

Frink stopped mid-stride, his pupils suddenly shrinking to pinpoints as his eyes went wide and his mouth froze in a grimace. The kids stared as he keeled over, stiff as a board.

Messinger turned on Mouse again, grinning maniacally. "That, Mouse, is what a voiding looks like. When you understand how Walters truly built OM, you realize there are all kinds of secret ways to override the system. Frink will be okay, eventually. No memory of this, of course."

As Messinger raised his hand and began spinning his fingers, the room was filled with an ear-splitting shriek.

"RAAZZZZZMMMMMAATTTTAAAAZZZZZ!" shouted Boone in an unearthly register. He barreled across the room into Messinger's legs and the two of them tumbled to the ground, disappearing behind one of the butterfly cases. Mouse didn't miss a beat, spinning her fingers frantically in the air. There was a brief, stunned silence, and then Boone's head slowly emerged over the edge of the desk.

"Guys. Um. Uh . . . I think he's dead . . . Ada, Mouse, I think I just killed Professor Messinger . . ."

"No. He's fine." Mouse grinned. "I voided him."

"You *what?*" It was Wendell this time, looking deeply confused. "You're not a sapient, are you? What are you talking about?"

"Don't need to be. I read Walters's thesis. It's simple. Remember the first thing I told you: Every connection is two ways. When Messinger attacked Frink it was simple; I just reverse-engineered the connection and *whammo*."

Eadric made a sound that sounded surprisingly like a sigh of relief. "I thought *I* was gonna be in trouble, but I think we just watched a Provi void a teacher who was trying to kill us in the middle of an illegal Botori session."

Gwenny giggled nervously. Wendell looked as if he was going to vomit.

Out of the corner of her eye, Mouse noticed some movement by Messinger's head. She saw that the glass case next to him was empty with no sign of its contents.

"Boone, get away from there," Mouse yelled as she leapt over the shattered glass. He skittered away as an enormous spider ambled up Messinger's neck and up onto his forehead. As Mouse slid to a stop over the unconscious body, she took a deep breath and looked at the spider.

She picked up the glass case and was about to swoop the spider safely back into it when she glared down at the unconscious figure of Peter Prophet. As she paused, the spider seemed to look up at Mouse with approval as it sank its fangs into his forehead.

Then she closed the case around the confused animal with a quiet nod.

The five of them stood silently in the semi-darkness of the now-quiet room. The only sound was a slight wheezing breath coming from the two voided professors.

The sound of footsteps pounding down the hall toward the butterfly room shook them out of their silent reverie.

Headmaster Garrick stood in the doorway, phone in hand. He waved his hand and the overhead lights blinked on, illuminating a bizarre scene.

He pointed at the floor. "I see six students in a closed section of the building, two professors lying in a pile of bootleg robotics, and it appears that a pair of Provis have just *won* a cancelled Botori! And, Mouse, you are *already* expelled. Explanations?"

Ada looked at Mouse and then back at Garrick. "Wait. What pair of Provis just won Botori? Who?"

"You did, Ada. You and Mouse." Garrick raised his phone so the students could see the screen. It displayed a slightly blurry picture of a small hand holding a white butterfly, with the text "Provis RULE" splayed across the image.

Ada looked over at her friend in confusion.

Mouse shrugged. "I promised we'd win. I don't break promises. Not to my family." She blushed.

Ada ran toward Mouse and grabbed her in a tight hug. "Um. 'Provis rule'? Seriously?"

Mouse's reply was muffled by Ada's shoulder. "Sorry, I was under a little pressure. I had to void Messinger while I was sending that message, you know."

Gwenny, Eadric, and Wendell had pulled out their phones and were staring at identical pictures that had arrived in their emails, time-stamped just two minutes earlier.

"*Enough.* I've called Nurse Wilkies; she'll be here in a moment to take care of this mess. You six. My office. Now."

As they walked out the door, Mouse turned around and added nonchalantly, "Garrick, by the way, Messinger was just bitten by a poisonous spider. Nurse Wilkies has two hours to get him some treatment or he'll probably die."

Garrick looked at Mouse, then at the spider, and raced off to find Nurse Wilkies.

As everyone else meandered away, Mouse stood there, fingers spinning by her side, staring deep into the Glass, puzzling over what to do next.

The walk through the empty halls of the Natural History Wing seemed to take forever as the students followed a visibly irate headmaster toward his office. Mouse caught up with everyone as they were walking into the headmaster's office.

She found it almost comforting to sit in the waiting room looking at dozens of Ms. Farnaby's dead plants as they waited to be called into the headmaster's office. After all, she'd spent more of her school career in trouble than out of it.

Mouse chewed contemplatively on her thumbnail and glanced at Boone, who was pacing in small, nervous circles in front of her as Headmaster Garrick emerged from his office.

"I'll speak to Gwen, Wendell, and Eadric first." He waved them in impatiently, and the three older students disappeared into his office. Before the door closed, Gwenny stepped back out and looked at Ada. "Thank you, Ada. No matter what happens, you helped free us."

Mouse whipped around as soon as the door clicked shut. "Okay. I can't stand it anymore. How did you figure out that Messinger was blackmailing them?"

Ada smiled. "I've been trying to tell you all along. It was their behavior. Gwenny was obvious; I mean she hardly knew Anna but was basically keeping vigil by the nurse's office to make sure she was all right. I had an inkling when we saw Eadric acting weird. I looked into it a little bit and found out that he'd basically stopped going to classes. Wendell was a bit harder. I only figured him out right before Garrick stopped Botori. I noticed that every Quant was involved in a massive Botori DDoS to try and stop us except one."

Mouse interjected, "Wendell Chilton!"

Ada nodded. "I finally confirmed it right before you kicked open the doors and ran away from the student archive. When you were looking up Cassandra and Tiresias, I checked a few things out myself. It turns out that only four students haven't bothered to pre-register for classes next year. Guess who?"

Mouse answered, "Wendell, Eadric, and Gwenny."

"But who was the fourth?" Boone asked.

Ada shook her head. "Who do you think?"

Mouse waved her hand. "I'm not wasting my time signing up for a bunch of classes I don't even need."

Ada sighed. "I just hope I have a reason to get angry with you."

A puzzled look came over Mouse's face. "Wait, but how did you find me? You didn't figure out the Botori clue. What made you think of the Natural History Wing?"

Boone blushed bright red. "Oh man, please promise you won't get mad."

Mouse looked at Ada. "What's he talking about?"

Ada laughed. "Boone has been tracking you the entire time. Like *entire* time. Since Botori started. He put a tracking device in your shoe, and one in your backpack."

Mouse looked at him, speechless.

"It was your idea. You told me to 'watch and learn,' remember? I'm sooo sorry. I just knew we couldn't compete with your code, so Gustaveson and I have been following your footsteps. Every one of your little adventures we traced, tracked, and followed. From your adventure in the Hall of Heroes, to your brilliant maneuver using Ada's whistle to crack the payphone. I knew what you were doing the whole time. We were always one small step behind you."

Mouse's gaze went back and forth between Ada and Boone until she finally exclaimed, "That is cool!"

Ada smiled. "Garrick's got to change his mind about expelling you now."

Mouse sadly shook her head. "Ada, I'm sorry, but that's not how these things work. I guess you'll be fine, since your mom works here. And, Boone, it's obvious we were just a bad influence on you. But I'm out of here. Nothing's getting me out of this mess. At least you guys will be safe. It's back to Blackwell for me."

Her stomach sank when she said Blackwell. *Messinger was right,* she thought. *Blackwell wasn't the problem. My foster parents weren't the problem. I was. I've always been the one starting trouble, never fitting in, attacking everyone who tried to help me.*

Boone started to protest, but Mouse shook her head adamantly. "I'll be out before you can say disappointment, and you two will get a slap on the wrist. I never belonged here in the first place."

She looked down, avoiding Ada's eyes. Just then, the door from the hallway burst open with enough force to make all three kids jump.

Standing in the doorway was Ms. Rote.

Before anyone could speak, Nurse Wilkies raced by them with Messinger laid out on a stretcher.

"That bite will leave a very nasty mark right in the middle of his forehead," she yelled as she raced down the hall. "But he'll live!"

Mouse sighed with relief as Ms. Farnaby followed, pushing a zonked-out Professor Frink. She looked at Mouse and Ada. "Oh, hello, girls. I'm going to stay with Erwin. I know he can be a bit grumpy, but he's been such a doll, bringing Gigabyte lettuce and other treats nearly every day."

Ms. Rote grabbed Ada's shoulder with a gentle tug, pulling her into a gargantuan hug. "What in the *world* is all of this?"

Then she reached over to touch Boone and Mouse as well. "And you two? Sneaking around all this time, secret detective projects! I never would have encouraged you if I had any idea where this would all lead."

Mouse's face was stony. "My idea. All my idea. I couldn't let Botori go." She stood up abruptly. "I'm really sorry I got Ada involved."

Headmaster Garrick popped his head out of his office.

"In here now, you three. I've sent the others back to their dorm rooms. I've also asked Trent Rayburn to be present while we work out what exactly happened. I feel that it's appropriate to have Ada and Boone's parents present, given the circumstances."

Mouse and Ada looked at each other with puzzlement at the mention of Rayburn. Was it possible he was still involved?

Mouse crowded around Garrick's sleek, silver desk for the second time that day. Ms. Rote stood with the three children, while Garrick and Rayburn took seats across from them.

"Well, now tell Headmaster Garrick just what happened. No fudging, no equivocating; we'll just sort this out from the facts." Ms. Rote nodded encouragingly at her daughter, who was staring uncharacteristically at her shoes.

"Okay, so, and we thought the voidings were about OM because Mouse is really smart, but it turns out Ada was taking notes the whole time—" Boone spluttered.

"Thank you, Boone," Garrick interrupted. "But from the beginning, please."

Mouse sighed. "It all began with a stupid hack on Rayburn Tech's servers . . ."

Nearly an hour later Garrick, Rote, and Rayburn sat speechlessly as Mouse finished by describing how she'd voided Melvin Messinger while inputting the final passcode into the Botori app.

Boone added as a final note, "We're really sorry, but isn't it good that Peter Prophet didn't kill Mouse?"

Garrick nodded slowly, repressing a smile. "Yes. That *is* good. While I wish you had left the investigation to the adults, I see that in this *particular* case your instincts were correct, but there's still one question I have: Mouse, why did you choose to complete Botori after you had been explicitly instructed not to do so?"

Mouse took a long time to respond, so long that Boone and Ada started to shift uncomfortably in their chairs, and Ms. Rote patted her encouragingly on the back.

"When we were in the archives. I . . . I found something out."

Mouse took a deep breath. "Cassandra and Tiresias, I mean Ella Lightly and Erik Walters . . . I think they were my parents. I think they *are* my parents. I found a note when we broke into the school's records about them waiting for each other in 'oorbit.' Erik Walters's last line. Well, if you change around the letters, it spells 'Botori.' I guess I thought that if I won, there would be some kind of Easter egg or some hack they'd left, like a witness mark to help me find them."

Mouse paused, and her voice shook. "Then I could ask them why they left me."

Boone and Ada stared at each other in stunned silence. Mouse kept her eyes focused on the floor, her expression carefully neutral. Suddenly, she heard a peal of laughter.

Ms. Rote had turned bright pink and was covering her mouth. "I'm . . . I'm so sorry. Honey. I shouldn't laugh, it's just . . . you're—"

"She's just like them." It was Rayburn now, speaking for the first time since they had entered the office. He glared as he spoke. "It's more than just her physical resemblance, even the way she codes. Mixing protocols, switching languages without a moment's hesitation, breaking down security without a blink. It's chaos, but so elegant that you'd never realize she broke every rule to get there. She's their daughter, all right. I'd already put it together before her little hack."

"Trent. You knew? Did you know all this time that Erik and Ella had a child?" Ms. Rote was glaring furiously. "Oh, Mouse." Tears welled up in her eyes. "I'm so sorry you had to find out like this, that you had to wait so long . . ."

"Garrick." Rayburn's voice was firm. "I believe that you, Mouse, and I should have a private conversation?"

Ms. Rote narrowed her eyes. "Trent, you and I have some things to get straight. Don't think you're leaving without an explanation. Ada, Boone, come with me." She pulled the two kids through the door, as they both stared back at Mouse.

• • •

"Sit down, Mouse. There are a few things you should know." Rayburn spoke like a man accustomed to being obeyed.

Mouse stared pointedly at the air between Rayburn and Garrick.

"Do you know why you're at Rickum, Mouse?"

She didn't look at him. "I'm here because someone made a mistake."

"No. I don't make *mistakes*. You're here because I put you here. I've heard you made the connection with the Concilium program. That gave me a simple way to get you into Rickum. You see, I needed to watch you, to see if he'd come for you. You were the bait."

Mouse's face registered a rare, genuine look of shock. "*You?*" Mouse quickly composed herself and laughed sarcastically. "With friends like that . . ."

Rayburn replied with a glare that Mouse realized held something much deeper than contempt.

"Oh, I wouldn't say we're friends, Mouse." He leaned toward her and whispered in her ear. "If it wasn't for *him*, I'd see you rotting in prison for your little hack."

"Speaking of *him*," Mouse scoffed, "I guess the bait didn't quite work. I mean, where are they? Ella and Erik. These super hackers."

He folded his hands carefully. "Ella is dead. Very tragic. She died just after you were born. And Erik . . . Oh, Erik Walters is everywhere. Even when he was in prison, if he was even in prison, he was somehow chiseling away, finding weak spots, attacking at every turn. Trying to prove that the code the Pericles Society created could make the world better. It wasn't enough that I built the biggest company in the world." His voice was a bitter growl.

Mouse wasn't looking at him. "Dead. My mother is dead? Well, guess that's about right. Just my luck."

She whipped around and addressed Garrick. "I'll be packing my bags then. I assume I'm still expelled. Please don't kick out Ada and Boone, though. It wasn't their fault."

Rayburn turned to Garrick. "I certainly agree. I don't think there's any need to keep this charade going any longer. Clearly Erik Walters would have made contact if he was remotely interested in Mouse. I think we've seen, yet again, why the Concilium program is so dangerous. Once a black-hat hacker, always a black-hat hacker." He turned and stared at Mouse again. "I must say, you are a talented coder. A shame you've got so much of *him* in you."

Garrick shook his head. "Your opinion is noted, Trent, but Mouse won't be packing any bags. At least not yet."

Mouse furrowed her brow in confusion.

"This has been an exceptional series of events. And I'm afraid that I've made a terrible mistake, and I think in some ways Mouse was quite right when she said that I have been too distracted by concerns about

Rickum's reputation. That ends this moment. We believe in Data and Performance here at Rickum. When Mouse arrived, we did not have much of either, but now we do. We have plenty of data to see that Mouse not only has some of the most remarkable technical skills I've seen in a generation, but has the kind of character we aspire to teach here at Rickum. After all, data and performance are nothing without loyalty, perseverance, and a sense of justice and commitment. All things that you've shown are at the core of who you are."

"But why would you want someone like me here?" Mouse asked. "I hurt people. Why would you keep someone who hurts people?"

Garrick raised his hand to stop her. "You haven't hurt anyone. Those voidings weren't your fault, as is now painfully obvious. All this time, you've just been trying to find out who you are. You are a child, just searching for safety." He took a deep breath. "And I should never have allowed you to be a pawn in this game. Though luckily, it brought you into our school, and now I intend to keep you here. Rayburn, is there anything else you wanted to say to Mouse?"

Rayburn stood and shook his head once, then paused and looked over at her. "I hate to say this, but I see why Boone cares so much about you. I . . ." He looked down. "I wanted Erik to believe in me more than anything in the world. If things had been just a little different, we would be working together." Bitterness clouded his eyes. "I just pray you don't hurt Boone the same way Erik . . ." He shook his head and left.

CHAPTER 29

Headmaster Garrick looked down at the students from the high stage of the Great Hall.

For the last six weeks, Mouse had been impatiently waiting for this day. Garrick had postponed his official judgment on the outcome of Botori until the end-of-year feast, claiming the situation was so unprecedented that it required careful consideration from the whole faculty. Most students were anxious to hear who would be added to the Hall of Heroes, but Mouse had other worries. She couldn't stop that little voice in the back of her mind saying that there was no way she'd really be allowed back at Rickum next year. After all, she'd nearly *killed* a professor. To make it worse, she'd done it on purpose!

She caught Garrick's eye and saw that same glimmer of stern amusement she'd seen the day that she'd voided Professor Messinger. She replied with a look of furrowed frustration and concern.

What if something's changed? What if they've decided to expel me after all? Now's their last chance before the year's over.

Garrick couldn't help himself and broke into an open smile.

"At Rickum we rely on data and performance, the twin bedrocks of our school. At every review, at every test, and with every breath we insist on the importance of those two beloved principals."

Garrick wiped his brow and sighed as he continued, "Yet this year we all learned that there's more to being a great student and leading a good life than just data and performance. We learned that family and friendship are why our performance *matters*. Without human connection and responsibility, the cold reality of data and performance can become a sickness."

He paused for a moment and looked offstage as there was a rustling. "Now, speaking of sickness, I'd like be the first to congratulate Professor Frink on his healthy return from the unhappy incidents earlier this year. I've asked him and Professor Bunyan to join me onstage for our next announcement."

Professor Bunyan lumbered onstage with her irrepressible smile as Frink responded with a dire frown.

"I'd also like to invite three very special students up to the stage: Gwenny, Eadric, and Wendell. I'm happy to announce that the discipline committee has looked into your transgressions and cleared you of all wrongdoing, given your bravery in risking your own reputations to help uncover the truth and protect other students from harm."

Students burst into wild applause and cheers. Of course, as they roared with approval there was still the unanswered question that had dominated the last six weeks of the school year.

"Now finally to a question I know you're all burning to ask: What about Botori?"

The students all sat up and listened with rapt attention. Since Mouse had sent that message, "Provis rule!" it was the most hotly debated topic on campus. Had they really won?

"As you all know Botori was cancelled, and cancelled for good reason. We are, of course, a school where rules *matter*! The school board has considered the situation very closely. It's clear that the school rules *were* broken. Naturally, the students have been given detention. A close reading of the rules of Botori, however, state clearly that only causing bodily harm to another student can disqualify a team. Since no other *students* were harmed through their actions, though they irresponsibly disregarded the *school's* rules, they did not break the rules of Botori."

He paused to look down at Mouse and Ada with a quick wink. "While we must recognize that Botori was cancelled, and thus we cannot have an official winner, we *can* recognize that sometimes true heroism cannot be measured in points, or represented by the winner and loser of a game. This year, while we don't have an official Botori winner, we have seen two students act heroically." He pulled a lever and a massive curtain swooshed to the side, revealing a new hologram for the Hall of Heroes, Mouse and Ada surrounded by a swarm of butterflies that swooped and swooshed around them.

Garrick clapped. Frink muttered, "An outrage."

"Mouse and Ada will be added to the Hall of Heroes as the first students who did *not* win Botori," Garrick said and smiled. "I think it's fitting that we've had to break some rules to accommodate Mouse for once. Congratulations. Now enjoy the graduation day feast!" For the next half hour, he handed out diplomas. Balloons cascaded through the air and confetti rained down as students celebrated.

Wurvil, who was still recovering, limped over to Ada and Mouse.

"Wow! I gotta say, I'm impressed. Almost impressed enough to forgive you for destroying Preying Mantis."

Mouse laughed. "It was for a good cause. Anyway, I made you a little gift, and this one's got a level of encryption that will keep even me out of it." She handed him a handmade version of Preying Mantis. "I call him Monarch and he's got a few surprises that even you wouldn't expect."

"Not bad," Wurvil replied. "Thanks, Mouse." Then his eyes caught something on the other side of the massive room. "Well isn't this a sight for sore eyes."

Boone ran over and yelped with excitement, "Razzmatazz! I see you got Dubloon up and running again."

Wurvil responded by unabashedly bundling Boone into a huge hug. "At least one of my creations survived the carnage. But, old chum, enough small talk. I know you were involved in some truly dramatic events earlier this year. I suppose you'll be needing a good long rest now. How's your father taking it? I know he had great hopes that you'd avenge him this year."

Boone smiled, "Let's just say my dad's learning to let me walk to my own beat a little more. I think he's worried if he pushes me too hard, I'll get even closer to Mouse."

After inhaling as many Twizzlers, Skittles, and Sour Patch Kids as she possibly could, Mouse walked out of the Great Hall with Ada. They bumped into Ms. Rote who was scouring the room.

"Aha! Just who I was hoping to spy with my little eye. Run along now, Ada. I have something to discuss with Mouse."

Ada looked at Mouse and then at her mom. "Okay, but don't get too schmaltzy. Mouse can only handle small doses."

"To the preacher she preaches." Ms. Rote shook her head in mock disapproval as Ada walked off.

"So much has happened to you this year," she said, shaking her head with a smile. "You know you look so much like her. Like Ella, I mean, I should have known all along. There were just so many secrets back then."

Mouse shifted uncomfortably. She had been trying to forget everything about that day apart from winning Botori.

"Ella Lightly was my best friend, and as close as we were, well I hardly knew Erik. No one really did except Trent and Ella."

Mouse looked at Ms. Rote. Now that she knew where she came from, she wanted to understand her parents to help understand herself. "What did she see in him? Why would she want to be with a guy who was so hard to understand? I mean, he abandoned me. Why would Ella be with someone who was so unreliable?"

"You see, Mouse, he was so kind. Almost like a child himself. He wrote those tenets in *The True Magicians* as mantras to himself, building a moral world he could believe in."

Ms. Rote's eyes welled up with tears. "When Ella got sick, no one except Erik really knew. They disappeared to the Berkshires, living all alone. A part of me thinks they were hiding from Trent. He'd started to change, and all the work they'd done together he was using to start Rayburn Tech."

"What were they doing?"

Ms. Rote shrugged. "I don't really know. I didn't hear from them until years later. When I arrived for her funeral, Erik looked as though he'd aged twenty years and lost fifty pounds. He looked like a ghost. He didn't even cry at the grave. He just stood there silently. Trent Rayburn eventually led him away. That was it. The last I heard about Erik until he was arrested. Without her, Erik put all his focus into trying to use technology to make the world free for True Magicians. He thought Trent was doing the opposite. Using technology without any purpose other than creating wealth. He poured all his sorrow and rage into trying to destroy him."

Mouse looked up at Ms. Rote and suddenly felt tears start to well up in her eyes. When they began to fall, she didn't try to hold them back.

"But what if I'm really the monster? Maybe . . ." Mouse couldn't believe what she was saying, but as soon as it left her mouth, she knew that it was a question she'd wanted to ask her entire life. "Maybe it was my fault they left; maybe it was my fault she died. I just hurt everyone everywhere I go. Even Ada almost got suspended because of me," she stammered.

Ms. Rote just pulled her into a hug. "Oh, my sweet girl. You're a child. Children can hurt those around them from time to time as they grow.

Just like code, you must test your boundaries, test your strength. After all, you did much more than just hurt everyone around you."

Mouse took a deep breath and pulled back. "Not really."

"Oh, Mouse. We can bring you through the desert, but we cannot foist you to the promised land." She shook her head in dismay. "You think that you only hurt the people around you? You know Ada ripped my Kraftwerk Live in Dusseldorf poster in half during a fight when she was six. Can you imagine?"

Mouse had to suppress a laugh and shook her head.

"Had a fully grown adult done that, it would have been quite strange, you see. But a child? Not so strange at all. Children act up, and then they calm down. You were never given a place that allowed you to just be you. You were in a system that treated you like a transaction. Of course, you tried to break free. After all, you really are a True Magician, just like Erik always dreamed of. Look how much joy you've given Ada. You're her best friend. Almost her sister. Look at her, even now."

Ms. Rote pointed to the doorway where Ada was hiding poorly and scribbling in her notebook.

Mouse quickly looked back and nervously asked, "So where do you think he is?"

Ms. Rote looked quizzically at Mouse. "Where who is?"

Mouse looked at the floor. "My dad?"

"I expect he's closer than we think." She smiled.

"Erik *chose* to be in prison and the moment he didn't want to be there anymore, he simply left. It certainly wasn't because he'd made some silly coding error to give himself away. Not Erik Walters. I imagine he's reemerged for one reason. Trent knew it too, and that's how he tried to trap him."

Mouse replied, "What could be so important that he'd break out of prison for it?"

"Well, I think that's quite obvious."

Mouse looked at Ms. Rote with confusion. "I don't understand. What?"

"Why you, of course."

Mouse shook her head. "Then why wouldn't he contact me? Why wouldn't he tell me who he was? It doesn't make sense."

"Doesn't it? I mean, aren't you a bit like him? Everything's a riddle. Even before the Pericles Society, the two of them created their own little universe. They even joked about it. Ella and Erik. Alpha and Beta."

Mouse looked up. "What did you say?"

"'Alpha' and 'Beta.' Their nicknames for each other. You know, the two brightest stars in a constellation. The two brightest stars in their own special world. Until, I imagine, there was a third. Gamma."

Mouse's eyes lit up, as they welled with tears.

"You see, Ella was already gone when Eric was arrested. His last message wasn't for her, Mouse. He was speaking to you. Erik's waiting for you in orbit."

Mouse felt a surge of happiness and replied, "Thank you, Ms. Rote. Thanks for everything."

"For what?" she replied with a grin. "I can't imagine."

EPILOGUE

Mouse sat down in the Hall of Heroes as the sun began to set. The coolness of the floor chilled her as she admired the row of holograms moving and shimmering in the early evening sunlight.

It does feel pretty good to see Ada and I among the greatest hackers that Rickum's ever produced.

Out of the corner of her eye, she saw a familiar hologram blink. Unlike the rest of them, this one had stopped looping and the boy had turned and was looking at her.

"Not so hard to find you anymore. 'Oorbit' really is a clever little Easter egg. I almost missed it at first."

The hologram laughed. "Well, you had a lot going on. I'm glad you know how to find me now."

Mouse nodded. "I know how you did it, by the way. How you took control of the local network without ever stepping foot on campus."

"Yes. I imagined you would. That and everything else. We have so many things to talk about," the hologram replied.

Mouse smiled.

ACKNOWLEDGMENTS

For someone who reads books and believes so deeply in the power of reading books, it's been quite wonderful to write one for a change. In no clear order, many friends and colleagues have contributed to *Mouse*—Danny Stedman and Kate Crassweller. Mikey, Barbara, and "Po" Stedman. Emily Lacouture and Micky Mcsorely. Eric and Ben Svenson, Dana Nielsen, and Aron Epstein.

I've been very lucky to have learned from a remarkable creative community over the years: Bill Abely, Sophie Hunter, Jesse Smith, Michael Bassik, John Stirratt, Sara Mnookin, Josh Derman, Dev Subhash, Lindsay Nelson, Janet Balis, Joe Wardwell and Katie Fitch, Ken and Celine Oringer, Jann Schwarz, Ilya Marritz, Dan Chiasson and Annie Adams, Michael Fanuele, Alex Hocherman, Cass Taylor, Michael Shields, Chris Casgar, Keith Johnson, Kara Block, David Morris, Whit Collier, Pat Cramb, Justin Nesci, Jeff Evans, Will Guidara, Michael Hendrix, Mikhail Iossel, Andrew Essex, Eric Kerns, Erin McPherson, Nick Thompson, Kelley Walton, Jeff Howe, Becca Parrish, Nick Burry, Lindsey Slaby, Ivan Kayser, Jeff Gordinier, Steve Rossi, Adam Kosberg, and the midday mischief crew, Annie Oh and Lisa Laich.

The wonderful team at Greenleaf—Teresa Muniz, Leis Pederson, Amanda Hughes, Jessica Reyes, and Lindsay Bohls. The book club boys: Fred Fogel, Paul Zei, Brook Rosenbaum, Jay Staunton, and Alex Baker.

Mouse is truly unimaginable without Emma Page—who put enormous effort and remarkable work into helping create this world—I cannot overstate my appreciation. Yasmine Jaffier, Sonny, Felix, and Louise—who inspired Mouse. Of course, Crystalle Lacouture, who's been my partner in everything I've done and will do. I'm very lucky to have such an inspiring crew rooting me on along the way and calling out my name to "keep going" when I'd get tired.

ABOUT THE AUTHOR

N. SCOTT STEDMAN is a writer who lives outside of Boston with his family. *Mouse* is his first novel.

Made in USA - Kendallville, IN
62647_9781632994523
04.20.2022 1536